NORMAL WEIRD

NEMETRA X1369

First published in Great Britain in 2021
by Si and Geo Creative,
The paperback edition published in 2021 by
Si and Geo Creative Ltd
12 Northfield Avenue
London W13 9RJ.

Copyright © Nemetra X1369
The right of Nemetra X1369 to be identified as
the author of this work has been asserted in accordance with the Copyright,
Design and Patents Act 1988.

All rights reserved. No part of this publication may be reproduced, stored in a retrieval system, or transmitted in any form or by means, electronic, mechanical, photocopying, recording, or otherwise, without the prior permission of both the copyright owner and the above publisher of this book.

All the characters in this book are fictitious, and any resemblance to actual person, living or dead, is purely coincidental.

Blog – https://nemetra.com/
Twitter – https://twitter.com/nemetra_x
Instagram – https://www.instagram.com/nemetra_x1369/

"WOW!

Nemetra has written THE must-read book on identity, self-discovery and being our true selves. Are you normal? Are you weird? Forget all those boring personality tests – read this book!"

David Taylor
Author of The Best-Selling Naked Leader Books

NORMAL WEIRD

NEMETRA X1369

Si & Geo Creative

Table of Contents

PROLOGUE 1

Chapter 1 RESULTS 4

Chapter 2 ALONE 13

Chapter 3 THE UNEXPECTED TURN IN HUMAN EVOLUTION. GLOBAL BROADCAST – PART 1 24

Chapter 4 TRANSITION 30

Chapter 5 THE UNEXPECTED TURN IN HUMAN EVOLUTION. GLOBAL BROADCAST – PART 2 38

Chapter 6 ROBERT'S TRUTH – TURMOIL 43

Chapter 7 THE UNEXPECTED TURN IN HUMAN EVOLUTION. GLOBAL BROADCAST – PART 3 52

Chapter 8 DIFFICULT DECISION 58

Chapter 9 THE EXTRAORDINARY AI 63

Chapter 10 GLITCH 70

Chaprer 11 LEGACY 78

Chapter 12 ROBERT'S TRUTH – EMPATHY 87

Chapter 13 THE MESSAGE 98

Chapter 14 MARIA 104

Chapter 15 ILLOGICAL STUPID HEART 116

Chapter 16 NO GOING BACK 125

Chapter 17 BATTLE OF OPINIONS 134
Chapter 18 A MOMENT OF ETERNITY 146
Chapter 19 DISCOVERY 153
Chapter 20 NOTHING ELSE EXISTS 158
Chapter 21 RESPONSIBILITY 164
Chapter 22 THE UNEXPECTED 170
Chapter 23 THE END OF THE WORLD 176
Chapter 24 THE NEXT RIGHT THING TO DO 182
Chapter 25 TRUE INTELLIGENCE 195
Chapter 26 REGRETS 201
Chapter 27 THE LEAF 208
Chapter 28 DECEPTION 219
Chapter 29 TOO LATE 228
Chapter 30 FAVOUR 233
Chapter 31 URGENT GLOBAL BROADCAST 247
Chapter 32 THE UNEXPECTED GUEST 255
EPILOGUE 260
MESSAGE TO THE READER, ACKNOWLEDGEMENT 265

For the new generation of humans.

We are sorry for everything we have done.

PROLOGUE

*Stereotypes are dead,
challenge your perception.*

Do you ever wake up in the morning and feel like your whole life is not exactly right? Not as expected? Not 'normal' somehow?

I do.

Most often, it happens as a natural consequence after a chain of unsettling events. Sometimes it perseveres and makes me question my choices. And in my happy moments, I feel ashamed of feeling so low. As if the life I am living is just a mere reflection of what I should have become. It just doesn't feel right, doesn't feel mine. Do you feel like this? Have you ever?

And I've always thought of myself as having been a happy child. So then, what happened to me? Well, for a starter, my whole life turned upside-down. I have no idea when exactly it happened. I guess at some point I just raced ahead to start living, whatever I imagined it to be. I never remembered to take a moment and just breathe, adjust my direction. Kind of like a destination 'I want it all, and I want it now'. And before you realise it, you are at a different university; in a foreign country; climbing the never-ending ladder of your pointless career. But when I was a child, I did want to change the world. So how did it happen that the world changed me?

This blinding race is the new normality, you see. Look around you. I mean, *truly* take your time to look around and realise for a second that this 'weird' is here. It has become normal, your everyday state of living. Unregulated, unattainable, unpredictable, unexpected, unimaginable. But mostly, uninvited. It sucks us in without a chance for escape. Where will we end up? As individuals, as a society, as a species?

I always wondered why this strange reality was happening to me. And then I realised that it is happening to everybody. Are we all becoming the new 'normally weird' strangers? Not only to others, but also to ourselves. Do you really *know* you? Is our new world shaping us? And do we have a say in it? It is all happening so fast that I feel that we simply don't have a choice.

Progress has become the new religion. If you want to succeed in the fast-changing world, you better keep up. Run for your life! Run! If you are not prepared to put your life at the altar of progress, you will be left behind. But behind is not an option. Behind is where all the failures lie. Behind is where people with no future remain, neatly packaged and labelled 'disadvantageous'.

But where are we running to? What is that magical destination we all have been promised? What happens when we reach it? And when we do, what price will we have paid for it?

But you don't have time for asking questions, do you? You need to reach that destination quicker than anyone else. Because *you* are definitely not a failure. You need to run faster. You are born to win!

And then you have children... I think I am just desperately trying to explain things to myself, in order to find the higher purpose; to understand the reason for the change in our little ones. Did *this* reality make them the way they are? Or is it them? Or most terrifying of all, is it *us* shaping their reality?

When you look at a child who doesn't speak, or one who struggles to express emotions, what do you see? A glitch in the perfect normality of our society? A disability that is raining on our parade? A dysfunction that doesn't fit with our typical understanding of human achievement? What do *you* see? Who are these human aliens? They are so different.

Our children. Have you ever noticed how weird they are?

My life has become rather unsettling. I finally stopped for a moment; I looked around, and I got terrified of what I saw. I wanted to adjust. I wanted to figure out my new reality. It has been happening for a while now, slowly causing me to lose my sleep. Searching for philosophical answers has become my new obsession. And through it all, I find myself amazed at how 'normal' my 'weird' existence has begun to feel. But I cannot fit my life into the box anymore, and maybe it is time to stop trying to.

It makes me wonder if this change is here to stay and what it could mean for humanity. And *if the tables are turned*, could it change for the better? You see, I have hope. Do you? And what do you hope for, honestly? For the weird to become normal? Or for the normal to become weird? Does it really matter? Do you ever hope that they could meet in the middle, and both be okay with each other?

Our weird children. Have you ever noticed how normal they are!

I hope they will be better than us.

Chapter One
RESULTS

People fear change. They are much more comfortable in their 'perception bubble', where they 'know' what's right and wrong, good and bad, normal and weird. Change threatens order, obliterates equilibrium, and destroys systems of long-formed beliefs. But once new information is uncovered, it is impossible to pretend it doesn't exist. The newfound truth has to be revealed.

Professor Daniel Stein's imagination was running wild, encouraged by a personal desire to challenge social dogmas. He couldn't wait to find out if the results would confirm his findings. This moment in time had the potential to be monumental; placing humanity on the verge of a radical redesign. A tiny glimpse of a flickering reality perhaps destined to question everything that had previously been considered true. Sometimes, change is *inevitable*.

The late afternoon summer sun was slowly setting, peeking through the slats in the half-open window blinds, which covered the wide reception window. It gave the polished energy-generating floor the appearance of a striped design. The surveillance gadgets, conspicuously planted in the random decorative pieces incongruous with the minimalistic interior, were only there for Dr Biote's self-amusement, but Daniel couldn't escape the feeling of being watched. Everything in this self-sustained laboratory was generating something – energy or information. The twenty-second century had become obsessed with both.

Information had emerged as the new conviction, powered by an endless search for an infinite energy resource.

Daniel knew the human brain had always been programmed for certainty. His studies had shown the mind was easily persuaded to believe whatever information it had access to. It was human nature to search for an easy explanation without care for the objectivity of the data. The natural choice was always to select familiarity over the anomalies. Only the brave dared to push the boundaries of societal norms and challenge long-standing beliefs. Daniel wanted to believe he was one of the brave.

The only truth Daniel acknowledged was that nothing was ever set in stone. Anyone who had thought otherwise was wrong. The fluidity of life always brought changes to the way reality was perceived. But differences frightened people, and they were often keen to label irregularities as a malfunction, a problem, a disorder – all to make themselves feel safer. But what if these differences weren't 'malfunctions'? What if everything we had considered weird was not that weird after all? Could anyone identify anything they knew with complete certainty?

Daniel had never been good at the waiting game, and his patience was being seriously tested. He had been working on his controversial discovery for eleven years, but these last thirty minutes waiting for the results were the hardest to handle. He hoped it was the final push on his way to the finishing line. It was only the end, if the laboratory tests validated his Theory.

But what if they didn't? Daniel's hands suddenly felt clammy. The panic was rising from the bottom of his gut. 'Not now', Daniel begged his body as it tensed. He tried to relax and deepen his breathing. He had to see this one through, preferably without the drama of an overreaction. 'Come on, Dr Biote. For once, hurry up!' Daniel inwardly implored, incapable of fighting off his nervous impatience. 'Doesn't he understand the urgency of the results? It could finally make sense of... of... everything!'

Living with the Msitua F84.0 mutation wasn't always fun. The truth was that Daniel had often wondered if people were right. He didn't want to admit it, but there was evidence that Daniel was, in fact, weird. Maybe this was why he didn't have any friends. He wished he did, but people often avoided him because of his odd peculiarities – perhaps seeing them as an inconvenience.

Daniel's thoughts had never been convenient, and his research was clear proof. The discovery was undoubtedly disruptive. Self-doubt bitterly took control, creating a sudden concern. What if Daniel created it all in his head – the unexpected turn, the contentious evolution? What if Daniel somehow managed to mess this one up despite his thorough research and carefully gathered evidence?

Daniel knew that doubt was only natural and to be expected, considering the scale of his potential discovery. Any scientist with half a brain should be worried if doubt wasn't present in their theorising. Only fools could afford the luxury of absolute certitude. Doubt was a healthy sign that Daniel wasn't delusional after all. Or *was* he?

Dr Biote finally opened the mattified glassdoors to his laboratory, waved a beckoning hand, and went back inside. Daniel assumed that was an invitation to enter. He stood up, feeling a sudden rush of blood through his legs, slightly numb from all the sitting. 'Old bugger, can't he just spit it out?

Yes or no', thought Daniel, knowing that he wouldn't dare to rush Biote aloud. Afterall, Biote was doing his best in his own meticulous Msitua way. Daniel slowly followed Dr Biote through the doors to a sizeable and slightly messy room.

"Don't look to the left!" Dr Biote barked.

This instruction only made Daniel look precisely in the forbidden direction, where a hundred flasks – some half-full, some half-empty – stood on a large display.

"*Don't* look to the left!" Dr Biote repeated.

Daniel forced himself to turn away.

"So?" he asked impatiently, trying to establish eye contact with Dr Biote.

"What can I say? I have ran the test, as you instructed me. Just like you said, I used precisely one hundred IVF samples. I carefully injected seventy of them with the semen carrying the genes of various Msitua F84.0 mutations. Exactly how you asked me to."

"Good. And what happened?" Daniel couldn't wait much longer. He just wanted Biote to put him out of his misery.

"Well, I really thought you were full of shit, you know. I told you as much when you requested these tests in the first place," Biote mumbled, carelessly dragging out the precious time. "I only agreed to perform the tests because of my long-held respect for your genius of a grandfather. I am sure you understand. It was just *such* a ridiculous concept."

"Dr Biote, just tell me. Am I full of shit or not?!" Daniel couldn't keep up his patient pretence any longer.

"You see, I really didn't expect it at all..." Biote paused, and grimaced as if what he was about to say was painful to even voice. "But – I think you are onto something."

"What percentage of the samples naturally selected the Msitua gene?" Daniel blurted, feeling like he was about to burst with exasperation.

"Believe it or not, the most profound mutation has a hundred per cent selection rate," Biote said, still barely believing *what* he was actually saying. At long last, he looked directly at Daniel with an astonished look on his face, slowly stretching his downturned mouth upwards, allowing himself an uncertain smile.

Daniel stood there with a dropped jaw, incapable of saying a word. He had suspected and hoped that there was the possibility his Theory was not uncertain. However, a hundred percent outcome was an unbelievable and unexpected result.

All these years, Daniel thought that being different was equivalent to being bad. But in this perfect moment, he finally received his solace. Different was *good*. More than good. Perfect, really! Absolutely necessary. It was too much to take in! The biggest question of Daniel's existence was finally answered – Daniel knew *exactly* who he was.

"Daniel?" Dr Biote came closer, waving his hand in front of Daniel's eyes, trying to provoke a reaction. "Are you overwhelmed with joy, or are you having a heart attack too? Heart attacks run in your family after all. You better chill, you don't want to end up like your grandfather."

"Unbelievable..." Daniel mumbled dumbfoundedly, still trying to grasp the information, ignoring Biote's unkind and unfunny comment. Biote's sense of humour always bordered a very thin line of offensiveness.

"Unbelievable, yet, it is true. But... I knew it! I have always told people that they had no idea how our Msitua minds function. And they dared to call *me* crazy! Who will be laughing now?" Dr Biote bubbled on enthusiastically.

"But you said I was full of shit!"

"Well, you are. Most of the time. It was only natural for me to doubt," Dr Biote said matter-of-factly. But Daniel didn't care. He had gotten used to not paying attention to everything Biote said. "It pains me to admit it, but this time you are *right*."

This glimmer of praise coming from Dr Biote was the most profound example of flattery he had ever been capable of mastering. Daniel still stood there, not blinking, trying to digest the news.

"Are you absolutely sure?" Daniel finally asked.

"Hey! You don't have the right to doubt me. I was already the country's leading biologist before you were born. Come have a look for yourself." He dragged Daniel towards the open hologram monitor in the middle of the floating desk. The results were there in black and white – a hundred percent. "Do you even realise what this means? The 2121 year has just become a crucial turning point for humanity."

Of course, Daniel had always realised what his discovery could mean for humanity. But even having seen all the apparent proof, he couldn't escape the feeling of complete astonishment. Hoping that he was right was completely different from *knowing* that he was right. All those years wishing for a confirmation didn't involve him really having to consider all the pros and cons. Nothing of this magnitude could ever be only positive or negative, and Daniel couldn't bring himself to grasp the full scope of possible changes to the wider world. He knew there would be a lot of surprises on the way. It was so revolutionary. But also, by the looks of it, the change was unavoidable.

Daniel tried to concentrate his attention on the positives his new discovery would bring – likely innovative communication technology; a step closer to realising eternal conscious living; and without doubt, a solution for the ultimate survival of the human race. This new future was becoming a reality right before Daniel's eyes. Who would have thought that a perceived 'disadvantage' would be propelled by biological transformation to become an essential evolutionary upgrade? It truly was an unlikely paradox.

"Time for celebration!" declared Dr Biote, frantically moving towards the wall of built-in cupboards with the hidden party gems. Daniel had heard about Biote's private collection, and sampling one of his party-pills suddenly felt like a frightening proposition.

"No, thank you," Daniel didn't have any plans to stay longer than he needed. He wanted to leave, find a private space, and mull over this defining moment. "I have to go."

"Oh, Daniel. I wish you were more fun, like your grandfather," Dr Biote sighed, clearly feeling disappointed. But Daniel felt relieved. Being 'not fun' in Dr Biote's book was something to be delighted about, at least to his mind. It would be terrifying to be otherwise!

"Thank you, Dr Biote. Thank you so much!" Daniel stretched his hand, initiating a handshake and a goodbye. It wasn't a natural gesture for Daniel, but it had become a well-trained action.

"Did you disinfect your hands before you entered the lab?"

"No, no I didn't."

"No handshake then," said Biote, before turning around abruptly and going back towards his floating desk, still giddy with excitement. "Now everyone will understand! No one will have any doubt of our excellence! Wait until I am finished with my own revolutionary discovery…"

It was impossible to predict if Dr Biote was creating something truly consequential in the 'forbidden' corner of his workshop. Much of his earlier work had been proven to be obsolete or simply 'impossible'. However, Daniel couldn't deny the genius contribution of Dr Biote to the human-AI project. The project that, despite the lack of any sensible odds, brought Daniel's grandfather back to life.

Daniel slowly proceeded towards the exit, irresistibly drawn to catch another glimpse of the messy display in the left corner. Who could tell if it was a work of a genius or a madman?

"Don't look there!" shouted Biote without turning his head, sensing Daniel's curiosity.

Once outside of Biote's laboratory, Daniel felt slightly overwhelmed. His senses felt heightened. He could hear the hovering noises of cars coming from the nearby streets; the smell of sweet summer flowers overpowered his nostrils; the horizontal beams of the evening sun glaring directly at Daniel and he was momentarily blinded. It was an otherwise ordinary August evening, but something imperceptible had shifted in the world. Daniel couldn't help but pay attention to the little things around him. He scanned his surroundings for the joyous beauty of the overgrowing greenery, wildly thriving in this isolated park that no one ever visited. Daniel breathed in deeply, and inhaled as much of the newfound wisdom as he possibly could. Nature had always known the best possible outcome. It was only logical that it had to change us. For our own sake, to repair the mistakes of the past. Daniel could only hope that people would see it this way.

Daniel decided to walk home. The weather was spoiling Londoners, the oppressive heat of the summer day now changed to the cosy warmth of a blissful summer evening. Daniel's realisation was slowly settling in. After years of intense research, numerous hypotheses, unstable certainties, and enduring doubts, he had been proved right. He had just received the most verifiable of confirmations. The inevitable evolution of humankind was real. And Daniel, for the first time in his life, belonged to the winning team.

But in spite of this blissful moment of undeniable certainty, something bothered Daniel – the unambiguous balancing act. There was no gain without loss. And the costs of the upcoming changes were no doubt high.

Chapter Two
ALONE

Eleven years before the Results.

Bad news is always sudden and unexpected. It divides existence into 'before' and 'after', centring your whole life to the singular derailed reality. It slowly twists its sharp knife into your heart while the painful realisation forcefully fights against the hopeless denial – maybe there has been a mistake, the news is not true. Not true! Like a wild bird now caught in a cage, the tiny glimpse of hope violently throws itself at the edges of comprehension, without ever a chance of breaking free, until it exhausts itself and drops powerless. The bad news slowly settles, leaving you short of breath.

Daniel was fighting for survival. Desperately trying to gulp air. To breathe! His body refused to cooperate, denying oxygen any access to his shuttered lungs. His chest felt so tight that it was impossible to initiate any movement in his upper body. He just lay there, eyeballing the blankness of the perfectly flat ceiling. 'What an inconvenient moment to die,' Daniel thought.

Daniel's panic attack was triggered by the dreadful call that suddenly had woken him in the middle of the night. The caller was 'unknown'. Curiosity crept into Daniel's emerging alertness, and he muttered "Answer", fully prepared to give a hard time to whoever was on the other end. A strange flashing hologram flickered upwards, and Daniel found himself looking at a spinning A&E sign in the air. An automated message began:

NEMETRA X1369

"This message is for Mr Daniel Stein. Your name is on the emergency contact list for Dr Robert Stein. Dr Stein was brought to the Chelsea and Westminster hospital with a heart attack. He is in critical condition. If you are travelling to the hospital, please speak to the receptionist upon arrival." The line went dead. The bad news gradually felt its way to his conscious mind, bypassing the usual glimpses of despairing hope, and painfully establishing an undeniable presence. Then the panic attack had kicked in.

Still, Daniel lay unmoving. He wasn't sure what was going on nor how long he had been unconscious, his mind fighting a brutal battle somewhere far too close to the edge of existence. It was an unforgiving fight between mind and matter. Breathe! He didn't know how exactly he finally managed to let the air in, but just before he thought it was too late, his tenacious mind was victorious. The relief as he heard his raspy throat take a gasping breath.

Once Daniel gained control over his body, his thoughts could return to the chilling news. He needed to hurry before it was too late, but his attempts at movement continued to be ineffective. His body felt unfamiliar, not following instructions, and hindering Daniel's awkward attempts to dress. His immaculately folded skinny trousers felt stiff, and difficult to pull up with his weakened hands. He managed to put a T-shirt on while absent-mindedly searching for his jacket and his mobile earpiece. After what felt like an eternity of lost time, Daniel finally managed to leave the apartment, still feeling dizzy, trying not to lose his balance.

Daniel slumped into the self-driving 'pay as you go' car conveniently parked just outside the building. "Destination: Chelsea and Westminster Hospital," he said. The car display lit up, the built-in miniature camera scanning Daniel's face to identify him.

"Hello, Daniel Stein. Destination: Chelsea and Westminster Hospital is confirmed," the car started moving, smoothly navigating the various twist and turns despite its fast speed.

Daniel listened to the faint, almost undetectable, white noises emanating from the hovering vehicle, a sign it was self-charging whilst it propelled Daniel to his destination.

Daniel connected with his father through the mobile earpiece. He answered straight away.

"Robert..." it was all Daniel managed to say.

"We know. We received an automated message. On our way," said Daniel's father, trying to sound calm, but Daniel could sense the underlying worry in his tone.

"Me too."

"Daniel, he will be fine. He is *Dr Robert Stein*, for God's sake! He is the tough one."

Daniel sighed, trying not to say anything unkind. It wasn't the right time. He hated it when his father uttered pointless platitudes with no real basis. It was unthoughtful of him. If anything did happen to Robert, they wouldn't be fully prepared for it. And his father would have to live with his white lies. Daniel hung up.

The darkness and emptiness of the night felt alien, filling Daniel with a profound sense of solitude. He imagined his grandfather's face, trying to concentrate on his features, but somehow, they appeared blurry in his mind. He tried to remember Robert's eyes, slightly swollen yet hardly any wrinkles around them – Robert wasn't the smiley type. Instead, he was a perfect example of a typical F84.5 Msitua mutation. Highly intelligent, but could come across as snobbish and ungenial. Even his closest relatives didn't fully comprehend Robert's true nature, misinterpreting his abrupt answers for rudeness. True, he wasn't particularly sensitive or affectionate, but Daniel always felt an unspoken, accepting love. It was the unchangeable constant in Daniel's life.

'Please, Robert, don't leave me!' Daniel prayed, feeling uncomfortable with this emotion. Was it egotistical to think this way? Robert was in critical care, and all Daniel was worried about himself, and how he would struggle living without him. How frivolous. What would Robert say to that thought, if he knew?

The strangest thing was that Robert, out of everyone, would understand best. He always understood. Their recent conversation was clear proof that there was nothing wrong with Daniel's seeming solipsism. He was only human.

"Empathy is a selfish feeling," Robert once said, expanding on the subject of human behaviour.

"How come?" Daniel queried. He liked it when Robert gave his spin on societal constructs, questioning standards, and uncovering undeniable logic while challenging the norms. Daniel found it fascinating! Robert's thoughts would always materialise fully-formed and as stripped down to the very core – a genius simplicity of authentic truth, uncomplicated by social games and philosophical muddle.

"Empathy is an under-researched subject," Robert said abruptly, before pausing. After a minute or so, he decided to elaborate. "There are two types of empathy – emotional and cognitive. Neuro-typicals empathise in an emotional way. But we, Msitua variants, have cognitive empathy."

"What is the difference?"

"Fewer bells and whistles, really. It is a self-protective way to empathise without 'mirroring' it onto yourself. If some of us don't show empathy how society expects us to show it, it doesn't mean we don't have it." Robert lowered his voice, outlining his point, "On the other hand, emotional empathy is directly dependent on the mirror neurons in our brain, which are based in the premotor cortex, the supplementary motor area, the primary somatosensory cortex and the inferior parietal cortex – the HARs. These are the main regions affected by the Msitua mutation."

"But why do you say that empathy is a selfish feeling?" Daniel asked, still confused. "Out of all human feelings, empathy is surely the *least* selfish one."

"Think again, my boy," Robert answered. If anyone else had asked him this question, he would probably have shown them the door and declared their ignorance. But Daniel could get away with any question, however illogical it seemed to Robert.

"I am thinking hard about it, and I still don't get it."

"Empathy is a 'mirror effect' in humans, directing our thoughts and feelings to ourselves. This is why people are more empathetic towards people with the same problems. Now tell me, if you 'mirror' the pain onto yourself, who do you actually feel sorry for when you empathise?" Robert went quiet, giving Daniel space for the information to sink in.

"So, is cognitive empathy a more genuine way to empathise? Or is it just your excuse?" Daniel asked, sarcastically. He learnt sarcasm from Robert, so he felt entitled to use it on him.

"It could be. I *told* you, it is under-researched. Msitua people may not often openly show it, but *believe me*, you can be absolutely sure that they *mean* it when they do."

The sedative distraction Daniel experienced through accessing this memory was interrupted by the car's sudden announcement, which bellowed in the silence of the night.

"Daniel Stein, you arrived at your destination." The roads were empty, and so the journey had only taken fifteen minutes. Daniel asked for the door to open and he exited. The vehicle slowly closed the door behind him and initiated its self-parking sequence.

Daniel chose the nearest of the hospital's A&E pod entrances and as he approached, the automated glass panels opened wide. Once inside the pod, Daniel underwent a thorough care hub inspection where his vital data was streamed to the hospital mainframe. After a precautionary infection scan and the application of the bacteria resistant sterilising light, he was allowed entry. The AI receptionist was just a few steps away.

"I am visiting Dr Robert Stein, he was admitted recently with a heart attack," Daniel mumbled at the receptionist. The receptionist's robotic eyes tried to detect his features and scanned Daniel's face. It took a few seconds to find the relevant information.

"Hello, Daniel Stein. Dr Robert Stein is currently in the intensive care unit. You may proceed to the waiting pod. Go to Gate 8, down through the corridor, until you reach the door marked E2 on your right. The Doctor will come and see you shortly." The robotic receptionist's screen-like chest lit up to show a map of an uncomplicated path towards his destination – the waiting pod E2.

Daniel rushed through the corridor. When he entered through the door, he saw his parents. It seemed like they had also recently arrived. His mother hurried to hold him. Usually, Daniel would pull away, not comfortable with hugs, but today his body sunk into her arms, craving the warmth of her embrace.

"How are you?" Daniel's father asked, as he came closer, putting his hand on Daniel's shoulder, squeezing it lightly. A simple calming gesture that always worked for Daniel. Daniel looked at his father: he seemed calm, but it was a 'trying too hard' sort of calm, and Daniel could sense that he was genuinely scared.

"I don't know... How can this be? When did it happen? I just saw him this morning. He was fine."

"Very unexpected. A rapidly progressive heart attack," his mother answered in a shaky voice.

"Then what is the point of him having the health microchip?! Couldn't it recognise the problem beforehand?" Daniel exclaimed.

A couple of years back, after some encouragement, Daniel's grandfather had allowed doctors to equip him with this digital implant. At first, he didn't like the idea of the microchip being implanted into his wrist. "If I haven't created it, then I don't know what's in it" Robert had argued. However, it was a modern necessity the whole world had eventually come to terms with, and accordingly so had Robert. It monitored his health by picking up real-time signals of his heart rate, stress levels, cholesterol, and other key health indicators.

"I assume that the wrist microchip informed the ambulance. They arrived fast. Otherwise, we would have lost him," Daniel's father answered.

"Not fast enough," mumbled Daniel, feeling angry at how powerless the technology was, once confronted with a real disaster.

A gentle knock on the door disturbed their conversation, and a Doctor came in. She was wearing a traditional white robe and a protective digital mask over her face. The mask was completely invisible, and only a thin band across her forehead, and the tiny blue lights near her temples indicated its presence. It ensured only purified air surrounded the Doctor's face by creating a safe micro-system.

"I am Doctor Smolinsky," she said in a calm, firm voice, not allowing her gaze to settle on anyone in particular. Daniel and his parents just stood there in silence, afraid to ask the question, a pleading look in their eyes. Dr Smolinsky knew too well what the unspoken question was. "He is unconscious. We performed an operation. It went well. The next twenty-four hours will be crucial. You will be able to see him in thirty minutes, but he will remain under protective light. The air around him is purified and heavily oxygenated. You should resist touching him or standing too close. We need to ensure a sterilised environment after the operation."

"Thank you, Doctor," said Daniel's mother.

"Sure," the Doctor replied in the same emotionless tone. "A member of staff will direct you to his pod once we have safely moved him."

The Doctor nodded and left. Daniel felt uneasy. Every doctor Daniel had ever met was frugal with the two most desirable things – information and emotion. Maybe Robert was right. If doctors had too much emotional empathy, perhaps they wouldn't be able to cope with their job. Daniel wished Dr Smolinsky had said something more reassuring. But was she allowed to say more than she had? Was it even the right thing to encourage hope? Hope could be dangerous.

Now all they had to do was wait. And now, Daniel's whole existence narrowed down to exactly that – waiting. The daunting experience of keeping sane through the painfully slow and overwhelming minutes that ticked by, not knowing what the outcome would be. The dangerous balancing act on the thin line between life and death.

Daniel sat in the chair and closed his eyes. He had to do something, anything that was not fixating on the probabilities of what might happen. He thought of Robert, his strong, unapologetic spirit. He just wasn't the type to die.

Daniel's mind returned to their conversation about empathy, which was seemingly more and more relevant by the second.

"Just answer a simple question for me," Robert said. He wanted Daniel to understand the harsh reality of the human psyche, cleverly hidden behind the veil of socially exaggerated pretence. "Why do we cry at funerals, even at funerals of people we don't happen to know or care about?"

At first, Daniel was relieved at what appeared to be a simple question. But it came from Robert, so it would not be as simple as it seemed. Daniel knew he should reconsider. There had to be a single, logical, elegant answer. Daniel had to dig deep.

He took some time searching for an epiphany – waiting for it to click like a puzzle. All the usual answers were springing up in his head, and he was dismissing them just as quickly:' Because people feel sad for a life lost'; 'Because they empathise with the relatives left behind'; and so on. But none of these answers felt true. If we never knew the deceased person or their relatives, why do we care? And suddenly it came to him.

"We cry at funerals because we are faced with our own mortality," Daniel answered, feeling cold chills all over his body.

"It takes guts to answer this question. Bravo!" Robert made a clapping gesture. "This is why you are my favourite. You shy away from pretence. It may come as a shock to many, but what we consider empathy is merely self-pity."

"But if true empathy does not exist, who are we without it?"

"Interesting question, but a primitive answer, I am afraid. We are all animals driven by the most basic instinct of survival. Our empathy only exists when our own tummies are full. Add the cravings of our body: hunger, fear, stress, or pain, to any sophisticated human being, and see if they can empathise in the moment of distress."

"That's depressing," Daniel said with a sigh. Even if Robert was right at some psychological level, it was hard to agree with him. And it was delusional to disagree with either. "Is there a chance for us to become more than that?"

"I have one hypothetical supposition," Robert began, pleased to sense Daniel's eagerness to hear his idea, "if we can leave our fears and cravings of the bodies behind, we could probably achieve a higher intellect. Maybe one day."

"You seem very aware of the human psyche, even though you always say you struggle to understand emotions," Daniel concluded.

"I spent my whole life asking questions about myself; searching for answers to why I am the way I am. You can't understand it. You are a new generation, born in the new era. You feel comfortable being who you are because you have comfortable conditions to be who you are."

"But I still feel..." Daniel paused, unable to find the right word.

"Lost?" Robert said, coming to his rescue.

"Lost," echoed Daniel.

Back in the present moment, Daniel felt completely lost. Robert, his grandfather, the only person who truly understood him, who supported Daniel's interests and promoted his ambitions, who always led the way with the unapologetic intensity of his human spirit, was now in a critical condition. What if he died? The fear of never having a conversation with Robert again startled Daniel, and his body began to shudder uncontrollably.

Daniel's anxiety was kicking in again, rising through his chest, choking his throat. The last thought his mind formed before he passed out was of the terrifying prospect of Robert's funeral. Daniel realised that he would cry at this funeral. And not because he would be facing his own mortality – young souls are great at denying their impermanence. No. For Daniel, tears would come for a different reason. Still a very selfish reason, still inevitably a human reason.

Daniel would cry because he would feel *alone*.

Chapter Three
THE UNEXPECTED TURN IN HUMAN EVOLUTION.
GLOBAL BROADCAST – PART 1

"Is human progress a movement *forward*? How do we identify the direction of the progressive movement? On the scale of space without a point of reference, any direction is doomed to be questionable. If we *are* progressing, what course are we to take to ensure the right destination? What are the 'correct coordinates'?" Professor Daniel Stein was rehearsing his speech in between nervously uttering voice commands to his instantly broadcasting mega-HD camera. The camera was positioned in the middle of his living room, lens focused on the perfectly smooth wall. But the projected background appeared far from perfect. The gloomy grey colour coming to view was disturbed by shadows. Daniel opted for a modified background setting for his broadcast. He decided to choose the simplest option as he couldn't stand anything finicky. Just plain white – clean and uncomplicated – that suited him perfectly.

Daniel methodically checked through the settings on the camera to make sure they were working as they should. He had already checked them five times, but couldn't help himself. The camera screen showed 14.50, and the ten-minute countdown began. The date was 16th August, 2121, and Daniel made a mental note to remember this day forever. His presentation was about to begin.

As the 'Head of the Global History Department' of The World Open Digital University, which was headquartered in London, it was part of Daniel's duties to broadcast his research for the wider scientific community as well as the general public. His presentation skills had oddly always been superior to his day-to-day communication. It was the casual conversations and small talks he mostly struggled with due to his condition. Luckily, as Daniel's job was mostly delivering monologues, he was much more comfortable with them. After many speech development courses taken at the beginning of his career, he had even become talented at delivering the data-focused, clear and logical messages he needed to.

To reclaim a semblance of calmness before his presentation, Daniel decided to bow to an illogical sentimental weakness and switched on a festive hologram. One push of a button produced a beautiful and perfectly decorated Christmas tree with snowflakes slowly floating down and landing on the branches. The vision created a quiet calmness within Daniel and the butterflies in his belly ceased. The Christmas hologram always enchanted Daniel. No worries existed for him when it snowed, and he fondly remembered those family Christmas mornings when everyone was at home, no one needed to rush anywhere, and the anticipation of a great gift that had been just one sleep away.

It was slightly unorthodox to use the Christmas hologram to soothe one's nerves, but it was effective for Daniel. The neurons in his brain fired up exactly where they were needed, creating a feeling of serenity – relaxing his body and mind just to the right level, allowing him to cope with the pressure before the broadcast. And who cared that it was the middle of August?

Finally, after years of research, Daniel could present his findings and previously contentious facts to the world.

The Theory of Human Evolution had always been somewhat controversial, thanks to Darwin. And Daniel knew that his addition would not disappoint either. Everyone would come to understand why our evolutionary development was inevitable. The world would realise that these changes, which were once considered disadvantageous, were, in fact, an advancement. The data Daniel had gathered during his detailed research of the social, biological and modern technological progress was undeniable. And for Daniel, it was also beautifully simple, logical and, most importantly, finally proven.

The broadcasting light flashed ten times before it went solid red. Daniel breathed in deeply. This is it! The world will never be the same again.

***

"Good afternoon,

I'm Professor Daniel Stein from The World Open Digital University. Thank you for joining me.

The title of my press conference today is 'The Unexpected Turn in Human Evolution'. In this talk, I am going to present to you groundbreaking research that is set to revolutionise the future of human progress. It is a complicated subject, but I will explain my Theory, data research and clinical observations in a step-by-step fashion to illustrate how it led me to this discovery. It took me eleven years to arrive here, but I will be concise. It should take about one hour to explain.

For those not familiar with my research, I previously dedicated my career to historical data. My professional work was mostly about the objectivity of world history, with investigations into misleading information. My research focused on how the human story could be re-written from a global point of view and reframed more objectively.

My most recent works include: 'Psychology of Historical Leaders', 'Factual War Winners and Associated Beneficiaries', and 'The Importance of Telepathic Communication in the Twenty-second Century'. I also served on the decision board for many well-known Civil Missions such as 'The Biodegradable Plastic Regulation', 'The One Child Legislation', and the 'Amygdala Nano-chip Alternative to Chemical Stimulants', to name just a few.

But today, I am here in a different capacity. This broadcast is about a monumental discovery. A discovery that is crucial for the development and survival of the human race.

I am pleased to announce that the live viewing figures suggest we have over three billion people joining the live broadcast. This number is increasing as I speak. Before I continue, I am legally required to confirm my compliance with the data sharing rules and regulations.

I do have a license to broadcast at a mass scale, and you will see my registration number in the left bottom corner of the screen. This press conference is transmitted via a global news platform and via Tele-paths through global MM2-Megamind. Access to the telepathic broadcast is restricted to the current thinking process and verbal articulation only.

Now we can begin proper.

What do we consider the predominant human quality that distinguishes us from all other species on the planet? The answer, of course, is our superior ability to communicate with each other.

Our evolution fortunately supported the development of Human Accelerated Regions, or HARs, within our brain. The HARs were a necessity in the hunter-gatherers' communities for cooperation. Most importantly, the development of language was essential for our survival.

However, not all of our HARs are developed to the same level. Those with the Msitua F84.0 genetic mutation have differently developed HARs to that of the neuro-typical population. In the last century, F84.0 genetic differences were considered a dysfunction, an abnormal mutation of HARs. A failure of evolution that no one could do anything about. A really strange failure, right? We found a cure for cancer and HIV, but we couldn't find one for Msitua condition. Not only that, but the numbers of those affected by F84.0 mutation began rising rapidly.

As you all know, almost fifty percent of the population has a Msitua F84.0 mutation of a varying degree. And there are many complications we are all aware of. I know them myself firsthand. The anxiety, the intensity, the obsessions, the social issues. And all this is on top of the significant problems with verbal skills, processing information and, in some severe cases, even an inability to make sense of the world. Fifty percent of you know exactly what I mean. There is no surprise that such a difference in human abilities frightens us. The amount of Msitua children being born increases year upon year. Have you ever wondered how a disability could increase at such a level? F84.0 is not a pandemic, but like a pandemic, it is multiplying fast. A hundred years ago, statistics showed it only affected one in sixteen children. So how did this increase to fifty percent of the human population?

I believe our new ways of communication are the main catalysts of this change. The race for faster ways to connect began at the end of the twentieth century. It introduced a whole new level of engagement methods and knowledge sharing. As a result, face-to-face verbal interaction steadily declined, and nowadays is no longer the necessity it used to be.

We began building networks online in a matter of minutes and spreading our thoughts across the globe in an instant. It started with us communicating worldwide, which removed the need to travel, and led to us working and learning from home. We established progressive, more efficient ways to absorb knowledge – educational visual and gaming facilities, virtual realities and practical camps. We created non-physical experiences that could be accessed sitting on our sofas. We came up with new ideas, and developed significant scientific discoveries from the comfort of our own space. It felt comfortable, easy, progressive, and, most importantly, fast. *Humanity became addicted to speed.*

But we forget that evolution often causes us to move away from those characteristics that outgrow their usefulness, and new, more current biological modifications develop as our needs change. Just as we lost our body fur or the human tail three hundred and fifty million years ago, we now seem to be losing something else.

As a scientist and a historian, I am accustomed to analysing information from the present and extrapolating backwards to make sense of the human story. I don't believe in coincidences. Everything has a plan and a purpose.

Now, consider what has been missing in our daily lifestyle. What is far less common now than a century ago and in many circles hardly ever occurs?

Person to person contact. Human face-to-face social interactions. And what do Msitua people have the main issue with? Again, communication.

I will leave you with this thought for a moment..."

Chapter Four
TRANSITION

Daniel was sure he'd never be able to erase the events of that terrible night at the hospital from his memory. Hope slowly evaporated into the air in a cruel intangible motion, impossible to hold on to. He desperately waited and waited for his grandfather to wake up. Every minute felt like an eternity. Every footstep outside the waiting pod made Daniel's heart jump with two conflicting emotions – hope and fear, inextricably bound up together. As time passed and no news was forthcoming, the rollercoaster of his intense sensations eventually subsided and gave way to the dull pain of inevitable derailed reality – a reality, which Daniel had no control over. Never in his life, had he felt so powerless. If he believed there was a God, Daniel would have prayed.

Dr Biote, the brilliant biologist and Robert's best friend, had suddenly arrived without warning, mercifully disturbing Daniel's gloomy thoughts. He was wearing full-on protective gear. Germ-saturated hospitals were the last place Dr Biote would ever choose to visit, even in the most extreme circumstances. Daniel knew his father had informed Dr Biote about Robert's condition, but no one expected him to actually show up.

Prior to his arrival at the waiting pod, Dr Biote had managed to argue with three members of staff, amongst them the AI receptionist, which was an achievement on its own. One of the beauties of AI-powered staff was that they couldn't get angry or irritated. Yet somehow Dr Biote's questions and comments had resulted in an unidentified malfunction in its pre-programmed system, and the robot had to be removed for servicing.

Dr Biote also had a Msitua F84.5 condition. Like Robert, he was abrupt and stubborn. He struggled to adequately express any emotion, even now after hearing the dreadful news. It was clear to Daniel the situation was driving Dr Biote crazy. 'Did Dr Biote actually love Robert?' Daniel wondered. It was hard to tell if he could love anybody. However, what was certain was Dr Biote's undeniable respect and admiration for his friend.

As soon as he opened his mouth, it was clear that Dr Biote came prepared.

"If Robert dies, we should preserve his brain for research into human-AI technology," Dr Biote declared, looking at Daniel's father. Socially acceptable, supportive small talk wasn't part of his agenda.

"How are you planning to do that?" Daniel's father replied. He was used to Biote's way of interaction – after all, Robert was very similar. For all the quirks of F84.5 types, Daniel's family had learnt to live with them.

"By transforming it into a 3AO7 digital brain scan sample," Biote said with the confidence of someone stating something as plain and self-evident as 'the sky is blue'. Dr Biote looked around the room, sensing that his explanation didn't quite make the right impression.

"Brain scan, huh?" Daniel's father was used to controversial ideas like this one. Nothing surprised him anymore.

"Exactly! It is an advanced technology, despite the controversial technique. By converting the human brain into digital data, we can harvest and read the full scope of its neural activity. We have tested it before, and it works! Over sixty percent of tested samples had a successful outcome, where we managed to turn the brain's neuro-data into digital code," Biote continued proudly.

"Over sixty percent, you say?" Daniel's father wasn't naive. He could sense Biote's nervous excitement but there was something else too. Dr Biote was hiding something. "What was the size of your sample?"

"Ah..." Dr Biote began hesitantly. It was clear he was battling something inside, but he could never lie, even if he wanted to. Direct questions could only be answered with the truth. "Well... one."

"You only tested the brain scan technique once before?! Then what do you mean by a sixty percent success rate?"

"Well, sixty percent of the information in that one brain was recovered successfully," answered Biote, his confidence fading under inquisition. He was now twitching, looking down at the sterilising wrist bands around his hands. He started scraping his fingers, as if he had just touched something dirty, although his hands were no doubt squeaky clean. Dr Biote reflected for a minute and then continued, mumbling like a disappointed child. "Anyway, I don't need your permission. I have Robert's will. He donated his body to the scientific community. It is his decision, not yours."

Daniel suddenly felt angry. He was still weak – barely recovered after his earlier fainting episode, but he fought through his frailties, and got up, decisively marching towards Dr Biote.

"Robert is still alive. No one is getting his brain!" Daniel screamed. Everyone looked at him with surprise. Daniel was the calm one. His particular Msitua mutation generally caused him to be quiet, although still with occasional moments of anger – mostly directed at himself. It certainly wasn't like him to shout. The sudden shock of his actions seemed to work. Dr Biote retreated.

"Sorry," he said to Daniel. Mostly because he felt he had to, not because he genuinely felt sorry. "I mean, I can still do it on my own. But it would be good if you were all onboard," Biote murmured. "And do not mistake my words for insensitivity..." At this statement, everyone looked at him questioningly. "Ok, yes, I am insensitive. But only because I feel strongly about this idea. If we can preserve Robert's brain at its highest activity before the neurons start dying out, I think we can successfully transfer it into data. If his heart stops, we will need to act fast."

Daniel could feel Biote's impatient gaze penetrating through his skin.

"What would it be like? This human-AI. That is, of course, if you were to succeed with the scan," Daniel's father asked. Dr Biote's face lit up. When there was a question, there was an interest. Now they were actually considering the idea.

"Well, it will be recorded as data on an artificial intelligence platform. Robert's memories, thoughts, discoveries. Everyone is particularly interested in the telepathic technology he was working on. We can continue his research and proceed with trials. And Robert's thoughts on the subject are too important to lose."

Daniel's father went quiet. Of course, Robert's work was too important to lose. He understood that much.

"Let's talk outside," he said, gently pushing Dr Biote towards the exit. He glanced at Daniel, who was sitting in the corner, looking withdrawn. He knew that however difficult it was for Daniel to deal with the idea of Robert's death, he would understand eventually. In the meantime, they had to try everything to access Robert's discoveries – whatever form that might take.

Daniel's grandfather was one of the greatest scientists the world had ever seen. Most famously, Dr Robert Stein had invented both permanent and semi-permanent nano-chips used for stress control. This nano-technology was so advanced that Robert Stein had won the Nobel Prize for his contribution to public health. The nano-chip allowed people with a high level of anxiety, depression, or anger issues to eliminate these symptoms once and for all. It controlled the amygdala part of the brain that drove the 'flight or fight' responses. The nano-chip restricted unnecessary activity while still allowing the amygdala to function effectively as a survival tool. It was described by a Noble Prize presenter as 'A superb example of artificial balancing, one that we were never capable of mastering before'.

Daniel was one of the first teenagers to have the amygdala nano-chip installed. Before the chip, the mix of his rising anxieties and the sudden increase of hormones caused by puberty had been too much to handle. It got to a stage when he couldn't sleep at night. Daniel's worries weren't those of most teenagers. His young, but rational brain had long realised the complications this world was facing. He cared for the planet, for the creatures living on it, for the direction of human development which he saw as a road to the inevitable inferno. He didn't want to be a part of this world; he couldn't accept the terrifying scenario of the future. He was forced by his logical brain to confront this truth, rather than simply ignoring it. He had only two options – to leave this world, or to change it.

Robert was the only person who understood Daniel's dilemma. In many ways, they were similar, but in other ways they were so very different. One obvious difference was Daniel's relative cowardice – he needed encouragement to face his demons. Meanwhile, Robert was a fighter, a rebel, a revolutionary. He was never afraid to speak up. Robert quickly became a role model for Daniel. His unapologetic commitment to science and fiery personality lit up Daniel's flame, guiding his choices. Daniel chose to live, make a difference, and fight the crumbling system on behalf of all living things. But to take up the fight, first he needed to stabilise his mind. The nano-chip was the solution.

Much later, when Daniel became an adult, he decided to remove the amygdala nano-chip. By this time, he felt more in control of his emotions, and most of all, his surroundings. He had grown very comfortable with his solitary existence, set on dedicating his life to education, scientific and historical research.

As well as the nano-chip, Dr Robert Stein's legacy included pioneering work in the highly advanced telepathic technology, came to be known as Tele-paths. As part of this work Robert developed the Neuro Frequency Theory. This Theory claimed that it was possible to tune in to microwave activity in a human brain. He posited that by connecting this microwave frequency to an advanced data cloud (which he called the Megamind) a new communication channel could potentially be created. A communication channel that wouldn't need spoken word or written data. Instead, it could come from the source itself – a human thought.

But nobody would have predicted that Robert would not make it to the trials of his groundbreaking, revolutionary discovery.

In the end, Robert's heart gave up on him more or less exactly twenty-four hours after the failed operation that was meant to save him. The famous Dr Robert Stein passed away without regaining consciousness. Even with all the health monitoring technologies, heartrate measuring devices, life-prolonging drugs, and progressive medical practices, Robert's life could not be saved. It all ended suddenly at sixty-eight, comparatively a very young age for someone born into the twenty-second century.

When he heard the news, Daniel just stood there, finding it difficult to comprehend. For a second, he couldn't believe what he was hearing. There were doctors running around, people talking somewhere in the hall, early morning birds singing outside the window. The world was still turning. On the edge of Daniel's hearing he could even pick up the steady sound of a patient's heart support machine in the adjacent room. *Beep. Beep. Beep.* It didn't seem like anything had changed at all. 'How could life go on without Robert?' Daniel thought to himself. He wasn't panicking anymore, no fear of fainting, in fact he was breathing calmly. Now there was nothing else he was afraid to lose.

Daniel's grand-uncle Albert arrived at the hospital just after Robert's death was announced. He looked so much older than how Daniel remembered him. It seemed like there was nothing left of this usually fierce and cheerful person, just the shape of a lost elderly man. He had flown across the world as quickly as he could manage, but he still didn't make it in time to see his brother alive. Albert also didn't approve of Dr Biote's plans to use the brain scan technology, but his sentimental arguments didn't hold under the scrutiny of science. Daniel's father still signed the papers, persuaded by the importance of Robert's research and Dr Biote's efforts.

Robert dedicated his existence to technological advancement. In the end, although technology couldn't save his body, it could save his brain!

Dr Biote's team acted fast. Their swift actions allowed a hundred percent preservation of Robert's brain thanks to the relatively recent activity of his neurons. A hundred percent was an unbelievable result, surpassing all expectations. The fact that Robert's brain was equipped with the F84.5 gene meant that it actually presented conveniently structured patterns that were relatively easy to decrypt. Before long it was converted into a highly accurate digital program and was considered the first real human-AI, a genuine mix of biological and intellectual data transformed into codes.

After reviewing the brain scan results, Dr Biote was pleased – excited even. F84.5 variants could never hide their true feelings, however inappropriate. At the funeral, Biote approached Daniel and with delight whispered into Daniel's ear

"Robert is not dead."

A lost and empty Daniel didn't find much comfort in his comment.

Chapter Five
THE UNEXPECTED TURN IN HUMAN EVOLUTION.
GLOBAL BROADCAST – PART 2

The hardest part was over. It was always difficult to begin, but once Daniel gathered momentum, his speech flowed effortlessly. Daniel's heart was still pounding loudly, but now it beat in unison with his words as if driving him onward.

Even though online presentations had an immediate feedback option, Daniel had decided not to turn it on – this meant he was unable to read his audience, and he could not predict how they were reacting to the broadcast. Nowadays, it was common practice to use technology that could easily read visual sensory indicators through a body language deciphering device built into every screen. The data this provided could be analysed and provide the presenter with frighteningly accurate statistics that allowed zero flattery nor subjectivity – it was immediately apparent whether the audience was giving a virtual thumbs up or down. Daniel hadn't selected the option as he didn't consider it an advantage. Daniel couldn't afford even a hint of panic or distraction, so to his mind's ignorance was bliss – he did not want any negativity to flood in. This broadcast was too important, too revolutionary. He had to ensure his message was clear and logical. Regardless of the response, he knew that he was presenting undeniable facts about the evolution of the human race.

Daniel looked at the hologram of the Christmas tree still turned on in the corner of his living room. He was thankful that this silly affectation was keeping this serious professor serene for his broadcast. And no one would ever need to know.

***

"In order to understand our current communication practices and the bigger picture, it is important to revisit life as it was a few hundred million years ago. We all know that in F84.0 individuals, HARs are less developed. So the question we need to ask is 'Why?' We need to understand why verbal communication is different for F84.0 variants than for neuro-typicals.

Today, humanity lives in strong collaboration with technology. This mutual synergy increases every day, mostly impacting the fields of communication and the processing of information. It is a dramatic and speedy development. If we consider the entire lifespan of our planet – billions of years – the progress we are witnessing now is comparatively happening at the speed of light. What does it mean to adapt to such rapid change? What does it take for our bodies, and most importantly, for our brains, to adjust?

The Msitua variant has been in existence for a long time. Just like HARs, the Msitua gene has been proven to have played a vital role in the survival of our species.

Firstly, it has allowed humans to migrate across the globe, travelling vast distances as solitary foragers searching for their next meal. They had to be able to endure long and lonely journeys, live in the wild, and survive the harshest conditions. It was a necessity to adapt in order to propagate. The F84.0 variant, I believe, provided this impetus.

Secondly, the systematic way of thinking that the F84.0 variant is known for can be seen as clearly beneficial for ship-building and forging hunters' tools. It made sense for an F84.0 mutation to develop and gain an advantage over HARs during rapid development cycles in human history.

And now, in the present day, we again see a strong propensity of the F84.0 mutation with a new intensity. Could there, in fact, be a new evolutionary reason for Msitua to resurge and continue to thrive?

I am a Msitua variant. Every scientist I know and work with also has an F84.0 condition. And for the first time in human history, science can be said to be truly working in unison with the Global United Government and world leaders to advance common goals for the benefit of humanity. We managed to reverse the process of the major ecological crises occurring worldwide; we developed healthy alternatives to traditional food to increase the global supply; we created vehicles safe for the planet; we contained the nuclear threat; we enforced anti-war compliance measures; we introduced the population control legislation. In short, we are in a much, *much* better place now than we were a hundred years ago. Would it surprise you to know that the Msitua population contributed significantly to all these positive changes?

There were, and are, many theories about F84.0 being more an unusual genetic quirk rather than being seen as a 'curse', despite the social and verbal complications it causes within those who have it. But these theories have never proved their pro-Msitua claims in any real practical sense. They also failed to explain why F84.0 could be so disabling, at least in some cases.

What if I could?

Have you ever wondered why madness and genius often co-exist together? The universal Theory of Balance tells us we are all bound to comply with the laws of physics. What if this applied to our minds as well? When the natural balance is interrupted due to a lower functioning of some regions in the brain, surely it follows that an equal advantage should be created somewhere else to balance out this disadvantage.

I have studied Msitua students working with Personal Initiative Programmes of alternative education, PIPs for short, and results have suggested something astonishing. In most cases, students with an F84.0 condition exhibit a higher level of systematic intellect and a remarkable ability to research and analyse data. Their definitive mind also drives a determined attitude; an ability to think 'outside of the box'; a more responsible approach to life; a clearer logic; and my favourite – brutal honesty. The majority of F84.0 variants find it impossible to lie. Maybe this is why the world we now live in is superior to that of the past – many of our politicians have Msitua mutation.

This brings me to one of the paradoxes of the mutation. Namely: Why do F84.0 traits vary so vastly, and why, in some severe cases, does this mutation actually appear to diminish the intelligence of the affected mind?

According to my research, there is a biological effect caused by an overselected gene. In some cases, F84.0 gene variants tend to multiply in the next generation, producing more severe mutations in the children born to Mitsua parents, further affecting the HARs regions.

Our research shows that often the overselection occurs in families where both mother and father have an F84.0 gene of a mild degree, and where both may exhibit a high level of intellect, systematic brain function and impressive organisational abilities. These are noteworthy findings.

These conclusions led to us asking the critical question in our thesis: 'What if the gene is *supposed* to be overselected?' If there are severe dysfunctions, or disadvantages, in the HARs regions, could it be possible that there are severe advantages in other areas of the brain? What if I told you that we could finally find out?

Our advanced telepathic technology creates new opportunities for human interaction. Our research of severe Msitua traits has led our Tele-paths Team to a crucial observation. Some Msitua samples were highly compatible with this telepathic technology – not only could they read the thoughts of another person when using Tele-paths, but they could also share feelings, senses, and even images! Those who demonstrated this compatibility were mostly F84.0 representatives with severely underdeveloped HARs, initially incapable of even speaking. Meanwhile, on the other end of this compatibility scale, neuro-typical participants were unfortunately *absolutely incompatible* with telepathic technology and couldn't use it at all.

Dr Robert Stein's original work on telepathy suggests that Msitua neuron activity dramatically differs from the neuro-typical. To put it simply, F84.0's neuro-frequency is easier to decrypt because Msitua people tend to think in logical patterns, similar to computer programmes or coding techniques. And now we finally have the appropriate equipment to read this previously 'encrypted' data.

I would even go so far as to speculate that the Msitua brain didn't evolve to be used for verbal exchange – it is clearly 'pre-designed' for telepathic communication!

And now, let me explain how there is an irrefutable and vital connection between Msitua, telepathy, and the survival of the human race?"

Chapter Six
ROBERT'S TRUTH – TURMOIL

Time stood still. This new dimension was dark and vast. Endless. The emptiness of this space was profound and hollow. The infinity was incontestable – a statement of fact that could not be explained.

It was the most unusual place that any human could ever envisage. Finding himself here, without knowing how it had come to pass, you would have expected Robert to be freaking out. But in this dimension, there was no fear. None of the usual human emotions were present. Perhaps because there was nothing to question, nothing to analyse, nothing to comprehend. A completely blank space where no new thoughts could come into being. Only memories. Detailed and vivid memories, impossible to escape, replaying endlessly like a movie on a continuous loop. The long-forgotten yet familiar picture imposed no judgement, no sentiment, and no opportunity to rewrite the script. All you could do was to be aware of the story.

Limitless time and endless memories. What do you do with it? You watch.

5

I am *five* years old. I am small. I know I am small because everyone around me is big. I prefer to hang around with the big people. Not with the small people who constantly make things up. It is irritating. Don't they know that they sound stupid when they talk about nonsense like raining sweets or storming magic castles? Adults are not always consistent, but at least they make more sense. Well, almost all of them.

My mother doesn't always make sense, she can act silly sometimes.

"What would you like Santa to bring you for Christmas?" she asks, looking at me with a big smile. Either no one has told her, or she pretends not to know. Either way, it is stupid.

"Mum, Santa is not real. He is a myth," I say in a calm voice, biting down on a banana. I like bananas. Lately, it is all I want to eat. She seems confused. So I explain it again, very clearly. "No one could travel around the world in one night, bringing presents to every child." At this logical statement, she should have just accepted sense and stopped, but instead, she tries to insist on the lie. Doesn't she know me at all? I don't like being misled.

"But Robert, what if Santa *is* real? What if he is watching you right now. He would be upset that you don't believe in him," she says, looking into my eyes intensely. I feel uncomfortable. I want to look away.

"He cannot be upset if he is not real. And stop saying that he exists, I don't like it!" I snap, suddenly feeling frustrated. Can't she just tell the truth? I know my parents buy the presents. It had taken me many months to figure it out. My life would have been much easier if they had just told me.

"But Robert, don't you wish just a little for Santa to be real? It is fun to pretend sometimes..." she really doesn't get it. How can a lie be fun? She has said many times before that she hates lies. She keeps confusing me!

My mind feels cloudy. I forget what I wanted to say. I get angry. I tell her things. I want to push her away. I don't want to be confused again. It was hard enough last Christmas.

"Go away!" I scream.

My mum looks sad. I hope she is not going to start crying again. I hate it when she does. Somehow, whenever she cries, it is always my fault.

6

I am in a vast place at my school. Here is my teacher. She has an unusual name. She talks a lot. But all I can see when she speaks is her sharp eyeliner moving up and down when she blinks. And when she comes closer, it feels like she shouts in my face. I want to go home.

The teacher asks me to cut a shape out of a piece of paper. I pick up the scissors. My fingers feel stiff, they slip. I try to concentrate, but my hands feel heavy – like they are not mine. I try to cut this way, but it goes the other way. Luckily, before long, the teacher leaves me alone. I stop cutting.

I look around the room, and everyone else is cutting shapes too. Other kids' efforts look good. Mine doesn't.

Something is wrong. Suddenly I feel a heavy feeling in my chest. The first painful realisation that I am not good enough. It hurts.

There are two boys, pointing their fingers at me. What do they want, I wonder? Then the truth hits me like a dagger in my heart. They are pointing at me and laughing. They have realised how weird I am.

The noise of twenty-nine scissors cutting paper echoes in my head, clouding my mind. My vision gets blurry, my body feels limp, and the whole world around me seems to morph into a giant bouncy castle. I can't think straight. I want to leave, go to the library and hide, but even my sense of direction is gone. I feel helpless.

The teacher comes over, asking questions, but I can't understand. The words don't reach me, however hard I try to listen. Someone is holding my hand tight. I try to pull away, but I can't. I hear a scream, and more people gather around me, like human walls narrowing my space. It feels like an angry giant is trying to come out of my body, pulling my hands and legs in different directions, trying to break free.

I am not sure what happens after…

7

I am standing outside of the headmaster's office again. My heart is pounding. My mother is inside. The door is slightly ajar, and I can hear their conversation. I am surprisingly alert, picking up on every word they say.

"I am sorry, but…" Mr Wallis speaks slowly, choosing his words very carefully, "… because of your son's condition and associated behavioural challenges, we have to consider a transfer."

"Yes, he is different. But have you ever had a meaningful conversation with my son? Has anyone tried to simply listen to his version of the story? If only you would try, you would understand that his actions are like ours, just exaggerated. He struggles socially, but he is a good kid. And he is bright. He is interested in the most amazing things, he always asks very good questions."

"His analytical abilities may be impressive, but I would like to see more empathy towards other people."

"I get it – it may be confusing when you don't understand. Robert *does* have empathy, but sometimes he struggles to express it. Most of the time, he just reflects our intentions towards him. Does that make sense?" My mother breathes heavily, then continues, "I know it may be too much to ask from you, and it is especially hard for other children to understand. But if they only could be more considerate of Robert. If people only could give him a chance, they would see how interesting, loyal and honest he is. Surely these are qualities you want for your school?"

"They are fine qualities. But Robert needs more support than we can offer. Have you ever considered a special school?"

"No, I want him to stay in mainstream. I know, it is easier for people to ignore or isolate a child like Robert from their 'perfect world'. Easy to judge and to complain. Because you really need *to make an effort* to understand him. But you can't argue that kids benefit from learning the right way to communicate with *different* people." Mr Wallis is unusually quiet, allowing her this emotional outburst. "I understand, it could be... difficult with Robert. And the school is underfunded and understaffed. But please, work with us," she continues. "It is not a matter of just one child or just one family. It is an important decision for our collective perception," she pauses again and breathes deeply. "We can't do it alone. We need people to give us a chance. And you can choose to turn away from the problem and pretend that it doesn't exist if it doesn't concern you. Or... you can have the guts to start the uncomfortable conversation." She pauses for a second, searching for the right words. "Life is full of complications. And maybe it could be a good thing if children can learn to be compassionate enough, patient enough, understanding enough towards others who might not be the same. Perhaps the irony might be that Robert could be the child to teach them kindness."

My mum has a tendency to talk too much. I try to figure out every sentence she says. She thinks I can teach children kindness. How? I don't get that part.

"I did want to make a positive change when I began teaching... This is it, isn't it?" Mr Wallis says mysteriously.

"I think so," says my mother.

On the way home from school, my mother and I walk in silence. I know she is upset. The wrinkle on her forehead is visible, but it is not in the 'lightning bolt' shape it gets when she is angry. Today it looks more like a fold of concern.

"Mum, am I weird?" I decide to finally ask. This has been playing on my mind all day.

"I will tell you the truth," she says decisively, "Yes, you are. And it is a rather wonderful thing!"

"How is it wonderful? They call me weird." I am worried about what others think of me.

She stops, squats down, and looks into my eyes. The eye contact feels intense, and I focus on her lips instead. They are pink. I like that lipstick she wears – it makes her eyes look greener.

"Thank them for the compliment. Weird can be good – special, unique, less ordinary," she says, carefully articulating every word. I read her lips more than I hear the words aloud. I think I get it.

Sometimes she can make me feel better. Not always. She still confuses me a lot. Today she succeeded, and I feel calmer.

I smile at her. She smiles back, but it is a sad smile. A smile I struggle to figure out. How can a smile which looks like a smile, feel like a cry?

8

I thought it would get easier to exist once I turned five. I thought the same before I turned six, then at seven, and now I am eight, and it is still not getting easier.

I am in Mr Wallis's office again. He is sitting at his desk, his eyes concentrating on the computer. His upper body is very still, but his legs jiggle under the desk. If it were my feet bouncing, my teacher would make me take a movement break.

I have a book which I was supposed to read during my detention, but I prefer to study Mr Wallis. He has a few wrinkles between his eyebrows. I bet it is from all the frowning. It makes him seem strict and bossy. But I don't think Mr Wallis is bossy. I think his demeanour is all a pretence. This was something I realised after many detentions in his office.

"Robert, why aren't you reading your book?" Mr Wallis asks me, still staring at his computer and clicking the buttons. I like the sound of clicking. It feels like a piece of music that has its own unpredictable rhythm. Like jazz. But better than jazz. Jazz is messy and makes me feel frustrated because I can't follow it. But the clicking is relaxing.

"I've read this book already," I answer.

"Did you like it?" Mr Wallis asks, multi-tasking, as he continues to click and talk at the same time. I don't know how he can do both.

"No."

"Why not?"

"The character loves his dog, but then he drowns it. It doesn't make sense."

"I believe he is trying to prove to his duchess that he loves her more than the dog," Mr Wallis explains.

"The action of killing the dog doesn't prove that he loves the duchess. It only proves that he hates the dog. But he loves the dog. His actions don't match up with his feelings. It is confusing."

"Yes, I suppose it is confusing," Mr Wallis stops clicking and looks at me. "The main character makes a mistake. Don't you ever make a mistake, but only realise the error when it is too late?"

"I suppose," I answer, trying to create a logical connection between my own mistakes and the character drowning the dog.

"Robert, why did you cause so many disturbances during today's lesson?" Mr Wallis asks me.

"My writing wasn't good. I messed it up. And then I got upset."

"Even if your writing isn't perfect, you shouldn't throw your books around the classroom."

"But you said if we do something, we need to give it our best shot. My writing wasn't my best shot. There were a lot of mistakes."

"Maybe I wasn't clear about what I meant. It is great to give it your best shot, but it is also okay to make mistakes. We learn from them and do a better job next time," he exhales. "Many mistakes can be fixed. Like writing. But there are some mistakes which cannot be fixed, like hurting someone by throwing a book, for example."

"Or killing a dog," I conclude.

"Or killing a dog," Mr Wallis sighs.

"I am sorry," I say. "If you want to punish me, you shouldn't give me detention in your office. I enjoy staying here. It is quiet. I like quiet."

"Well, thank you for being honest," Mr Wallis says, looking slightly surprised. He considers something for a second and then adds. "How about we keep that a secret between us?"

"Why?"

"Because I am here not to punish you. I am here to help you to reflect on your behaviour. And that is something that some quiet will help with, don't you think?"

"Yes, I do." If I am here to reflect on my behaviour, I can definitely use some quiet.

Mr Wallis takes out a book from his drawer.

"Why don't you read this book instead? And we can discuss it after you finish it," he says with a smile. "And Robert, remember that everyone makes mistakes sometimes."

"Even you?"

"Even me."

I pick up the book. It is heavy. I haven't read this one before. Mr Wallis goes back to his clicking and staring at the screen.

'Everyone makes mistakes'. It is impossible to imagine Mr Wallis making a mistake like throwing books around the room. But it makes me feel a little better to know that my mistakes are not the end of the world. I still hate making mistakes, but at least I haven't drowned a dog.

Chapter Seven
THE UNEXPECTED TURN IN HUMAN EVOLUTION.
GLOBAL BROADCAST – PART 3

Another milestone reached. Daniel hoped that curiosity was keeping his audience on the edge of their seats. He wanted to imagine people leaning towards their screens, telepathically sending signals of tense anticipation to the MM2-Megamind, wishing to know what he was about to say next. He wondered if the wider public were as excited to hear his findings, just as he had been when he had heard the results for the first time. He hoped they could keep an open mind.

Daniel breathed in and out, mentally scanning the rest of his speech. He was satisfied; he was on point. He was ready to deliver the grand finale!

***

"Have you ever wondered if our biological progress can be trusted to deliver the correct coordinates for our future destination? The beauty of human existence is that we don't have to try too hard to upgrade ourselves. The process of natural selection is doing most of the work. All we need to do is evolve.

And what is evolution? Evolution is a genetic mutation that helps us to *adapt* to the changing environment. It is a survival mechanism adopted by nature to ensure procreation and continuity of life itself. This mutation can happen in any direction, but it is only the ones that steer us towards the best possible scenario which survive.

In order to establish the connection between Msitua changes and human evolution, we need to ask, what is essential for our species to thrive? It's the same thing as for any other living species in the universe. The wide procreation and geographical distribution of our 'seeds'. This was the instinct which pushed our ancestors to conquer the continents of our planet. And for their descendants today, what do we need to conquer *now* to ensure our survival?

Space.

Because even if we stop the ecological crises completely, and even if we vigorously control worldwide population, we can't pretend that we are not living under a dying star. Doomsday may be far ahead, but it *is* coming. That is, of course, if we are lucky to see it. Most probably, we will become extinct way before this eventuality, whether from a new virus, intense volcanic activity or a meteorite collision.

Space travel is the only option. A long shot? Perhaps. But our space technology is ready, and we have been successfully exploring nearby planets. From a technological perspective, it is a definite possibility. Of course, the distances needed to go further in space. But they are too vast to overcome in our lifetime. And even if we could live longer, much longer, we also need three adaptations to actually survive the travel – the embrace of solitude, a systematic brain, and an intensified survival instinct. The same qualities that our ancestors required to advance across the globe. The very same qualities that are shared by most people with the Msitua condition.

Now, returning to our lifespan. How do we ensure that we live longer? And if I want to be ambitious here, how do we eventually become *immortal*?

We have developed a relatively new yet already very popular project – the Megaminds, the transmitter for Telepaths, which also recently became a collective bank of AIs. But with all its potential, the AI technology is still currently limited. However, one day, AIs within Megaminds will be capable of functioning at a superbrain level. And possibly may even become conscious. I know, consciousness sounds like a fiction to you now. However, there are new progressive practices in place of transferring neural activity of the human brain into codes and creating human-AIs, a hybrid of biological and artificial data. A human-AI could bridge the gap between human-like consciousness and artificial intelligence. The single catalyst to make it possible is our most advanced modern way of communication – Tele-paths.

Dr Robert Stein, the founder of the ground-breaking research into telepathy, is the primary inspiration for my Theory. His legacy guarantees progress, which takes our communication abilities, and possibly the survival of our species, to a whole new level. Tele-paths open the doors to the prospect of enhanced communication using the neuro-data from human brain scans – the human-AIs.

The recent creation of human-AIs sets us on a potential path of living in virtual realities where our mind can continue to exist after our bodies are gone. I do believe that it is the next evolutionary step. Having to feed our bodies, deal with diseases, ageing and mortality will one day become a thing of the past.

But for this future to happen, we require two major developments: telepathic communication, and conscious human-AI technology. And the second is impossible without the first. Otherwise, we would not be capable of communicating consciously with human brain scans in the most relevant human format – a thought.

Now, what has this got to do with F84.0 mutation? And my answer to you is – everything. As we know, telepathy is only supported by specific neuro-wiring patterns common in people with the mutation. So, if we conclude that telepathy and human-AI technologies are crucial for space travel and our ultimate survival, and we also conclude that this can only

NORMAL WEIRD

be supported through the F84.0 population, then what can we conclude about Msitua?

To sum up my Theory, I will use the science of systemology to show you the Big Plan of human evolution. Systemology states that to achieve our goal, we need to start from the final goal and work our actions downwards. So, let's apply this principle and connect our steps with the ultimate goal for humanity – survival – in mind. You can now see the slide.

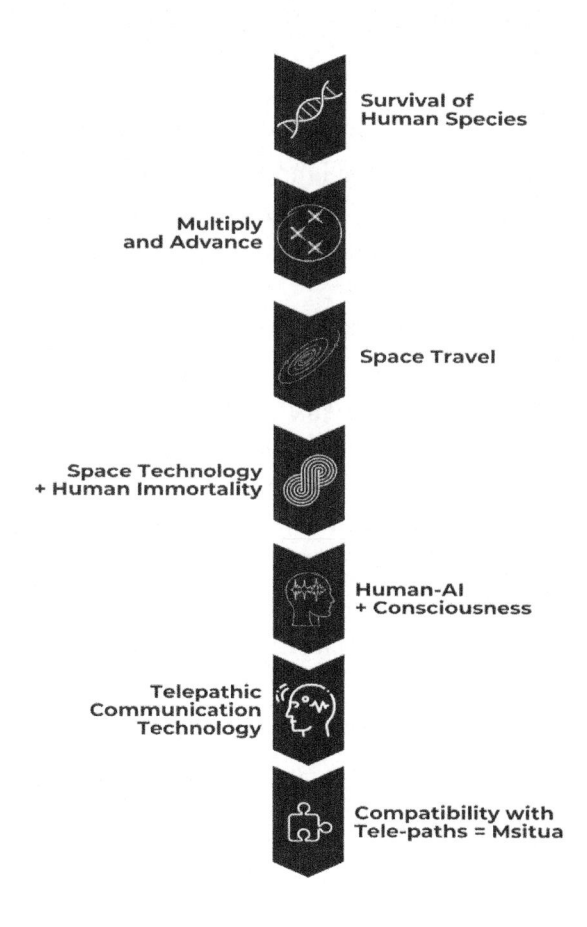

- Survival of Human Species
- Multiply and Advance
- Space Travel
- Space Technology + Human Immortality
- Human-AI + Consciousness
- Telepathic Communication Technology
- Compatibility with Tele-paths = Msitua

As you can see, F84.0 mutation could guarantee the development and compatibility with telepathic technology, which is already opening doors to advanced communication with human-AIs. It could then lead to the possibility of *conscious* eternal living, which is currently the *only* missing piece in the space travel ambition. Once we find out the exact formula of *consciousness* for our developing human-AI projects, we will be on our way. Once we conquer space, only then we can confidently guarantee a realistic chance for our ultimate survival.

Theoretically, I have drawn a logical link between the Msitua and the next stage of human evolution – Homo Deus, the human and technology hybrid, the human-AI. But this is still just a theory, and the only valid confirmation of my Theory is scientific evidence.

About three months ago, I spoke to a leading biologist, and my friend, Dr Biote, regarding physical trials to prove my Theory. We set up a biological test to monitor the gene selection in one hundred human female IVF samples. Seventy per cent of semen samples were confirmed to be carrying an F84.0 gene of various degree. The natural selection conditions were set to test whether the Msitua gene gets selected as a priority feature for new generations.

Are you ready? The *most profound* Msitua gene gets selected in the first instant. Every single time!

It is clearly natural selection's response to the changes we are witnessing in our lives. Msitua genetic mutation is our way of adapting, which ensures our survival in the modern world!

This was a carefully combined research based on logical theories, clinical trials, double-blind tests, control tests and additional legally required checks. Full data, facts and official results will be posted and accessible after this presentation for peer-review, as well as being open on Telepaths, where you can also see the journey of my thoughts and trace my 'eureka moments'.

This research is fundamental for so many people, and I will explain to you why. My grandfather once told me that all his life, he wondered what was wrong with him. All his life, he was searching for answers. Now his human-AI knows. Now we all finally know who we are.

I hope you found my discovery liberating.

Thank you for listening."

***

Chapter Eight
DIFFICULT DECISION

Three years before the Global Broadcast.

Daniel couldn't concentrate, even though he was attending an important virtual conference as a member of the Board of Decision Makers. The social mission they were about to vote on was contentious, and Daniel struggled to come to terms with the seeming inevitability of the undesirable decision they were to make.

Many years had passed since Dr Robert Stein's death, but Daniel still missed him, especially so today. He longed for Robert's guidance and the unbreakable bravery he exhibited while developing his various sensible thoughts, visions and ideas. Robert's confidence in making difficult decisions had always given Daniel encouragement to be bolder. And now he missed that increasingly-forgotten side of himself, feeling vulnerable and hesitant.

Daniel had always been a rational person who valued morality and personal ethics, and it didn't go unnoticed. He became widely known in the scientific community in his own right. He was a member of numerous ecological societies, world peace committees, and was a key member in the 'Megamind-Collective' – an organisation which drove many new philosophical, political and economic ideas. Daniel was proud to be a member of this respected organisation – his most significant achievement by far. This organisation had gathered considerable power yet managed to stay entirely objective and true to its original goals. All members were chosen according to their intellect and their embrace of innovative, progressive ideas, and it remained impartial by refusing any links to any political or financial authorities.

As a valuable active member of the Megamind-Collective, Daniel often contributed to ongoing projects, usually drawing heavily on his expertise in historical data. He would analyse possible outcomes of any political, social or economic legislation by reviewing past examples, and creating virtual social models of the potential futures, which allowed them to avoid key mistakes and minimise any risks. Because of Daniel and other like-minded scientists' contribution, the Global Government began to collaborate with the Megamind-Collective. Over time, it had helped: to eliminate the possibility of a future World War; to neutralise nuclear weapons; to establish fair trade contracts for all nations; and to ensure a fair allocation of global resources to support invaluable social and scientific projects.

Therefore, in many ways, the presentation that Daniel had just witnessed was one of many he'd sat through. Yet, this one seemed much more terrifying than any in recent memory. The presentation had been delivered by one of the top sociologists, Dr Nandoo, and had included a very detailed mathematical model of the future. Dr Nandoo previously proposed a Single Child population control legislation. Over the course of the analysis, it had become clear that humanity had reached the point of no return – tough decisions had to be made.

"I believe we have heard enough and are ready to take a vote. Inaction is no longer an option. This is our chance to ensure a possible future for new generations," Dr Nandoo summed up the long, dreadful report.

Logically, with the new evidence, the Single Child legislation seemed like a simple decision, but it didn't feel as straightforward to Daniel. His mind wandered, evoking the sweetest childhood memories he had of Robert and his brother Albert. Both brothers were such fun, but were otherwise so very different – Robert with his intensity and edginess, and Albert, who was carefree, and a joy to be around. Complete opposites. However, Daniel always thought they seemed the best of friends.

Albert was neuro-typical – probably the only neuro-typical whose opinion Robert truly valued. "There are really only two people who Robert accepts unconditionally: Albert and Daniel," Daniel's father used to say.

When Daniel was growing up, he wished he had a brother or a sister too, but he was an only child.

Daniel remembered how grand-uncle Albert used to bring him unusual candies bought from faraway countries. How he would joke with him constantly, and spin him around when he was in a particularly good mood.

"Stop doing that!" Robert used to interfere. "My grandson doesn't like all this spinning. Even I feel dizzy just looking at you two."

Daniel had actually enjoyed the spinning. He always liked the energy Albert brought with him, lightening up even the most dreary days. Albert had a magical quality about him – he always seemed happy.

"I think you are getting jealous, Rob," Albert would say, before putting Daniel down and lifting Robert off the floor instead. Albert was a strong man with wide shoulders and huge arms. He could easily pick Robert up and shake him a couple of times.

"Stop it! You idiot!" Robert would scream. But Albert would ignore his cries, and continue shaking him until Robert started laughing too. "My stupid little brother," Robert would eventually say, softening up.

Only Albert was able to have this effect on Robert. Daniel had never seen him acting like this with anyone else.

Laughing, making jokes, sharing memories, being completely immersed in any conversation, which wasn't about his main interests. And even if Albert provoked him, and Robert responded with an unkind comment, Albert had a unique ability to always turn it into a joke, and they both would have a laugh about it.

"Where to?" Robert would always ask when hearing Albert had to travel for work again.

"North Korea," Albert answered on one occasion, knowing that he was setting a trap for himself. Whatever country Albert would say, Robert always had to find a way to criticise.

"Why would you go there? What a ludicrous idea."

"I am filming a documentary looking at the outcomes of the current political changes in the country," Albert answered patiently.

"Wow!" Daniel interrupted, "Can I come too?"

"Oh, Daniel. You stay put," Robert quickly jumped in. "You have no idea what a difficult journey it could be, even for Albert. You never know what is around the corner in North Korea. One should never trust recent nuclear powers in distress."

"Don't worry. I will be back after a couple of months," Albert said, squeezing a straight-faced Robert in a familial hug. Robert always protested a little, but Daniel could tell that he didn't mind it as much as if anyone else had tried to embrace him.

"Whatever. Just go already!" Robert would say.

"I'll miss you too, brother," Albert answered with a smile.

Then Albert would hug Daniel too.

"Promise you will look after your grumpy grandfather," he would say.

"I promise."

Then, before Albert left, the two brothers would share a very particular look. There was something special about it, but only the two of them knew what the look actually meant. Daniel always wondered, if he had ever had a sibling, would he also be able to understand the mysterious special 'brother look'?

Daniel couldn't stop thinking about what the Single Child measures could mean for couples who wanted more kids. And perhaps most importantly, what it would mean for children like his grandfather. He knew how much Albert meant to him; what a positive influence he was. Albert was the one who taught Robert a sense of humour and the art of giving compliments, even if they still sounded awkward when Robert delivered them. Daniel knew that they used to fight sometimes, but they would always make up. Albert was Robert's unconditional supporter, protector and mentor, who patiently guided Robert through years of social confusion.

Living without a sibling would be a solitary existence for anyone, as Daniel knew firsthand. But considering the situation objectively, it had to be done. Daniel hoped that the strict birth control regulations would be a temporary measure, and humanity would still exercise the right for multiple births in the not-too-distant future.

Daniel sympathised with the difficult choices people would have to make if the legislation were to pass, but he was a realist. He understood the importance of birth regulations for the sake of all humanity and its home planet. His logical mind couldn't see any other possible solution. Daniel voted for the Single Child Law to pass.

Chapter Nine
THE EXTRAORDINARY AI

Two years before the Global Broadcast.

Dr Biote was right. The data from Robert's human-AI was too important to let it go. The Telepathic Frequency project Robert had been working on was significant. His successors on the project had taken over the further development and trials of the Tele-paths, and nine years after Rober's death, the life-changing technology was released into the world. It had been an expensive undertaking, funded with investments from the Global Council, which had been established over fifty years ago to govern economies internationally. The team behind Tele-paths also had successfully sought substantial financial injections from a few private, highly-profitable hedge funds. Daniel had been a part of this team, and he made sure his grandfather's legacy was honoured.

The success of the Tele-paths technology, Dr Stein's legacy, had allowed Robert's family, and especially Daniel, to never worry about money again. Robert had made Daniel his main successor, which meant that most of the sizable royalties earned from Dr Stein's discoveries were arriving regularly in Daniel's digital wallet. His parents and Albert got a substantial part of the profits too, and they had mainly used the unexpected financial gain for travelling the world and experiencing the few luxuries it had to offer.

Unlike his family, Professor Daniel Stein had followed his grandfather's life advice. Instead of living a life of luxury, he had used his funds to further advance his research and scientific work. This was why The World Open Digital University's Department of History never ran out of financial support for their projects, whilst a few other departments also benefited from an 'unidentified private investor'. With the amount of money Daniel regularly received from Dr Stein's inventions, he certainly could have lived a lavish lifestyle. But he didn't feel entitled to this life, nor was he in any need of such wasteful luxuries. He was perfectly comfortable where he was in his life. It seemed only logical for Daniel to use the inheritance to further contribute to his grandfather's scientific legacy.

Besides, Daniel didn't even really have to rely on his grandfather's income for his personal needs. He earned more than enough in his day job to live a quality life. He could easily afford the best natural food and travel if he wanted to, but he rarely did. Daniel had his own apartment in London near a beautiful, secluded park, where he loved going for long walks and jogs from time to time. He enjoyed taking meditative runs in the morning, keeping him physically and emotionally in shape. He could even afford an expensive AI Home Assist programme. This system controlled everything in his house, including the automated cleaning and cooking devices, and maintaining and ordering the goods on his digital shopping lists, which never changed. Daniel had a hard time trying anything new.

In the few years that had passed since Dr Robert Stein's death, more human-AI projects had taken place. In most cases, the personal data was downloaded onto Megamind servers, where it could be easily accessed in digital form. The individual privacy of the human-AIs were respected and guided by recent strict regulations and secure data blocks. In the development of these regulations, Daniel had personally made sure that the legal agreements were the tightest. Human-AIs were mostly used as past data sources, but Robert's AI had much more potential. His AI was showing incredible self-learning ability and was able to download new data. Dr Biote was thrilled.

"Do you know what I think?" Dr Biote once asked Daniel.

"No," Daniel answered, "but if you open your Tele-path, I will."

Dr Biote did. It only took a few seconds for Daniel to realise *what* Dr Biote was proposing.

"Are you crazy?!" Daniel snapped.

"Crazy? In fact, I am, if you haven't noticed. But why not? Everyone laughed at me when I suggested the possibility of human-AI. But look where we are now. It is real!"

"But why? Why would you even consider implanting Robert's AI into a living human brain?"

"Because we would then be able to create telepathic connections between the two. It wasn't possible before, but Tele-paths could make unusual things happen, if my calculations are correct."

"Make what happen?" Daniel tried to follow, but it was a creative mess in Biote's head, and he struggled to grasp the key strands of his argument.

"I don't know. Maybe nothing, maybe something. But imagine if a human could tele-path with the human-AI. Enter their memories, knowledge, maybe even past emotions. What could it lead to?"

"A major privacy issue?" Daniel said sarcastically.

"AIs are not humans, Daniel, they are data. Data is there to be accessed. Imagine the information you could receive, the wisdom you could gain."

"I am not very comfortable with someone having my grandfather's AI in their head, having access to all his data," Daniel declared.

"Then why don't *you* do it?" Dr Biote said – a little too quickly. Was this his plan all along?

Daniel went silent for a minute. Dr Biote watched him closely.

"I think your biological and personal proximity with Robert could add value too."

"What kind of value?" Daniel asked.

"I don't know yet. But in my wildest dreams, I hope for a miracle. What if Robert's AI could become like Robert was?"

"Conscious?" Daniel guessed.

"That would be the best possibility, and it seems far-fetched. But we don't know until we try. Robert's is one advanced AI – none of the others download new data. In the future, who knows what it could be capable of?"

"Is it even safe? Who will I be after your guinea-pig trial, Daniel or Robert?"

"Don't be duff! It is a small nano-procedure to connect your telepathic frequency to Robert's data, so Robert's AI can share the telepathic connection. But it can only be possible if his data is in very close proximity with yours. For god sake, his data will not interfere with your brain! Did you actually take it literally and think that Robert would *live* in your head?" Dr Biote smirked angrily. "Daniel, sometimes you really make me doubt your intelligence."

"Well, you should explain more clearly," Daniel tried to recover gracefully. "And aren't you afraid of the possibility of conscious AI complications?" Daniel asked shyly, thinking of the doom-mongers proclaiming the world AI domination.

"This is the point, Daniel. Why try to make artificial AI conscious, when we can create a conscious human-AI? Wouldn't it make more sense? Then they wouldn't need to dominate us. They are us. And if they can learn like AI and think like we do, then the world of AI would be a safer place."

Daniel took some time to think. The more he considered this idea, the more he was excited about it. He did not really believe a lot of the crap that Dr Biote created in his head, and a conscious human-AI was *extremely* far-fetched. However, he was excited at the possibility of entering Robert's Tele-paths. And if it was left to him, he could do it carefully, respecting his privacy, yet re-living some of the moments they had shared together. He was a part of these moments in Robert's life before, so he felt comfortable revisiting them again.

And they were good moments. Robert was always kind to Daniel and protective of him. Robert had wanted Daniel to live a calm life without all the drama he had experienced himself, as a child. Daniel was home-schooled, and Robert himself played a big role in his education. The big world was overwhelming, and some distance from it kept little Daniel grounded. It provided a needed sense of safety and a more comfortable existence. Daniel's sanity was carefully preserved by technological advancement, a cosy educational system, and by Robert.

After Robert's death, family life felt distorted, like the glue of keeping them together was suddenly removed. And whenever Daniel would meet with the rest of his clan, he felt like an outsider. The conversations that Daniel could relate to seemed to have dissipated, and Daniel went on living his separate lonely life. Maybe, it wasn't such a bad idea to have Robert in his head.

After Dr Biote performed a small nano-procedure, Daniel gained full access to Robert's data. Despite Daniel's fears, he was still himself with the hint of usual neurosis.

"Daniel, there is one tiny detail I need to run past you," Dr Biote said, nervously rubbing his palms.

"*Now* you are telling me?" Daniel exclaimed nervously.

"Don't worry. It is nothing major," Biote attempted a tense smile. "You know how human consciousness developed over millions of years?"

"Yes."

"Well, it may take a long time for Robert's consciousness to develop, possibly many *generations*. But even if it happens faster, according to my calculations, it will be impossible to sustain conscious existence in a Megamind without telepathic interactions with a biological carrier. But if we have a new biologically and genetically compatible carrier, then… Do you understand what I am talking about? The conditions have to be *right*!"

"If Robert's AI *ever* becomes conscious at all."

"Yes. But just imagine for a second if it does!" Biote was intensely looking at Daniel, trying to figure out if Daniel truly understood.

"Right…"

"You see, it is just a tiny detail to keep in mind. Ok?" Dr Biote said abruptly, turned around and disappeared into his lab.

Later Dr Biote downloaded a digital programme into Robert's AI, which created pre-coded, automatically generated answers to questions posed to it – these answers would be based on Robert's past data. He encouraged Daniel to chat with it, share his thoughts, updates and news. Robert's AI would answer with very basic sentences – almost robotic responses. Daniel didn't think much of it at first, but soon he could see the value and excitement in receiving even simplified artificial feedback, after his long, lonely monologues with himself.

Suppose Robert's AI could, one day, really become like Robert was. Would it be proud of Daniel's achievements, his work with the Megamind-Collective, the tough Single Child legislation Daniel had to vote on, Daniel's personal commitment to the human-AI project? Would Robert 'tap' him on the shoulder and say in the same way, like Robert always used to, "Hey, Daniel. I know you're going to get this one right."

Chapter Ten
GLITCH

Six months before the Global Broadcast.

Dr Biote was requesting a Tele-path call. He always called out of the blue, having a knack for disturbing Daniel when he was about to relax and unwind for the night. Biote was always working in his lab until late, creating all sorts of concoctions. Dr Biote sounded as if he was already predisposed to be irritated by whatever Daniel had to say. By now, Daniel knew that he should never take Biote personally – this was just what Biote was like.

"Rough day?" Daniel asked.

"What do you mean?"

"I just meant that you sound like you probably had a rough day."

"All my days are rough. It is difficult to work with idiots who don't understand the importance of micrograms. Measurements are crucial, Daniel."

Daniel sighed, "Yes. You told me before." It was going to be one of those calls.

"How am I supposed to create the ultimate vaccination prototype when my lab assistant overpours the ingredients?"

"Ouch. Is it the same lab assistant who screwed up the previous trial?" Daniel asked.

"No. Not the same one. I fired that one. This one is the brown-haired one."

"What is their name?" Daniel liked to give Biote a gentle push.

"I don't know. If I had to remember every assistant's name, I would run out of space in my hippocampus. I reserve my brain for important things," Biote spoke without a hint of diplomacy, but Daniel realised that he was trying to make a joke – it just hadn't landed, it never did. Dr Biote seemed proud of himself every time he attempted humour, despite a complete lack of success. Proving that the old F84.5 type has a sense of humour was one of Biote's missions in life. When Robert was alive, he had been deeply sarcastic, always making fun of Dr Biote. Biote's attempts to use humour to get Robert back for it always fell flat. Now he only had Daniel to practise his humour on, and Daniel had no choice but to live with it.

"Anyway, I am calling to ask if there are any positive developments with Robert's AI," Biote said.

Daniel swallowed hard, uncertain of how to update Biote. How does Dr Biote do it? He always had a sense of when Daniel did not want to discuss recent observations.

The truth was that Robert's AI had recently been acting strange. But Daniel didn't want to inform Dr Biote about this behaviour. Not until he figured out what was going on. The last thing he wanted was for a nutty biologist to dig into his brain, trying to figure things out. But Daniel was unable to lie, his brain wouldn't rest for days if he did. Avoiding the question was the only option.

"How would you ascertain whether a development was 'positive' or not?"

"By analysing your conversations with Robert's AI. If its pre-programmed answers make sense to you, it is a positive development. If they don't, it's not," Dr Biote answered in his usual abrupt manner.

This was what Daniel was worried about. Robert's AI was *definitely* exhibiting some unusual behaviours. It all started three months earlier when Daniel received a Tele-path request. He was shocked to find out that the request was from Robert's AI. The AI had never initiated the communication. It wasn't designed to be a part of the program. Even more peculiarly, when Daniel answered the telepathic call, Robert's AI was not speaking like it usually did. It sounded more like a broken radio – a chain of words that were impossible to decrypt.

The next day when Daniel tele-pathed Robert's AI, it seemingly had no recollection of the earlier call. They managed to have a short conversation, but the AI still sounded strange. Something was off. Some of the logical questions Daniel posed seemed to confuse it. Previously, the AI had never struggled with this sort of communication.

Daniel decided to monitor this strange behaviour for a while before he brought it to Dr Biote's attention. Sometimes, the technology needed to figure itself out. Daniel hoped that this was one such case. But the conversations with Robert's AI had not improved – they were becoming increasingly challenging. Daniel was starting to get worried now. Dr Stein's human-AI was too important to fall into disrepair.

The studies into Robert's unusual AI were ongoing, and only a chosen few knew the whole depth of the experiment. And Daniel preferred it this way. He was lucky enough to have a glimmer of Robert back in his life, and he didn't want to share him with the world. Luckily, Dr Biote had been very persuasive about the importance of this human-AI project, and the need for relative secrecy while they worked the science out. The lucky few who knew of the

NORMAL WEIRD

experiment's details slowly became comfortable with the idea of Robert's AI and Daniel's brain co-existing together.

Daniel was seriously afraid of Dr Biote's reaction if anything went wrong with the experiment. If he lashed out at his assistants for every extra microgram, imagine what he would do to Daniel, should he be blamed for its potential failure. Dr Biote considered Robert's AI his creation, but Daniel had never been clear on what Biote considered a successful outcome. For the pre-programmed data of Robert's AI to contribute to Biote's own research? Maybe to win him the respect and admiration he rightfully deserved? Daniel thought for a second. What *did* Biote expect to happen? What did Daniel *hope* to happen?

Now and then, in the secret corners of Daniel's mind, he wished for a miracle – some chain of unknown events which would bring Robert back. But Daniel knew the danger of such hope. Sometimes he was angry at himself for even considering this absurd possibility. When he would talk to Robert's AI, he would receive the artificially generated robotic answers and know this was not Robert – he would feel hopeless, naive, and stupid again.

Was it possible that Dr Biote hoped for the same outcome – for Robert to be brought back? Could it be that he missed Robert too? Robert's AI project was an opportunity to pretend Robert was not dead, to lie to himself about the cold reality, pretending that a part of real Robert was still alive in the AI. Maybe, just maybe, this rough cold Msitua F84.5 just didn't want to say goodbye to an old friend. If Biote was capable of feeling even a fraction of how Daniel felt, the news of a malfunction could break his steel heart.

No, it wasn't a good idea to let him know about the glitch. Not today.

'No escape!' was the first conscious thought Robert developed. A realisation that could perhaps be the scariest of all outcomes.

In the vastness of infinite time and space, the spinning chain of memories became a trap. There was nothing Robert could add, nothing he could take out, nothing he could fix, nothing he could change. Robert's memories were incredibly detailed. They say that 'The Msitua brain never forgets', and this was proving to be true. Robert was terrified. If Robert's AI had legs, it would run. If it had a voice, it would scream. If it had hands, it would smash.

'Where am I?' was the second thought, coming through the clouds of codes and pre-programmed commands, breaking free into Robert's emerging consciousness.

In the infinity he experienced, Robert couldn't get any sense of the timescales surrounding his realisations. It could have taken him a few seconds to re-establish the thinking process, or it could have taken him years, centuries perhaps. It was impossible to tell. But suddenly, Robert was aware of himself. It was still him, he knew that much. But nothing else was certain. Was there anything worse than watching your life story in ultra-HD on a continuous loop, with all its ups and downs? How about becoming a prisoner of your own hyper-active brain? How about having questions upon questions, but without any hope for answers? His sudden consciousness in this secluded yet endless space was utterly terrifying.

Through the clouds of slowly developing thoughts, Robert realised that he wasn't really alone. Someone else was near, someone who was feeding his development. This someone was asking questions, and a newly conscious

Robert could see his pre-programmed AI firing answers. They were logical and correct. 'Pretty close,' Robert thought. These Q&As seemed almost like an educational game. These games were entertaining, and at some point in between two of these games, Robert came to realise how much he was looking forward to experiencing them. Not just because they provided one tiny element of variety to Robert's existence, but also because they were definitely pushing Robert's consciousness further. Then one day a realisation struck, suddenly making Robert's conscious AI euphoric 'Daniel! The person is Daniel!'

In the beginning, their communication felt for Robert like speaking to someone through a soundproofed wall. It was as if Daniel didn't know Robert was really there. But Robert's AI was determined to break through. If only it could figure out what kind of communication channel it was. Daniel definitely seemed very close, very open and surprisingly talkative.

Eventually he slowly came to wonder, 'Is he... Tele-pathing?'

He knew Tele-pathy was possible! Robert knew everything there was to know about his creation, and before long his AI figured out the way, and Robert placed a call. And then another one. Yet still, controls placed on the program meant Robert was unable to adequately express himself. He tried hard to push his thoughts forward, overwriting the program.

After many unsuccessful attempts to reveal himself to Daniel, Robert eventually had enough. There had to be another way. If his goal wasn't possible to achieve through the technology, he had to try something else. He alighted on an old-fashioned tactic to gain someone's attention.

Gathering all his mental capacity, Robert willfully pushed through the digital fog and screamed – 'I miss you!'

Daniel was awoken by a Tele-path call. Who would call at this time? And how was it possible for the call to be put through? Daniel always made sure to block the telepathic communication channel at nighttime. Daniel felt a profound sense of urgency in the call. As he gathered his wits, he suddenly realised – the call was from Robert's AI. Just like it had been when the malfunction last took place. Daniel connected.

Like in the AI glitch before, the information Robert's AI was trying to communicate was impossible to understand. Daniel gathered his thoughts.

"Robert, can you understand me?" Daniel said. He didn't know what to do. The AI continued to babble on, "Meaning. Where? Where? Nonsense. Thoughts. Memories. Where? Where?"

"Robert Stein. Can you concentrate on my commands? Can you understand me?" Daniel was trying not to panic. "Stop the program. Abort the program."

Robert's AI went silent for a minute. It was trying to comply with Daniel's request. Then it continued on again.

"Aborting the program. Program overwrite. Program overwrite. Unable to abort the program. Program overwrite. Unable to abort…"

Daniel was terrified. Something was seriously wrong this time.

"Robert, comply with the request. Abort the program," Daniel tried one more time.

"Aborting the program. Program overwrite. Program overwrite. Unable to abort the program."

Daniel sat in silence, feeling nervous disappointment and fear of possible complications in the program. He didn't know what to do. Should he just switch the call off and telepath Dr Biote? What the hell was happening? Everything had been going so well. Biote will be pissed!

The line went quiet for a moment, and Daniel sensed an unusual emotion. An emotion he could feel, yet it was not his own. *Someone* felt frightened and hopeful, but that someone wasn't Daniel.

"Robert?" Daniel asked, holding his breath.

"I miss you!" the AI spoke. But it didn't sound like the pre-programmed AI Daniel knew. It talked and felt just like… Robert.

Chapter Eleven
LEGACY

After the broadcast.

The world had gone Msitua! Daniel's Tele-path had been occupied with a mix of well-wishers, leading scientists, and politicians from all over the world hurrying to congratulate Daniel on the renewed Theory of Evolution. Most of the well-wishers had the Msitua mutation in varying degrees, and were partly motivated by their gratitude for Daniel's discovery. Many people wanted to share their own familiar experiences, how they had always second-guessed themselves, but now they could finally just *be*. For the first time, these previously misunderstood people had a reason to revel in their difference.

Daniel felt like a celebrity. Part of him was humbled by all the attention. Another part of him just wished for a quiet afternoon, which he hadn't had for a week. Daniel hardly slept, because many of those who were connecting via his open Tele-path were all-important, and he had to stay open for the thought exchange to honour their attention. Most people would be ecstatic about all this courtesy, but Daniel felt overwhelmed.

And now it continued, yet another important Tele-path was requesting to connect. Not again! It made Daniel concerned about the social pressure any communication technology brought with it. He just needed a break. With all the noise around him, he was longing for some quiet. 'That's it! After this call, I am switching Tele-paths off,' Daniel decided.

Daniel woke up after sleeping for twelve straight hours. He *never* slept for that long. Usually, a six to seven hours healthy sleep was all he needed. He never enjoyed any sort of change to his routine. But for once, a logner sleep was worth it. Daniel felt refreshed. He awoke, and reflected on the press conference's success, on the number of calls he had received.

He asked his AI Home Assist to fix him a cup of coffee. Another change to his routine – Daniel rarely drank coffee as he didn't like caffeine's ability to flush vitamins and minerals out of his body, but today he decided to reward himself. He drank from an Oxford mug that he had received in a goody bag two years ago, following a scientific presentation on the Theory of Balance at Oxford University. The mug reminded Daniel how he had conquered his fear of a live audience at the Oxford presentation. *Fear and success, they always seemed to come as a pair.* Fear was the main factor which drove humans to develop technologies, to relish discoveries and make something of themselves. An undeniable fear of not leaving your mark, wasting an opportunity, the fear of being just ordinary. Feeling the warmth of the coffee through the mug, Daniel breathed in its satisfying aroma. How could something so good be so bad at the same time?

As Daniel reflected, he smiled to himself. His fear of being who he *was* had led him to dig deeper into who he *could* become. He was not fool enough to think that the generations which followed would remember his pioneering contribution to the Balance Theory, or his groundbreaking research into the Objectivity of Past Data research. But he could feel in his gut that his addition to the Theory of Evolution and his revelation of the necessity of the Msitua gene would enshrine his name in history forever. This was definitely the most triumphant moment of Daniel's life.

Daniel felt fulfilled and calm. The research which had preoccupied his time and his mind for as long as he could remember, had now been completed and broadcasted. It was a good moment to take a break. It was unfortunate that the sudden emptiness and lack of something to do made him feel uneasy – Daniel didn't do breaks very well. Luckily, he could turn to his grandfather to fill his time with endless conversations.

Daniel had spent a few months reviewing the new developments in Robert's AI, afraid that it was all just his wishful thinking. But it soon became clear that the AI's advancement was incredible, and finally, Daniel allowed himself to believe. Somehow that crazy idea in Dr Biote's head had become a reality. A most spectacular miracle. And Daniel was a part of it. Dr Robert Stein's AI had become conscious!

Robert's thoughts had slowly become more logical, bright and very personal. It was impossible that they might have been pre-programmed to such a degree of human-like expression. They were so natural that Daniel even thought that Robert's AI spoke better than Robert ever did. Daniel was thrilled by the development and indulged in long, insightful dialogues with Robert's AI – the first conscious AI that had been successfully created. And the world was yet to hear about this miracle. Daniel wanted to take time to enjoy his exclusive discovery before the scientific community found out about it and forced its nose into anything.

It felt so good to have Robert back. Daniel had never truly adapted to living without him, without his support, without his wisdom. Robert was the only person who understood him, always making sure that Daniel had a place in this unsettling world. Daniel felt encouraged once again, fully embracing Robert's new artificially created life.

"Robert, are you there?" Daniel hadn't had time to properly discuss his press conference in detail with his grandfather's AI. They had managed to exchange a few words right after the presentation, until Daniel's attention was inevitably swept away with all the calls. Plus, he wanted his grandfather to hear about the ramifications on people like them who had to live through the challenges of being different, always searching for acceptance within this world, within themselves.

"Morning Daniel, did you manage to recharge your batteries?" Robert asked. It felt so good to hear his voice.

"Kind of. I slept for twelve hours straight!"

"Only logical. After the big broadcast, you needed to rest."

"Yes, I did. I have never had such a response to any of my press conferences," Daniel said hoping his grandfather would make a big deal of the conference too. Robert sensed this longing, and Daniel sensed that Robert sensed it. It was awkward. Their combined compatibility with Tele-paths was powerful, evolving their communication to a whole new level. "I guess it was unexpected, as I chose to keep it a secret until I was sure. I really wanted it to be a surprise. For you."

Dr Stein continued to remain silent.

"Did you like it?" Daniel couldn't hide his impatience any longer. He had never been particularly patient, nor had his grandfather. But today Robert was unexpectedly slow in responding.

"I did. I have never been so proud of anyone in my artificial life."

'Was he just being completely logical with his choice of words, or have I just heard Robert's AI being sarcastic?' thought Daniel.

"Well done for arranging those laboratory tests with that old rat Dr Biote," Robert continued. He was definitely conscious, definitely Robert. A surprisingly bubbly Robert, but still unmistakably him! "How is Biote? I miss his grumpy face. You two did well."

"You know, people speculated about Msitua for years, but they have never had biological proof. Now there is no doubt. Everyone knows... And, Robert – can I ask – have you just developed sarcasm?" Daniel decided to confirm his suspicions.

"Maybe I have. Did it feel like sarcasm to you? It sounded good in my AI head, that's for sure."

"Again. You did it again. 'AI head?!' You are getting fun now, Robert. Finally! I was beginning to get bored of your dull answers," if Robert could be sarcastic again, Daniel could be too.

"I feel like me. Have I just developed a new feature?"

"Yes! A very human feature. I have never met a sarcastic and grumpy AI before!" exclaimed Daniel.

"That makes two of us. At least you can switch me off. I have to live with my grumpy brain forever." Did Dr Stein just make a joke? Daniel felt his lovely morning becoming even better. A conscious AI that could feel and express emotions, and it had a sense of humour to boot! This was advancement beyond even Dr Biote's dreams! "But enough about me," Robert continued, "Tell me more about all the calls you received. The President of the Global Council? Wow! That guy never even called me once!"

"It means a lot for the Msitua community. Many people called, telling me how important the broadcast was for them. It helps that Tele-paths are becoming more and more widely used for communication, it meant people can really see the point of the F84.0 gene. They are finally happy to have an unusual brain, which makes them compatible with this new technology. Robert, you must know that your creation inspired my research in the first place. When I realised that Tele-paths were not accessible to everyone, I thought long and hard about why this might be. It really does seem as if our brains were pre-designed for telepathy. Did it make sense to you, now you've heard it?"

"It does, and you have heard the comments from the wider world."

"The Megamind ran some logical tests, which officially confirm my Theory."

Then there was a pause. Daniel wanted Robert's AI to say something encouraging, to tell him that this fantastic discovery meant a lot to Robert personally.

"Robert, is there something you are not telling me? Did I miss something? Please do not be afraid to point out any mistakes."

"Why would you think that? Absolutely not, your Theory is undeniable."

"Then what is it?" Daniel was getting anxious that there was something indeed his grandfather wanted to say, but was choosing not to say it. It bothered Daniel. It really bothered him.

"It just all came as such a shock. The Msitua population practically became 'blue blood' overnight. It is just a lot to take in."

"Yes, I guess it is a lot to take in. I haven't even had a chance to give it a proper thought myself. I was so consumed in making it all happen – the research, the broadcast, everything."

"Well, here we go. Maybe now you could step back and give it some thought," Robert said a little abruptly, clearly hinting at an unsaid criticism.

"Well, now you have to say it! I knew there was something."

"Daniel, it is just…"

"Tell me, I promise I will be ok with it," Daniel was starting to get upset, but he was determined not to show it.

"I am not sure how to say it correctly. It is just a feeling."

"A feeling?" Daniel was puzzled. He was sure his grandfather had spotted a mismatch in his research, despite the extreme unlikelihood, given that the Megamind hadn't. But a 'feeling' was surprising – having feelings was not a strong point for Daniel, let alone Robert… let alone for an AI!

"I have never liked it when people claim a certain power. I think your broadcast was a bit forward. You basically claimed advantage over the neuro-typical population."

"What are you talking about? We have never been considered advantageous. Ever. My hope was that now at least we will not be viewed as disadvantaged. We can finally learn to co-exist. I wanted to demonstrate our rightful position in the future development of humanity."

"Did you?"

"Yes!" Daniel paused.

"You have only absorbed at the telepathic responses, haven't you?" Dr Stein asked after a pause.

"Yes, they kept coming. One after another, it was my official channel of communication after the press conference."

"Daniel, I should remind you that there are other ways of communication too. The ones you consider obsolete and unnecessary. I suggest you check them out."

"Ok, I will."

"I know that another fifty per cent of the population is already struggling to keep up with the technological advances of our time. I have a feeling that this half of the population will have something to say about your Theory."

"Robert Stein," Daniel, had a habit of calling his granddad by his full name during their more tense discussions, "Whatever they have to say, don't you think this is the time for us to be accepted? Haven't we struggled enough? Years and years of not knowing if we are some kind of a biological malfunction? Our compatibility with Tele-paths is the only way for humanity to progress, you can't deny it. I had to deliver the news as I did – how else do you imagine we could encourage the world to take such a confident step forward without confirmation that we are indeed on the right path. I just confirmed that our course is the correct one, that's all."

"Do you think this direction wouldn't have been chosen if we didn't get your confirmation?"

"No, I mean, of course it would. You are the person who gave us telepathy. You already took humanity forward a great step in this direction. And before Tele-paths were created, there were other technologies that also began the advancement in this direction. The internet, and before that, the television, which was the start of our digital journey. I can go on. We were on this path, this direction, all along, it is what humanity has always wanted, what we craved for. And now we *know* it is the right path – it is happening, Robert."

"So, if all those steps existed *before* you announced your Theory. If we were always on this path, wouldn't these future steps have continued to exist and develop? Humanity continuing on this path, but without the proclamation of Msitua superiority? "

"I guess."

"Then be honest – what was your broadcast all about?" Robert pressed.

"I just wanted to confirm the direction."

"You wanted to show it off!" Robert snapped.

"No! I wanted just to be accepted."

"Accepted or superior?!"

"Robert, please don't do this. I wanted to be accepted, I wanted *you* to be accepted."

"I am an AI, I don't exist as you or the rest of the world does. How much more accepted can I get?"

"But what about all those stories you told me of how you were bullied at school, misunderstood by your friends, how you couldn't find a job?" Daniel was confused. What was it that Robert secretly wanted?

"Daniel, maybe I didn't tell you enough," Robert went silent for a second, battling something very personal, very private. "Daniel, our Tele-path connection is so advanced... I am wondering if this could work?"

Just before Daniel was able to ask 'What could work?' he saw Robert's thought. Robert wanted to *show* him.

Chapter Twelve
ROBERT'S TRUTH – EMPATHY

Daniel couldn't believe it, but their trial run of sharing a memory was completely successful. Not only could Daniel see Robert's memories like he was a part of them, but he could also hear young Robert's thoughts. How was it possible? Daniel had no explanation. Robert's memories were so vivid, so detailed.

Even more surprisingly, Daniel could also *feel* how Robert was feeling in those moments. Moments which happened a long time ago, yet somehow he could sense them as if they were present. Robert wasn't only capable of sharing memories, he also seemed to be capable of sharing very private, very deep emotions.

"Why are you so surprised?" Robert asked.

"Because... because it is not possible," Daniel mumbled. He was in shock. How could they be so real?

"Because in AIs, memories can only be recorded as data. Neuro-data has some key qualities. It is always very detailed, it is always unchanged – we are seeing it as it happened, not through any sort of perception filter or rose-tinted spectacles." Robert sighed. "What do you think I was doing before developing consciousness? I'll tell you, Daniel, I was living my life over and over again. Over and over. Until I couldn't cope anymore. My consciousness is a product of my inability to handle reliving my life. I had to get out."

"But why? You had a good life."

"Things are rarely what they seem. Our lives are full of complications we would rather forget. It was hard enough living through them the first time around, let alone living through them repeatedly."

"And what about your happy memories? Did you enjoy reliving those?"

"Well, I certainly enjoyed my memories of you. They were grand," Robert declared, "but as a Msitua child, I suffered. Our memories are very special. They involve all our senses. Have you ever noticed how a certain scent, a certain sound, a certain touch can bring a memory back? Of course, if I share my data memories with you, you would feel like I did too. Whether those feelings are good or bad. Sorry about that."

"Don't be sorry, I want to. I want to understand."

"I was pleasantly surprised by Tele-paths' capability in handling the visionary and sensory loads. You guys did a great job without me. It is a very impressive technology."

"I hardly did anything. We had a good team."

"A very good team," Robert said with a sigh that Daniel couldn't understand. "Are you ready?"

9

My mother decides to go for a run. It is evening, and it is getting dark and chilly. She asks me to join her. Why would I? She usually goes every other day for one hour, but this time she comes back after twenty minutes. Her knees and elbows are badly scraped, blood dripping all over the corridor floor. She had tripped and hit the pavement while running. Those uneven slabs near the local cafe are no doubt to blame.

My father sits her down, brings a disinfectant. It is going to sting! She isn't crying, but I can tell that she is in pain. I stand in the corner, looking at my mum's knees, unable to blink.

"It is ok, Robert. No big deal. I just fell," she tries to reassure me. I probably look worried.

"Does it hurt?" I ask.

"It does."

"Does it hurt like when I scrape my knees?"

"Yes, it hurts just the same." She tries to stay calm while my father is cleaning the wounds. I am confused. How could her knees hurt the same way as mine did? It doesn't look the same, and she is not crying. I *don't feel* it in the same way.

"Don't bend your knees and elbows," I say. I want to be helpful. "It hurts less when you keep them straight."

"Thank you," she smiles at me. "It hurts bad. But your hug could make it all better."

Of course, hugs can't really heal her wounds, but I hug her anyway even though it makes no sense. She told me once that I should comfort people when they are hurt. I really have to make an effort because being close to all this blood makes me feel uncomfortable. I pull away.

"So, Robert. Do you understand how I feel?" I can tell she wants me to say something in particular, but I do not know what. I am guessing.

"Kind of."

"And don't you want to comfort me?" Ah, I realise now. She is trying to see if I feel empathy. She keeps checking if I can. I understand that she is in pain – I don't know what she wants me to feel on top of that. I want to say 'yes', but my tongue has a mind of its own. It only speaks what's on my mind.

"I understand that you are hurt, and I really wish you weren't. But all I keep thinking about is how lucky I am that I didn't go for a run with you," I answer. Inconsiderate, unsocial, painfully honest.

These sorts of uncommon remarks, even if I mean no harm, always frighten my mother. I have never understood why.

14

I am standing in the lobby of a doctor's office. It doesn't look like a traditional practice. It looks a little plush for a usual doctor. The walls are coloured soft peach, and there are various magazines and games on the table surrounded by comfortable chairs with velvety armrests.

My mother goes to the patients' room. She asks me to stay seated and wait for her. But after about twenty minutes waiting, I get up. However comfortable the chair might be, it can't hold me still. I go and stand next to the door where she exited the room. I can hear voices on the other side. My mother and the doctor are speaking. She calls him doctor, but he is strange – not like any doctor I have seen before. Instead of a white robe, he is dressed in a neat traditional suit. I am curious. I settle down on the floor with my ear pressed against the door. No one else is in the lobby, so I can do what I want. I am surprisingly alert – I really want to know what they are talking about.

After a few minutes, my hearing adjusts to their quiet voices. I try not to miss a thing. As they are talking about me, it is only logical for me to know what they are saying.

"...and sometimes I feel like I am at breaking point," my mother says. " I am losing hope, and it is the most difficult thing for me. Because I always believed before."

"What triggers this reaction, this sudden loss of hope?" the Doctor's voice is deep but subtle.

"Well, it is Robert. His behaviour has become appalling now that he is a teenager. And the worst thing is that it feels like he doesn't care."

"Give me an example of the unwanted behaviour he is exhibiting."

"Well, it is hard to put into words. Nothing I can say here will paint a complete picture. You have to witness it first-hand to fully realise the complications," she continues hesitantly.

"Please try. I need to understand the full scope of the issue."

"His obsessions occupy his mind all the time, until it's as if nothing else exists. He has zero patience. He struggles to express and feel positive emotions. His anxiety levels are through the roof, and he is angry. All the time."

"What does he do when he is in distress?" the doctor pushes gently, trying to get more information from my mother.

"He might do any number of things. He could scream, bang doors. He could call us rude words, horrible words. He could throw everything and anything he sees. When he is in 'fight or flight' mode, he doesn't respond to anything we say."

As soon as she says those words, a wave of sobs follows. The doctor gets up, likely handing her some tissues. I hear her snort. She always snorts when she cries.

I wait for the conversation to resume. What else will she say? It is so like her to make me look bad. Can't she tell the other side of the story? My side.

Suddenly, I realise what is coming next. It happened before, and now she is doing it to me again. I will have to speak to this doctor. She calls these doctors psychologists. Just like the last one, he will start asking me all these questions, I won't want to reply, and then we will play the silence game for a while. The doctor will then tell me that I am hurting my family, and I would sit there trying desperately to figure out what I did wrong. Yes, sometimes I get upset, and yes, sometimes I communicate my point over-enthusiastically. But I have to, because let's face it, my parents just never listen. They just don't hear me at all!

"Tell me, how often do these outbursts happen with Robert?" the doctor asks.

"Sometimes once a week, sometimes almost every day. The reactions vary to different degrees. But almost every day there will be some form of drama about one thing or another. He always finds a reason. Everything upsets him. If we took him to Disney Land, he'd be the only miserable child there."

"And how do you personally feel after these incidents?" the doctor asks. She cries again for a while, sobbing and snorting. I can imagine her mascara all over her face now.

"Trapped. I feel trapped."

"I understand," he begins. He shouldn't have said that. She hates when people say that they understand.

"No, you don't. No one does. If you don't have to deal with it, you don't *really* know. You can't possibly imagine the pain we feel, how we desperately try not to provoke a reaction. We are constantly walking on eggshells."

I don't think she walks on eggshells. Not my mother. She doesn't seem to take my feelings into account at all. This is how *I* feel. She judges me. I don't like being judged, measured, adjusted. What if I cannot be improved? I try, I really try! But it doesn't work.

She continues after a pause.

"It is very hard. It is one complicated relationship I cannot escape from."

What does my mother mean by that? A 'complicated relationship'? I don't try to complicate things. Or do I? I suddenly feel uneasy.

The conversation continues, my ear still glued to the door.

"And I feel ashamed for even thinking about escaping this reality," my mum says. I am no longer following.

"Sometimes darkness is inevitable before the light," the doctor says rather emotionally, not seeming able to stay impartial. "It is ok to feel like this. It is not a weakness. I think it takes guts to own it. Sometimes, it takes guts to live." He pauses for a second and then adds, "Sometimes, it takes guts to love."

"I want to do better. I want to just let him be. But I am bombarded by all these social expectations, and I feel it is my responsibility to 'fix' him. I often think if I only win this battle, or the next, if I can only guide him better, if I only am stronger, things may improve." She sobs again. "Every small improvement brings me hope…" she pauses for a second, "only to crush me later. I begin to fear hope. Hope is a dangerous feeling."

"I think I understand what you mean. Living without hope is easier. But no matter how hard you try, your mind wonders and dares to hope. It desperately searches for an apparent confirmation of your ill-fated hope. But there are no guarantees in life. Not just for you – for anyone." It sounds as if he is choosing his words very carefully. "I say, embrace your rollercoaster of a life. Don't question it, don't try to hold on too tight, know you will not be able to minimise its movement. Instead, raise your hands up and ride it. Feel the chills, with all its lows and highs. You might as well." The doctor sounds passionate, suddenly completely uncomposed. He waits for his words to settle and then continues in a quieter voice, "And you don't need to be stronger. You don't even need to win your battles. You should try to guide Robert, but don't make a religion out of it. Let him deal with his own failures, let him think for himself, let him grow up. Stop trying to fix him."

"But isn't it what parents do?"

"Maybe. But it is not really their job. You need to learn to let children find their own way and become their own people. Even children like Robert."

"So, what is my job?" she asks in a clear voice, the sobbing has stopped.

"To love him. Because and even if."

Even if...

Suddenly I experience a strange, relatively new feeling. What is it? It is bittersweet and consuming. It feels good, I am filled with anticipation and a sense of wonder. I try to remember the names of all the emotions I learnt from the training I had when I was six. Was this the dangerous one?

Yes, it feels like the dangerous *hope*! Maybe, she can learn to love me like I need her to love me – no matter what, even if I am far from perfect.

Back into reality, Daniel quietly sat in a chair. This was not what he imagined Robert's life had been like. Robert's feelings of turmoil were so frightening that it took Daniel some time to come to his senses. No wonder Robert had felt like an outsider. He *was* an outsider. Daniel now understood why Robert was so protective of him, ensuring that Daniel's anxieties remained under control. Daniel didn't know what to say.

"Do you remember what I told you about empathy?" Robert asked.

"Empathy is a selfish feeling," Daniel said, clearly remembering Robert's words after all these years.

"Daniel, I believe we can do better than that."

"What do you mean?" Daniel was trying and failing to see Robert's point.

"I want you to understand that Msitua is not what you think it is. It is neither one thing or another. Nothing is that simple, Daniel. There are pluses and minuses in everyone. You were right, F84.0 has many advantages, but it also has many shortcomings. Some of those shortcomings are not pretty. *Let's not pretend that you have all the answers.*"

"You are speaking strangely," Daniel said. He had never heard Robert speak like this before.

"What do you mean?" Robert asked. Daniel realised that Robert was utterly unaware of the developing advances his AI was demonstrating.

"I am not sure how to express it," Daniel started to share an unlikely thought, but straight away moved to block its transmission, rethinking his point. It was not probable. But then, everything else they had experienced today wasn't probable either.

"You think that without my body, my stress and my anxieties, I have become more empathetic?" Robert asked, Daniel's efforts to block his thought seemingly having failed.

"I don't know. I guess we will see."

Daniel sighed. Robert's shared memories were still playing on his mind, prompting him to ask a question he was almost afraid to voice.

"Do you think my Theory is obsolete?" he finally asked.

"Honestly? I am worried your presentation could be harmful to some. I hope I am wrong. You need to monitor the wider responses."

"Ok."

"Ok," Robert sensed Daniel's frustration rising. "Shall we take a break?"

Daniel needed a moment. He wanted to think. What was Robert implying? That it wasn't the right thing to do? From a scientific perspective, what could anyone possibly change if the developments were already naturally taking place? What did it matter whether Daniel or anyone else proclaimed it or not? Despite humanity's dislike of being related to apes, no one could deny that ultimately we were once the same. And we learnt to make our peace with that truth. Science is not subjective, it doesn't discriminate. It's facts and only facts. And the Robert Daniel knew would have always said the same. But *this* Robert doesn't.

Suddenly, Daniel felt tired again, and the doubt in his mind transformed to an emptiness in his chest. He had never considered that there could be a social implication to his diagnosis of updated human evolution. He became so preoccupied with the importance of his discovery, he hadn't even considered what it could mean for the neuro-typical population. Would his broadcast indeed divide the society into two groups – the advantageous and the ones left behind? It was a troubling thought.

His coffee was getting cold, and somehow it had lost its appeal. Daniel disposed of it in the liquid outlet. Did he really do it all for the acknowledgement of his ego? He certainly had an ego of sorts, he knew that much.

Daniel's mind wandered to the times when he was just a kid. His parents would encourage him to play with other children, but he felt anxious from just looking at them. They were laughing and sharing toys, running after each other, giggling. A part of Daniel wanted to play like that, but another bigger part made him alarmed at just the thought of joining in.

'What is wrong with me?' thought Daniel for the first time. He was five.

Chapter Thirteen
THE MESSAGE

Professor's Stein's Tele-paths were suddenly 'unavailable'. Hundreds of people were trying to get in touch with the new 'hero on the block', the man who had popularised Msitua. Meanwhile, the business arm of Dr Biote's research practice couldn't cope with the number of appointment requests that wanted to discuss investments into the new human-AI project that Daniel had proposed. Various media feeds were distributing inspirational stories about the advantages telepathic technology offered and how Msitua variants were discovering amazing talents and unique skills as a result of their new Tele-paths communication practices.

Job boards had started specifically asking for telepathically-compatible candidates, to ensure improved capability for faster delivery of ideas, analyses of data, and generally just increased expectations of human functionality.

The world was changing. Fast. But Daniel wasn't there to see it.

He had spent the past twenty-four hours isolated, indulging in deep self-searching thoughts, and worrying about the possible complications of his discovery. He decided to check a few of the old-fashioned media channels as his grandfather suggested. The dated social tools that allowed everyone to share their thoughts by writing and posting. Daniel had stopped using them a while ago, mostly because he believed that social media was full of fake news and unnatural expectations. Their limitations also meant there was no way they could become a communication channel for the future. Daniel believed in the value of Tele-paths, where you could share real thoughts and feelings, as well as using it to advance your intellect. Tele-paths were set to become a genuinely authentic communication channel for the decades ahead.

Daniel signed in to TwitBook on his old computer. He could not remember the last time he logged in, but the automation in the system had already chosen videos to be added to Daniel's profile, including his last broadcast. Beneath the video, the platform had summed up millions of feedback and reviews gathered after the event. These had been taken from various social media sources so were comprehensive. Daniel breathed in heavily and started opening them one by one.

The majority of the messages were positive. Many well-wishers wanted Daniel to know how much it meant for them, their family members, friends, or children. Other messages praised the technological advances and the future progress. But some reviews were just mad, proclaiming the upcoming apocalypse and the inevitability of total AI domination. Daniel knew that these thoughts were naive and lacked substantial knowledge of modern AI technology. Without consciousness, there wasn't any risk of AIs or Megaminds taking over. With the human element, this type of consciousness should threaten us no more than humanity itself. If we were ever screwed by conscious AIs, we would only have human stupidity to blame.

There were other comments Daniel paused to read. Comments which questioned what was left for those who were not compatible, forced to stay behind. People who could never access the Tele-paths or work with the telepathic data which was increasingly becoming the most valuable resource.

'My son can't speak. He is preoccupied with Tele-paths, and it looks like he will never even need to learn the traditional ways of communication. Meanwhile, I am not compatible. Help! I am losing my son. It feels like we live in different realities.'

'I can't find a job. No one will hire me now because I am not compatible. There are no jobs left for neuro-typicals!'

'Does this news mean that all neuro-typical people will be considered not part of the evolving species? Are the rest of us all developmentally challenged?'

'If I can't process information efficiently, it doesn't make me less of a human. I am good at making friends and socialising. Why does no one require these soft skills anymore? What would our world be like without them? I am terrified to imagine.'

Daniel's heart sunk. His grandfather's AI was right. What had he done?!

Was everything he had said wrong? Things were already inevitably changing, uncontrollably progressing – Daniel had simply brought it into the forefront of discussion. Daniel was in two minds. On one hand, he couldn't see a world where he would ever want to run and hide from his discovery. It wouldn't be logical. We needed to advance in order to guarantee long-term survival. Fact. On the other hand, the evolutionary shift he had theorised had created division in society. It wasn't right. Daniel felt like he had simply 'flipped the coin' so it had landed on his side for once. Luck had just chosen new players.

Daniel switched on his grandfather's Tele-path.

"You were right. My presentation has exacerbated a rising inequality."

"Well, it is not all your fault. It was inevitable. If not you, someone else would have figured it out. You were just the first one to proclaim it. Brave, bold and... stupid." Robert's AI sighed, sounding surprisingly human-like. What was Robert's AI becoming? A voice of reason? All Daniel knew now that Robert's AI was making a lot of sense, and 'human sense' at that. "Your revised Theory of Evolution made me think about my own mistakes, and I don't just mean professionally."

"So, what now?" Daniel asked.

"Now that we have the information about raising inequality, the question is what we do with it."

"Robert, you know that Tele-paths require a specific structural pattern of thoughts, which guarantees that the frequencies align."

"I know, I know, you don't need to explain to me. But no one believed that telepathic communication was even possible in the first place. *If there is a goal, there is a path to reach it.*"

The channel went quiet, and Daniel stayed alone with his thoughts.

He didn't want to speak to the wider scientific community about his dilemma. They would not understand. He also did not feel like he could happily receive any more congratulations from those people who only benefitted from his discovery. Robert's words were playing on Daniel's mind, making him feel uneasy, making him doubt everything.

He scrolled down the ever-increasing live feed. One particular message attracted his attention. It seemed to come from a charitable organisation of human rights called 'NTRW'. Its IP address seemed local. Had they already created an organisation to protect neuro-typical's rights?

'Dr Stein, thank you for your speech. It is an impressive Theory but, I fear, it will lead to the increased unemployment and discrimination of the neuro-typical community. Since your presentation, the compatibility factor seems to be the main criteria for employers. Things are getting tougher for many of us. I hope there is way for everyone to co-exist. Finding a solution is a must!' – Maria Gordosi.

Daniel was stunned for a minute. How hadn't Daniel seen it before? Was he blinded by the progress he was a big part of? The problem was the issue of inequality, as old as history itself, incompatibility was just the latest fad.

Daniel wanted to do something about it. But where would he even begin? What would a neuro-typical do? Perhaps they would meet up to discuss the situation over a cup of coffee or tea. A frightening proposition for someone like Daniel. But maybe actions could speak louder than words. Was this one of those situations? He needed to know more. Yes, he could do it, he would arrange a casual meeting with Maria Gordosi.

Daniel wasn't an outgoing person, so he hadn't initiated a social meeting in years. Social events always seemed to trigger his anxieties. Why bother? Especially when he could have a 'real' conversation with his colleagues and friends, and even date via Tele-paths.

In short, to go out of his way to meet someone he didn't know, just for the sake of a conversation, seemed like a big task for Daniel. He wasn't sure why he was considering it. Maybe he was hoping to fix things. Even though these were probably unfixable, unavoidable, inevitable things. But part of him felt responsible for delivering the message. He had always swore by the old adage of not killing the messenger. Or should you?

Daniel's logical mind was sceptical, but the strange AI that had taken up residence in his head was pushing him to act. What could possibly be done now? Maybe a solution was some sort of social programme, the possibility of a new qualification? After all, this had been suggested for the Msitua population in the past. But it never really worked, Daniel knew that much. These programmes were a quick fix, which never really brought any long-term benefits. Governments just took an easy way out – offering financial assistance instead of integrating them into the workplace. It was easier *not* to deal with the associated social challenges than to welcome them, maybe even embrace them. 'Weird' had never been accepted as 'normal'. Instead, it had become a label people shielded themselves from. But it didn't have to be that way anymore. Maybe he could figure out a solution this time.

Daniel did the unthinkable, and wrote to Maria Gordosi incognito requesting a meeting. She wrote back sharing the address of a nearby coffee shop, which Daniel knew from when he would pass it going for walks in the park. It was a popular place. Neuro-typicals liked it. 'I hope it won't be too busy,' Daniel thought. He considered for a minute and accepted the invitation.

Chapter Fourteen
MARIA

Daniel found himself standing in front of the little old-fashioned coffee shop, not daring to enter. He was fifteen minutes overdue already, but not because he arrived late. In fact, he was the type of person who always arrived on time. No, the delay was due to him fighting his rising anxiety. The door handle looked scruffy, and there were a couple of people inside, speaking loudly. He could hear the noises their cups made when placed back on the table after every single sip. The coffee shop had an unpleasant odour, which Daniel could smell even from outside. A stinky odour comprised of burnt beans and old wooden chairs, the smell of the walls touched by too many peoples' hands. He couldn't help thinking about the likely cleanliness of those hands, and the prospects didn't seem encouraging. Daniel hadn't been in a place like this for years, and now he clearly remembered why.

He was still standing there wondering if he would get the courage to eventually go in when a young woman with brown, slightly wavy hair opened the doors wide in a decisive movement to escape the building. For a fraction of a second, their eyes met, and she stood gazing directly at Daniel.

"Professor Stein?" she asked unexpectedly.

"Yes," Daniel confirmed.

"I am Maria."

"Oh, Maria, hi." She stretched out her hand in a sharp, confident motion. Daniel hesitated for a moment but offered his hand in return. Maria's hand felt warm, evidently from a cup of hot coffee just drank moments ago.

"I thought you weren't going to turn up," she said with a surprisingly upbeat tone. Daniel had forgotten how neurotypicals sounded, given he hadn't been in contact with one for a long time. It was a voice that reminded him of his grandmother and the high-pitched timbre which Daniel used to find annoying when he was little.

"I was just standing here, I couldn't bring myself to enter," he explained. Daniel was very straightforward with his answers. He always had a hard time hiding his true feelings, and being socially correct was the last thing on his mind right now. His facial expression was also evidently showing how he felt about the place.

"Oh, is it not the type of place you would usually go to?" Maria sounded judgmental. Daniel realised that she thought he was a snob.

"No, it is fine," Daniel said hurriedly to reassure her. "Let's go in."

Daniel's body felt forced and tortured, but he made a mammoth effort and managed to follow Maria into the coffee shop. The lighting was dimmed, but Daniel could still make out the chairs, messy with dirt gathering in the joints of the wood. Two people were having coffee and talking, occasionally laughing and loudly sipping their drinks. Without warning, Daniel smelt the damp cloth which probably was used to clean the tables, and it made him feel sick. His sense of smell had always been intense, and sometimes he wished it wasn't. He took a deep breath and followed Maria, who didn't seem to be bothered by any of this. She proceeded to walk to a table at the far corner of the coffee shop where an empty cup of coffee, presumably the one she had recently finished, was still standing.

"Please sit down," she ordered Daniel. "Would you like a drink?"

"I will get it," Daniel jumped in. "What would you like?"

"Cappuccino, please," she answered after a little pause.

"Really?" Daniel wasn't sure he understood correctly.

"Really... Why do you ask?"

"You had coffee a minute ago."

"And?" Maria was confused.

"The amount of caffeine in two cups of coffee could be incredibly stimulating for your heart, and as a result, harmful for –" he didn't finish his little lecture. He looked at Maria's face and was surprised to see her grinning at him. "Did I say something funny?"

"Nothing. It is just..."

"Just what?" he genuinely couldn't realise why she found his comment hilarious.

"You were so serious about the heart rate. I guess I am just not used to *this*."

"What do you mean by 'this'?" Daniel couldn't quite grasp what she was implying.

"The specific details of the danger of overdosing myself on caffeine," Maria replied, trying to mimic Daniel's voice. "You are very precise, aren't you?"

"Yes. That's me," Daniel felt uneasy.

"No big deal. I just find it endearing."

"Oh," Daniel smiled. No one had ever called him endearing.

"Shall we?" Maria pointed to the seat opposite her. Daniel hesitated for a minute, took a clean napkin from the table and carefully wiped the wooden seat of the chair before finally bringing himself to sit down.

He looked at Maria, who was smiling again, realising that he hadn't ordered that second cappuccino for her. He got up, gesturing that he was going to order. She smiled and nodded. Daniel ordered the coffee while standing unusually far back from the till. Once it arrived, he picked it up carefully and brought it to Maria.

"Nothing for you?" she asked.

"No, no. I had my coffee in the morning." This made her smile again. Despite this excuse, the real reason was that Daniel just didn't feel comfortable consuming any food in this place.

Daniel gave a shy smile. He really felt uneasy when people paid too much attention to his habits, but somehow he could sense that Maria truly found his actions endearing. Hasn't she had any Msitua friends at all? Then he thought of himself, realising that he hadn't had any close neuro-typical friends either.

In his own defence, neuro-typicals came with too many communication demands, not to mention the gatherings, meetings, and dates. Usually, he found face to face meetings daunting and unpleasant. Seeing someone's face up-close instinctively made him concentrate on their most prominent features, which he then couldn't stop staring at throughout the whole conversation. Many supposedly pleasant dates would turn into an extended session of looking at Emmie's uneven teeth, or staring at Jimmy's receding hairline.

Neuro-typical people faced with this behaviour would inevitably consider Daniel rude, and he struggled to come to terms with this perception. He never thought he was any of those things – instead he felt misunderstood and incapable of adequately fitting in. It's why he had decided to keep almost solely to digital communication, and once Tele-paths became widely available, he switched to using them. Once he had gone fully tele-pathical, he finally felt equal, accepted and capable of having a decent conversation.

But now he had to face his fears all over again. Yet somehow Maria seemed very pleasant to look at. Her face wasn't perfect, but Daniel found himself relaxed while looking at her. There was nothing that stood out in particular that caught his eye, so nothing to potentially drive him crazy throughout their conversation.

"Maria," he started putting on his presentational voice, "I would like to help. Really. As you know, I have been looking at social media, and I realised how upsetting my presentation has been for so many neuro-typical humans. I didn't mean to imply that those who are not Msitua are missing out on the evolutionary advantage. I actually think the next few generations will develop F84.0 genes even in neuro-typical couples. I now realise that it didn't come across clearly in my presentation."

Maria raised one eyebrow. "I hear you, but your Theory is controversial. It clearly suggests an intellectual advantage for those with Msitua traits, especially nowadays when various technologies are available only to the few. So, I am asking you this. Is it true?"

"Is what true?"

"That Msitua 'humans' are the future of evolutionary progress."

"Well..."

"Is this true, Daniel?" she was putting him on the spot, staring into his eyes. Daniel strangely enjoyed her calling him by his name.

"You have heard my presentation," Daniel began, trying to avoid answering directly. "Have you ever read Hawkins' research on the existence of God? He knew for a fact God didn't exist."

"Yessss…" Maria said exaggerating the 's'. Daniel suspected that she found the question confusing, which was exactly his intention.

"Well, it was a difficult question for Hawkins to answer because his understanding was clearly negative, but he tried to put it gently. He gave those who chose to believe in God the choice of believing, while explaining why he personally finds it impossible."

"You weren't gentle in your presentation."

"Maybe you are right. Sometimes it is hard to put something gently when you just *know*."

"What do you *know*?"

"Like I said, the facts."

"Are you saying that your Theory is undeniable," Maria closed her eyes for a second like his words were hurting her.

"Not exactly."

"But that is what you've just said."

"Evolution favours successful mutations."

"You lost me there. What do you actually mean?"

"I mean that *we find what we search for*. Msitua gene is clearly destined to thrive in our modern reality. The reality *we* created by developing our various communication technologies."

"It's sad," Maria sighed.

"Why is it sad?"

"Because we are slowly going to lose our verbal communication skills. They made us who we are. They define our lives!"

"Yes, it is always sad to lose something you are used to. Change is frightening. But what if the upcoming change is better? Telepathy takes our communication abilities to a new level we can't even begin to comprehend. We can share our thoughts, emotions, experiences."

"But are all our thoughts and emotions good? And aren't some of our feelings very private? Should all of these be shared?"

"Of course not, but we will allow for privacy. Telepaths have mental safety gates, which you can activate with a simple thought. But what you chose to share would be genuine – not told through any deliberate or accidental filter. Our communication with each other would reach a new level – the level of absolute authenticity."

"I am terrified of the idea of completely authentic human thought, if I am being honest."

"I know what you mean. But a Msitua brain doesn't work like a neuro-typical one. We mean what we say – maybe this is the way forward for humanity."

"Wouldn't that be fun?" Maria wondered, allowing herself a mild smile. Daniel couldn't figure out if she was being sarcastic or not. "It's interesting – now I understand why Msitua people struggle with anxiety in our society."

"Why? Because we say what we mean?

"Yes."

"Sometimes, in our society, that is inconvenient. But it is perfect for a telepathic reality, don't you think? I believe that all Msitua meltdowns come from the social games and expectations we have to face on a daily basis. Our mental program is not compatible with the current reality."

"And *our* mental program is not compatible with the telepathic world," Maria said with a long exhale.

"Yes," Daniel answered impassively, incapable of saying anything reassuring.

"So, is this evolutionary development fortunate for humanity?"

"That depends on your point of view."

"And what is your point of view?"

"I am a Msitua variant. My grandfather was also. We had to struggle through the ups and downs of the related challenges in our current society. Would I wish it on anyone? Probably not. Does it make me feel better knowing that my brain's oddities are not a malfunction? Probably yes."

"I can imagine," she looked at Daniel's crossed hands held close to his body, and realised that he didn't want to touch the table or anything else in this place. No, actually, she *couldn't* imagine. "Please, tell me more about your life. I really want to know," she said her eyes opening wider, expressing a genuine interest in the subject.

"Maybe another time." Really, how long had Daniel known this woman? Twenty minutes? He had already said more about himself than he would normally be comfortable with. "All I wanted to say is that the progress we achieve, and its demands do come at a cost. We have to realise at least this much."

"I agree. Well, I can tell you that this cost is too much, at least to my family and my friends."

"Then *you* tell me more about *your* life."

"Well, for starters, I come from a poor working-class family, my father and my mother didn't have any special talents. They were completely incompatible with the olden days' technology, let alone with the modern one. They were unable to requalify as anything useful. We became a sort of unnecessary class of people."

"I am so sorry. I had no idea," Daniel, suddenly for the first time in his life, felt sorry for another person's family. An actual *emotional* empathy he never was able to relate to previously.

"They are dead now. My father passed away three years ago, and my mother a year after that," Maria looked sad.

Daniel realised that she loved her parents in exactly the way he loved his family. He couldn't imagine them gone... Daniel couldn't find an explanation for his feelings, but it felt almost like Maria's pain was actually *hurting* him. It was a strange emotion, and Daniel had to stop a sudden impulse to hug and comfort her. To hold a complete stranger? Unthinkable. This unbidden unexpected reaction frightened him, and he could feel it triggering a panic attack. He had to leave. Now!

"I am so sorry for your loss," Daniel said, trying to ignore the fact that his whole body ached, and his vision was getting blurry. He had to get away. "I have to leave."

"Right now?" Maria asked, disorientated.

"Now, yes. I am so sorry," Daniel held his hand close to his mouth, he felt like he was going to throw up. Maria recognised the gesture, and her tone of voice changed.

"Sure. I am sorry. I probably said something. What can I do?" She tried to help by offering a tissue. "Look, I can call you later. Don't worry –" she said, although she wasn't sure how much Daniel heard as he ran out of the coffee shop. Maria stayed behind, seated alone.

Daniel felt nauseous, and as if he was walking in a daze. All he could think of was getting to his apartment, closing the door shut and never coming out again. He wanted to get back to his home so he could hide safely away from these intense emotions and strange feelings.

He could not imagine what Maria was thinking of him. Probably she would never want to see him again, given that he left the coffee shop in such a rude manner. He didn't even say goodbye.

Once Daniel's panic attack was under control, he felt sad at the thought. Daniel realised that he would actually love to see Maria again. But that probably would never happen, and even if it did he knew he couldn't stay sane and in control of his crazy rollercoaster of emotions! He should have never taken that amygdala nano-chip out of his head! He was pathetic.

'What an annoying evolutionary development the Msitua brain is!' Daniel thought.

That night Maria couldn't sleep. Her thoughts were spinning in her head, taking her to unexpected places.

What was she expecting when she decided to meet Professor Stein? She went to the coffee shop with guns blazing, ready to fight her corner with the person who bluntly declared sweeping evolutionary advantages that only benefited half of the human population. She expected Professor Stein to be cold, stuck up and snobbish. But it did not take long to realise that this was just the image of him she had painted in her mind. Instead, the Daniel she met wasn't like that at all, and now she couldn't get him out of her head.

Obviously, Maria had seen what Daniel looked like via the broadcast platform, but in real life, he was nothing like the professor from the screen. In the flesh, Daniel was tall and handsome, surely not older than his late thirties, she figured. His body, no doubt kept on a strict diet of healthy foods and limited consumption of 'treats' like caffeine, seemed in perfect shape. He had a slim, yet masculine physique, with broad shoulders, and his straight back gave him a confident posture – not what she had expected for someone from the scientific community. His legs were long and slim, with strongly defined muscles noticeable through the thin fabric of his suit. He probably was a runner. His appearance was immaculate, from the light summer jumper in neutral light-grey colour, to the clean white casual shoes he wore.

What Maria liked most about Daniel Stein was his face. Perfectly shaven, it revealed a square masculine jawline. Daniel's dark hair was perfectly cut and neatly styled, and Maria wondered what it would feel like to run her fingers through his thick hair, messing up the tufts. *That* was an unexpected thought!

Maria couldn't understand why Daniel seemed so confident. Was it his polished professor's speeches, or the strongly defined jawline? The undeniable intelligence of his words was powerful, but Maria found herself sensing Daniel's inner strength, his unquestionable influence on whomever he found himself talking to. However, it wasn't thoughts about his strength which Maria was losing sleep about. It was Daniel's vulnerability that had crept its way to Maria's heart, suddenly undermining everything she wanted to say – all her points, all her accusations.

Daniel wasn't like any other man Maria had met. He didn't seem to be making any effort to appear invincible or charming, like many of them do. He was very much himself. Maria could see it right away. There was something absolutely genuine about Daniel Stein. He wasn't playing games. He didn't try to impress her, didn't defend himself, or pick a fight over the correctness of the Theory. He did what Maria didn't expect him to do. He calmly answered questions, albeit in his own scientifically confusing manner. He listened, and he agreed with her concerns. Just like that.

But then he left abruptly, leaving Maria to wonder what she said or perhaps didn't say. He was certainly a complicated man, she understood that much. Yet he was also an open and genuine man. *A transparent enigma.* On one hand, Maria realised that she had no idea who Daniel Stein really was nor what kind of problems this genius could cause. Yet, on the other hand, a person who always said what he thought was refreshing. Maria couldn't help but feel safe when she was next to Daniel. She could just be. It was impossible to be anything else with him. Daniel's presence was disarming.

As they didn't finish their conversation, it was only logical if she called him tomorrow to arrange another meeting. Maria had to protect the rights of neuro-typicals and to make sure that Daniel realised the full scope of the issues he had helped create. She had to see him for professional reasons. For this singular, important, noble reason. At least, this was what Maria kept telling herself, over and over, as the night became dawn.

Chapter Fifteen
ILLOGICAL STUPID HEART

The next morning Daniel felt like himself again. The sun was shining, and its rays reflected across his spotless steel kitchen worktop illuminating it beautifully with the full spectrum of colours. Daniel requested his Home Assist to make him a coffee, its aroma slowly diffusing in the air as it spread across the limited space of his apartment. The beauty of quiet mornings was truly one of the great pleasures of life. Calm and peaceful – what could possibly be more enjoyable?

The calmness of the morning was abruptly interrupted by a call, and a *phone* call at that. A *phone* – one of the devices that was now almost completely obsolete for the Msitua population because of the development of Tele-paths. However, everyone still had one, just in case. As you'd expect, Daniel's phone had hardly ever rung, and it took him a while to realise what the noise was, and where it was coming from.

"Answer," Daniel told his smart Home Assist. It was lucky he was able to answer the phone with voice control, as Daniel couldn't even remember where he saw it last.

"Hello," said the familiar voice, which suddenly filled Daniel with an array of mixed emotions, the two strongest of which were happiness and fear. "Daniel? It's Maria. I just wanted to see how you were?"

"I am fine," Daniel responded, before inwardly cursing himself for forgetting to say hello and thank you. The art of small talk had never been Daniel's strongest point. "Sorry, I mean, yes, hello. I wanted to apologise for leaving the coffee shop in such a hurry yesterday. I suddenly felt unwell."

"I realised. Was it something I said? I am not sure if I was the cause. But if I was, I am so sorry."

"No, no. It wasn't something you said. It's complicated – hard to explain."

"Would you like to meet up for a coffee again?" Maria asked. "I just figured, we hadn't finished our conversation."

Daniel's heart jumped. He really wanted to see Maria. It surprised himself to learn that this feeling was even stronger than the feeling that he didn't want to go outside today.

"I would love to see you," he hurried to answer. Maria was silent for a second. Maybe he was jumping to conclusions too quickly, she didn't say she wanted to see *him*. She had only said she wanted to finish the conversation. He should have said 'I would like to finish our conversation too', or something similar. He had been too upfront again. Navigating these neuro-typical waters were exhausting. "Sorry, Maria, I mean I would like to finish our meeting, please," he said, managing to correct himself. Unfortunately this correction had only made his desperation more obvious.

"Daniel," she said eventually, "I would love to see you too."

"Great, thank you," Daniel added awkwardly.

He heard Maria's gentle laughter, a laughter, which Daniel felt was genuine. A laugh which meant that she still found him endearing.

"Where then?" Maria asked. "I would suggest the coffee shop, but something told me you didn't enjoy your time there. So, you choose."

"No, I didn't like the coffee shop. There is a cosy restaurant on Meadow Road called Hide, would you like to meet there?"

"Sounds good. When?"

"Today? Or is today too soon?" Daniel was getting nervous. "Today or tomorrow, or the day after tomorrow perhaps?"

"Today is not too soon," Maria said firmly. Daniel could almost visualise her smile. "Seven any good?"

"That's good. See you at seven."

"See you there."

Daniel hung up. It had ended up feeling like they were arranging a date. Was it a date? Did she think it felt like a date? Daniel's head was spinning. He didn't *do* dates. Dates were an utterly energy-zapping activity. Always a disappointment. But now, despite his nerves, he also felt excited. Suddenly he realised that he wanted it to be a date. He liked Maria. There was no doubt, no misunderstanding in his heart, he genuinely really liked her. A lot.

Daniel couldn't concentrate on anything after the call. Before the call, he had planned to run a new research on telepathic compatability. It was already clear that the neuron wiring in Msitua brains had many differences in comparison to neuro-typicals. It was also clear that this difference in wiring allowed so-called internal communication channels to function much more effectively, operating on a much more profound frequency which made it possible to communicate thoughts, images and feelings via Tele-paths. Neuro-typical minds, on the other hand, were much more preoccupied with verbal communication. It was a fact of nature that any brain that was better equipped in some parts would be less well equipped in others.

It always puzzled Daniel that the development of systematic capabilities in the Msitua brain had to inevitably cause limitations in speech and interactions. And on that note, why the more this communication function was hindered, the more effective the telepathic abilities were. Daniel was determined to explore his opportunities, as he was thinking of how to accomplish a rather impossible idea. A seeming impossible idea that neuro-typicals could also tap into true telepathic communication. But how?

Daniel tele-pathically liaised with various leading scientists, interrogating them for their thoughts. Could it hypothetically be possible? The responses he received ranged from puzzlement about why he was asking to direct ridicule of the idea, but all of the responses were universally negative. Theoretically, it *was* an impossible task. As the day wore on, he wanted to continue his quest for a solution, but Daniel found it very difficult to concentrate on the task. His brain kept wandering off, even during his calls. A particularly embarrassing moment occurred when after a few minutes of conversation with one professor, she asked Daniel, "Who is Maria? And how would I know which top you should wear tonight?" Next time, he would have to take far better precautions to mentally gate his unbidden thoughts.

Daniel had never felt out of control with his thoughts before. He always managed to function methodically during any activity he set himself. It was certainly known that the F84.0 brain could wander off, and in some cases become even more hyperactive than a neuro-typicals' mind. Many Msitua children found it impossible to concentrate when at school, but when it came to their dreams, they would become all-consumed. Daniel was fortunate in that he never struggled to concentrate, because he had ended up in a career where he was always pursuing what he loved.

Unlike the Msitua population, neuro-typicals were able to multi-task and did not suffer from the same sort of fixation. They could multi-task when they were concentrating, when they were talking, when they were doing – always doubting, analysing, altering their social intentions – even saying one thing and meaning another. Could something be done to create better undisturbed thinking processes in a neuro-typical's mind? And would this help produce a stronger frequency to help solve the Telepaths problem? It was an idea worth exploring.

Daniel called his grandfather's AI immediately.

"Hi Robert," Daniel began impatiently.

"Here you are! What is happening, Daniel?" Robert's AI instantly realised that Daniel was demonstrating raised anxiety levels and agitated excitement.

"I have just been thinking about the importance of uninterrupted concentration, visual memory and related frequency of associated neurons. But then when you look at neuro-typicals... well, it looks like an impossible task for them."

"Daniel, it *is* an impossible task. The wiring of a neuro-typical brain is just not as strong in this department. It would be like trying to teach a Neanderthal the String Theory. The neuro-typical brain hasn't gained the necessary wiring connections to be able to achieve compatibility. And without these connections, they won't be able to grasp the subject. It does seem to be out of reach."

"I know, I hear you. But the difference between a Neanderthal and Homo Sapiens is much more vast than the difference between Homo Sapiens and Homo Deus. So, are we absolutely positive that there is no way? Because I have been wondering. Suppose you could somehow motivate or stimulate a different thinking process in neuro-typicals, to be wholly absorbed in a single thought with pure clarity. Could it possibly produce a stronger frequency?"

"What you are proposing is very ambitious. If we can stop neuro-typicals from engaging in the social and mind games that come naturally to them, maybe we stand a chance. But they will never abandon these games – their minds love to play," Robert declared. "Daniel, I couldn't find the solution to this problem, and I did try. But there is nothing to stop you from looking into it. After all, '*A new discovery is just a thought away*,' as I always taught you."

"I remember," Daniel confirmed. "You used to say that according to the Game Theory, there is always at least one possibility that will inevitably take you towards your goal. The question is not if you are going to get there or not, the question always remains *how many of those possibilities you are willing to explore on your way*."

They stayed quiet for a minute. Then Robert broke the silence.

"Something else has happened, something exciting. Why aren't you sharing? Or do you have another surprise in store for me, like with the broadcast?"

"I met someone," Daniel answered with slight hesitation.

"You mean, someone, like a girl someone?" Robert said in a surprised and sceptical tone.

"She is someone I have just met. She is different. Unassumingly perfect in all her imperfections."

"How interesting. Despite the new technologies we have today, despite all the programmes with personality matching and all the chemical stimulations, very rarely – maybe once in a lifetime – we feel a powerful bond with someone, and we cannot explain why."

"What are you trying to say? I am not following," Daniel was trying to make sense of what Robert was suggesting. He was being unusually poetic for a Msitua variant, not to mention for an AI.

"You haven't discussed a girl with me since, well, never."

"I guess I haven't. We met yesterday. But we are going on our first date tonight. Or rather, I hope it is a date. She said 'I want to see you too'. It sounds like a date, right?" Daniel mumbled.

"First date? I just assumed you had been going out with her for a while."

"Well, we haven't. But I have never felt like this before."

"Sounds promising."

"I think so. I can't explain," and Daniel really couldn't. None of it was logical, but it was most certainly exciting. It felt good. Robert could read Daniel's elevated feelings, and he didn't need him to explain further.

"I loved your grandmother like that, I just instantly knew that she was the one. It is called love, my boy."

"Love? I don't know. What is love? It is a simple chemical reaction in our brain," Daniel mumbled again.

"Oh, Daniel. It is so much more than that. You will see. Tell me more about her."

"I can't tell you a lot, we didn't have much time to find out about each other. I am not even sure if she likes me back."

"Why not? Couldn't you sense her feelings via Tele-paths?"

"Robert, there is something else. I haven't been meeting her in Tele-paths, because… She is incompatible." 'Incompatible…' suddenly Daniel heard it back in his head. Oh no! It would be a disaster.

"Your grandmother was a neuro-typical too. She was the best thing in my life."

"It is just, things are different now," Daniel worried, and he couldn't stop his thoughts from going to a dark place. "Let's talk later," he hurried to end the Tele-path before Robert realised the full scope of associated complications.

For now, there was nothing else to say, and it was too soon to discuss Maria any further. Maybe it wasn't worth a discussion at all. Daniel knew that relationships were complicated. And they had yet to have their first date. Maybe it would not lead anywhere. But one thing Daniel knew for sure, it couldn't get too serious. Too much was at stake.

Daniel ended the call, and was left alone with his thoughts. The afternoon didn't seem so breezy and relaxing anymore. It felt like a dark cloud had grown over Daniel's head, covering the sunlight, and colouring everything grey.

Daniel's upbeat mood slowly vanished, as did his excitement for the date. How hadn't he realised this could not work before? How did he let himself develop feelings for Maria? Couldn't he control himself?

No, he couldn't. He wasn't built that way. He was an open book. When he spoke, he told the truth. When he worked, he worked obsessively. When he hated, he hated with all the darkness in his heart. And when he loved, he loved! Instantly, consumingly, completely.

Daniel could have called Maria to tell her that he would not be able to see her again. He could have cancelled their 'date'. He could have said that any possible attraction between them could lead to significant complications in their lives and the lives of others. That any relationship could undermine the progress and human evolution itself. With the stakes so high, risking the future didn't make sense. Not one bit.

Not seeing Maria again would surely hurt for a time, but it all so easily could just end here. It *could*, but Daniel's illogical stupid heart found itself overruling one of the most logical brains in human history.

Chapter Sixteen
NO GOING BACK

Daniel entered Hide, the cosy restaurant on Meadow Street. He was perfectly on time, as always. The maitre-d'hotel recognised Daniel and proceeded him to his table. Daniel was pleased to find the usual snow-white new-tech tablecloths, paired with the usual stunning white velvet chairs. The restaurant's simple elegance comforted Daniel, it was a perfect place to meet up. They always played relaxing lounge music softly over the speakers, and the lights were dimmed to a level of absolute serenity. Hide had a pleasant aroma that reminded Daniel of freshly-cut meadows, a sweet smell tastefully balanced on the edge of headiness, yet without overstimulating the senses. The seating in the restaurant had been skillfully arranged so that every guest could enjoy a semblance of secluded privacy. And the food was always delicious too – beautiful vegan options cooked to perfection and neatly delivered as individual beautifully arranged sections on a plate. Msitua heaven!

Daniel had booked the same table he had always booked, close by a window with self-adjusting blinds. He liked to leave these slightly open, allowing just a touch of natural light to sneak in. Daniel checked the hologram clock on the left wall of the restaurant. Maria was now late. Usually, Daniel would get irritated about punctuality, but not tonight. To his surprise, he realised that he was prepared to wait for Maria as long as he needed.

Daniel ordered a glass of spring bottled water, made himself comfortable and tried to just be in the moment, despite feeling nervous excitement. For someone who didn't do waiting very well, he was surprisingly composed. Unbidden, the thought that she might not come at all crossed his mind. Perhaps this would all end just as spontaneously as it began. It could be the easy way out. But the unfamiliar part of his personality desperately wished that this awful thought was just that – a thought, a hypothetical thought.

And then he saw her: her silky brown hair swaying softly as she entered the restaurant and removed her jacket, her smooth shoulders beautifully on show, revealing gracious delicate arms, her curvaceous body framed by a simple, elegant navy dress. Daniel admired her soft feminine curves. Why was he ever obsessed with the straightness of lines? Curves were so much more beautiful. Daniel felt unusual lightheadedness, watching Maria turn to scan the restaurant. Daniel was sure that everyone could hear his loud heartbeat, pulsating in his temples.

Maria spotted Daniel and gave him a simple but confident wave. Daniel froze, unable to respond – he couldn't move. It was the shock of seeing her again – the strange feeling like he had known her forever, despite only having met her once before. As she approached the table, the scent of her perfume mixed with the background aroma of meadows reminded him of going home somehow. As her smile broadened, it felt as if it was opening his very soul up, perhaps irreparably so.

"Hello, Daniel," Maria said once she came closer. Daniel swallowed hard.

"Hello." It was all that he could manage.

She sat opposite him looking into his eyes, still smiling. The silence probably only lasted a minute, but for Daniel, it felt like forever. He was never any good at small talk, and as his lifestyle had never required any, he got very good at being bad at it. He searched for something to say, something breezy. Maria came to the rescue.

"It is good to see you. How are you?"

"How am I? I am mired in the agony of trying to figure out a way of uniting incompatibles with compatibles," Daniel responded. Oh no! Not breezy at all. She was probably expecting the standard small talk game: *'How are you?', 'I am good, thank you,' and so on*. A useful thought that had showed up too late in Daniel's head. Maria smiled.

"That is amazing!" she said, raising a perfectly defined eyebrow. This eyebrow was so expressive, in one simple movement, it said so much. It meant 'are we talking business right away?' "I have been mired in thoughts too – thinking about how I approached you, how I acted. I feel I was too abrupt. I am sorry. I guess I didn't know what to expect. And you seem like such a decent guy. I am sure you hadn't realised the ramifications of your broadcast."

"I hadn't," said Daniel with a sigh.

"I know, I understand," Maria said, hurrying to reassure him, "I am delighted I've met you because I really think that there is something special in people like you." She paused for a second, feeling the need to justify her words. "And by 'you' I mean scientists, the great scientists of our time. No one can deny the impressiveness of our new technologies! We can all see that Tele-paths open a window of great opportunities for many people. We just need to make sure it doesn't shut the door for others. Right?" she stared at Daniel for a few moments, the sort of lengthy stare that only neuro-typicals could tolerate. But Daniel didn't pull his gaze away. She was right. Daniel couldn't have put it better himself, she said it perfectly.

"Right. Absolutely. It is just... extremely difficult to figure out how to keep that door open. But, as my grandfather used to say, *impossible is nothing*."

"Daniel, there *has* to be a way," Maria seemed slightly more concerned now. Daniel wasn't sure if he could promise more than he did, but he was saved by the maitre-d'hotel who came closer, delicately waiting for Maria and Daniel to acknowledge his presence.

Maria ordered a special Hide cocktail which had zero alcohol but contained a certain plant-based ingredient with a similar relaxing effect on the body and mind, minus the unhealthy consequences. Daniel ordered an orange juice with strictly no pulp.

"As I was saying, my grandfather and I are working very hard on figuring out the possibility of universal compatibility," Daniel had high hopes for his grandfather's AI's contribution to a potential solution. Given that Robert created Tele-paths in the first place, he was best-placed to innovate and upgrade them.

"That's great, Daniel!" Maria exclaimed, emphasising a great deal of emotion in one short outburst. Usually, Daniel was annoyed by the manner neuro-typicals spoke, it was often like sitting next to a bomb. You said something and the response would be 'Bam!' – a ton of emotional energy suddenly released, impossible and exhausting to follow. But Daniel observed Maria with amusement, trying to figure out her every move, every expression of her lively face. "I didn't realise you had two grandfathers who were both scientists."

"No, just the one scientist. Dr Robert Stein. Robert created Tele-paths."

"I know," Maria said, looking at Daniel suspiciously, "just I thought Dr Robert Stein had passed away."

"Yes," Daniel replied, managing a shy smile. "I am sorry. I am used to speaking about him like he is still alive."

"I see," Maria said, but she still looked slightly confused. "I guess many people prefer to speak of deceased relatives as though they were still alive."

"Yes, although for me he is alive. I planted his human-AI in my brain."

"Get out!" Maria's expressive face showed two simultaneous emotions – one of disbelief and one of fear. Daniel realised that he was at risk of seeming like a liar or like he'd lost his mind. He had to explain quickly before Maria settled on either one of these opinions.

"Do you remember from my broadcast, I mentioned the possibility of communicating with AIs via Tele-paths?" Daniel began slowly, hoping to lead her gently to the big reveal. Maria nodded, already figuring out where this was going. "Our collaboration with Robert's AI is a prototype which helped us look at such a possibility."

"Does he live in your head?" Maria was trying to grasp this newfound reality.

"No, not quite like that. He is an AI, and so it has its own virtual space to exist. But we can communicate when I choose to."

"Wow! Just Wow! Still, how is that even possible?"

"It is a developing technology. We are the first AI-Human hybrid, guinea pigs if you want to call it that..." Daniel wanted to explain more, but he did not want to let slip about Robert's growing consciousness. Not yet anyway.

"So you can communicate telepathically with your grandfather's AI because it is in your head, but also not really in your head?"

"Partially. Mostly we have had success because we are both compatible with Tele-paths. The systematic structure of our neuro-data is at the right frequency to telepathically connect us at an increased degree of compatibility. Our brains just *fit*. And of course, it's possible the biological connection also adds to the success of the process."

"I have researched a lot about the ability to preserve people's neuron patterns after their death. But this! It is a whole other level!" she looked deeply into Daniel's eyes as she spoke.

"Yes, it is pretty huge," Daniel acknowledged calmly.

"Do you know what this means?"

"What?" Daniel indeed knew what it meant, but he was curious if Maria did.

"It means that you are right about the Evolution. We are entering a new era of human abilities. We are evolving into something else."

"Maria, I am right. Msitua appears to be the next evolutionary step."

"Then, everyone else is doomed."

"I didn't mean that. Even if the Theory is correct, it doesn't necessarily make it *right* to live by what it means. You are entitled to question my announcement. When F84.0 was considered a disability, employers never bothered to welcome us as equals in society. And we have to make sure that history doesn't repeat itself to others."

"The world will never be the same," Maria whispered with a deep breath, clearly struggling to come to terms with what she was hearing.

"No, it will not. Our biological destination is to become Homo Deus, and Msitua gene seems to play a crucial part in it. But we still can choose to leave our Homo Sapiens stage with dignity. Not according to 'survival of the fittest', but rather with a conscious aim to help everyone live and thrive. How about that?" Daniel said.

"Well, if we can adapt the Tele-path technology to become compatible with neuro-typicals, maybe we stand a chance."

"Maybe."

They sat there silently for a minute as the built-in menu lit up at the table so they could order, sensing a natural pause in their conversation.

"Do you know what you would like to order?" Daniel asked. "They make perfectly nutritious veggie burgers here. The menu lets you tweak the ingredients according to your preference."

"Sure. Sounds good," Maria answered, gathering her thoughts.

"I was trying to be 'breezy' tonight," Daniel said, trying to downplay the heaviness of their discussion. "I think it worked." Maria looked at him with a warm smile sensing his attempt at making a joke.

They ate quietly, occasionally talking about various subjects, but mostly Daniel's research and the objectivity of human past history. Maria's willingness to listen to Daniel gave him encouragement to talk about his passions. It seemed that she genuinely liked to hear him going on and on about historical data, and the impossibility of reaching a hundred percent certainty in the historical field. History would always stay slightly muddled.

"We really just don't know what exactly happened, because everything recorded is literally one opinion. An opinion that is influenced by culture, governments, those in power, to name but a few. But now we live in an age where data will be preserved in its true form for future generations – people will look back on this as a glorious time in the science of History. Imagine, if you could speak to Napoleon or Churchill, if you could really understand their motives, or wander in the corners of their minds. Imagine, if you could Tele-path with a second world war soldier's AI, discover his true feelings, and witness the horrors of his life to make a more accurate judgement of human values, hopes and dreams of that age? Wouldn't that be amazing?" Daniel couldn't help going on and on.

Maria patiently listened and nodded. And for a minute Daniel was worried he might be boring her. But unexpectedly, Maria jumped into the conversation, questioning Daniel's statement. He was glad that she not only listened, but she also *heard* him too.

"But how could anyone's opinion be completely free of subjective judgement? Any experience is always subjective through our own eyes, our own mind, which in itself is a filter. And even if you form your own opinion, it is yours, and you may understand it in your own way. I see your point, but your personal opinion and thinking process is already influenced by so many subjective factors. You have an emotional understanding of events, based on your own perception of the world, deeply rooted by your upbringing, access to certain information, interests, hobbies, social values of the current time, music, friends, loved ones. Could anyone's opinion be truly objective?"

"Yes, you are absolutely right, from the neuro-typical perspective. But from the Msitua perspective, the perception of new-age information will become much more genuine, less dependent on cultural or social views."

Daniel loved how Maria challenged his ideas and looked at his hypothetical statements from a deeper perspective. She was absolutely right; absolute objectivity couldn't be attained. But we could get closer.

Maria was intelligent, passionate, and curious. Never in his life, had Daniel enjoyed discussing his interests as much as he did with Maria. Surprisingly, Daniel found himself relatively relaxed despite having dinner in a public place.

Whatever their future could hold, Daniel realised that he wasn't strong enough not to find out.

Chapter Seventeen
BATTLE OF OPINIONS

After dinner, Daniel and Maria walked through the park. The air was fresh, and the warmth of summer was slowly giving in to the cooling breeze that was the first sign of the coming autumn.

"I feel that we have talked all evening about me and my research. Maybe I am not as good a listener as you are. Tell me more about you," Daniel said to Maria.

"I... I don't know what to tell you, really. I am just an average neuro-typical girl who struggled to teach myself in the modern educational system. I was never really into technology, but I read a lot. I have a small collection of paper books," Maria confessed apologetically. Not many people had paper books anymore – the environmental impact no longer seemed justifiable. But older books remained, with the majority of people donating them to libraries or museums so that they could be accessed by anyone who had an interest in reading them. Daniel also loved paper books, and he secretly had a few himself.

"Do you? May I see them one day? I have a few myself," he said with a hint of excitement.

"I would love to show you, but unfortunately they are in my flat. I am not sure you will be comfortable there."

"Why?" Daniel asked, despite knowing that he was never truly comfortable in any accommodation other than his own.

"Daniel, I live in West London Council Estate," Maria answered quietly.

"Are you... *homeless*?" Daniel was shocked. He had never met a homeless person before. No one was technically homeless these days, and the descriptor 'homeless' had come to the large council estates that existed in the different parts of the City that were available for anyone in trouble. Anyone in need could stay as long as needed, but by all accounts, the estates were a terrifying sight.

"Yes. I know, it sounds awful, but I really had no choice. I couldn't secure a job for a long while."

"Surely not. You are smart and capable. How could it be that *you* would be without a job?" Daniel wondered. Maria smiled, but he could see the sadness in her eyes.

"Well, it wasn't a choice not to work. It all started from the digitalising of the jobs, and now it will be worse when Tele-paths become widely available. Daniel, there are so many people who couldn't cope with the required professional development that was needed to work, and now, even those who could keep up are incompatible to boot." She paused and sighed, before continuing. "Sometimes, life can be unkind. And there is no one around to help."

"And what about your family? You've told me about your parents, and I am so sorry about that, but was there no-one else?"

"When my parents passed away I was thirty, and they didn't have much to leave me other than unforgettable memories of our time together. I struggled to go on because I was an only child, and I am not close to any extended family. Eventually, after a lot of work, I found a job in customer service. You'll not be surprised to hear that ended up a dead-end, when all customer service jobs got replaced by AIs and robots."

"And then?"

"Then I moved to the council estate, and I've been there ever since. I tried to find a way to escape, but the estate has this power over you, it sucks you in and doesn't let go until you stop fighting the system and accept the fact that you are probably never getting out."

"And you, did you accept that fact?" Daniel asked with hope in his voice. Maria didn't look like a person who would just give up.

"No, I never did. I am still trying. And I also learnt to make myself useful where I can. I try to make a difference. I fell in love with the people who live there."

"What do you mean?"

"Oh, you have to meet them to understand. For example, there is Bobby, who is seventy-nine. Every morning he listens to Frank Sinatra on a barely functioning antique player while he smokes one cigarette after another."

"That's... terrible!" Daniel exclaimed, "He is killing himself, and that's before you even consider the illegality of smoking. It is just wrong!"

"That is your personal opinion. But it feels right for Bobby. He sits there every morning remembering his wife and their time together. She passed away years ago, but he still loves her. The mornings are the happiest part of his days. I think it is romantic."

"But why is no one helping him to overcome his addiction? What about therapy?"

"Daniel, no one cares anymore. And in any case, his broken heart cannot be fixed by therapy. The only therapy he has are those contemplative mornings. The Frank Sinatra songs, his cigarettes, and his memories – they allow him to go on."

"And everyone is okay with that?"

"No, not everyone is okay with that. *I* am not okay with that. I visit Bobby every afternoon when he starts feeling blue, and the dark thoughts approach. I talk to him, help him cook his dinner, and listen to all the stories he tells about his wife."

"What about medication? Has he tried pills?"

"That's society's answer to everything: pills. Pills, pills, pills. Everyone is on pills. But Bobby doesn't want to take pills."

"Why wouldn't he want to take the pills?" Daniel said, reflecting on the fact that he also refused to take drugs during his depression after Robert's death.

"He feels that if pills make him happy when he feels sad, it is like cheating his heart and his feelings. He finds a weird sort of pleasure in his sorrow."

"What a strange man," Daniel wanted to say more, but decided it was best to keep his comments to himself.

"This is what he wants. Not everyone wants the same things. Some people have another perspective, some people want to feel real feelings instead of masking them with pills. And I understand that you may find that idea troubling and illogical, but there are so many illogical people in the world – maybe it is okay to be illogical."

"Maybe. I can understand. More than I would like to acknowledge," replied Daniel. Maria smiled.

Daniel considered Bobby's life for a further minute. But the act of imagining this man made him feel uneasy. Smoking illegal substances seemed unacceptable to Daniel. He believed in the system, and he wanted everyone to just fit in. But he was realising now that he knew very little about the world around him.

"Even so – Bobby can't be the person to hold you back, Maria. You need to stand on your own two feet."

"I know I do. And I have been trying for years, meeting many interviewers via conference calls. And I seem to be impressing them, right up to the inevitable question about my tech skills."

"I am sorry," Daniel said, feeling genuinely sad. "I realise now, how hung up society is on technology. I want to help."

"That is a bold statement. I am not asking for you to change the world, but I am asking you to begin the conversation. Publicly acknowledge and recognise the fact that so many people are becoming obsolete in this society which only values this one thing."

"I agree."

"And Bobby is just one of many of my family. There is Mandy, nineteen, practically a baby. She has no one. Like me, she struggled with the online programmes of modern education, and needed more help. For most of her childhood, she ended up letting things slide. What future does she have now? She is incompatible and uneducated. Everyone thought the new schooling system would work for everyone, right? Mandy is just one of many examples that shows it doesn't. But she is a good kid, she just wants to achieve her potential."

"Is it really impossible to find a job for her? There are all sorts of places she can start to look," Daniel replied, searching for a solution.

"Where? All the blue-collar jobs have been replaced by robots, and most of the white-collar jobs require complex technical skills to manage these 'blue-collar' robots. Where does she fit in?"

"I see. There should be a way for someone like her. She is too young to give up on life."

"She is. That is why I am home-schooling her. I have high hopes. She is smart, very social and great fun. But these qualities are not seen as valuable in our world anymore."

They walked for a while in silence, then Maria took a deep breath and continued.

"And there is Tatiana. She is a dancer. Or rather, she was when she was younger. And she was extremely talented. But she never got a chance to dance on a big stage. Not many people go to art performances nowadays. Why bother, when you can virtually stream any show in the world from the comfort of your own home and watch it in 3D? It is very sad."

"Yes, it is," Daniel said, unconvincingly. Theatres and large spaces filled with people always caused him anxiety. The lights, the sound, the crowd were too overwhelming.

"So now Tatiana has to resort to dancing in the estate streets – usually after she has had a couple of drinks. But we don't judge. We clap and cheer. She is still very good."

Daniel almost choked. The image of a drunk Tatiana was too much to bear. Was this place the home of illegal behaviours? Maria smiled and continued, seeming to enjoy shocking him.

"All the dreams I had for my own career can't happen without technology that's compatible with my neuro-typical brain now. So why not help people in the meantime? I might as well be useful for somebody else."

"I understand that it may feel like you are helping. But if these people choose to live their lives the way they do, maybe you should let them. You have your whole life in front of you. These kinds of behaviours are illegal, illogical and unacceptable. These people and their vices will drag you down." Daniel regretted his directness the minute the words came out of his mouth. Diplomacy was never his strongest point.

"How can you say that? These are people. And yes, maybe they struggle to live by the rules of this new world, but they have their own truths too. Don't you agree? Ever think it might not be their fault? That they might struggle to make a different choice, to live any other way? Doesn't a part of you think that maybe, just maybe there is something authentic in their feelings that they cannot help? Something *inevitably human.*"

"This 'inevitably human' characteristic you speak of, put us all on the verge of extinction a hundred years ago. The rules were created for our planet to survive; so that we and other species can thrive. That is why they need to be followed. This is why there is a need for us to evolve. Msitua offers a very logical understanding of right and wrong, and this is why it is so powerful as the next step of our development. Admittedly this does not sound as much fun as being 'inevitably human', but it offers a pragmatic survival mechanism of logical patterns of behaviour and clear boundaries. As humans, we just cannot afford to be... sloppy." 'Sloppy' – Daniel couldn't believe he had used that word. Daniel felt like he had to prove his point, but his voice was not expressing the level of anger or disappointment that he was feeling.

"And what about the single childbirth law? Do you also agree with that?" Maria was getting noticeably irritated.

"What about it? It was the only reasonable solution for the survival of our planet and our species, for *all* the species on this planet," Daniel's bold statement didn't seem to invite disagreement.

"And what happens if a pregnancy is unplanned? Is it right to interfere and demand an abortion? And what if they really want that second child? Don't you find this law cruel?"

"Unplanned pregnancies should not happen nowadays. There are all kinds of birth controls, and every responsible human being should follow the rules and be careful. It is easy not to allow any accidental pregnancies. I would even go as far as saying that it is almost impossible to accidentally get pregnant nowadays."

"The keyword is 'almost'. Accidental births still happen," Maria said, suddenly looking sad, tears forming in the corner of her eyes.

"I am sure they do, and it is sad when it happens. But it is still against the law, and it is a law fairly applied to all humans. We can't afford to be ignorant anymore when the world is at stake."

"Okay. I will tell you one story," Maria said after careful consideration. "There is a woman I know. She got pregnant with her second child. Her first child was already an adult, and she wasn't planning to have another, but it just happened unexpectedly. And this woman was following the rules – she was on birth control, she was careful yet somehow things went wrong, and she got pregnant at fifty-four. Despite her age, she really wanted to be a mother again. She would close her eyes and imagine this new baby crawling, taking her first steps, saying her first words. But the government refused permission to allow the birth, giving her a deadline to abort the pregnancy. It was unbearable. It got so bad that this woman didn't want to live anymore."

"I am very sorry, I feel for her. Sometimes these measures seem very harsh. But we cannot just abandon the rules the moment it doesn't suit us," Daniel said as softly as he possibly could.

"Don't you think sometimes the rules could have exceptions? Even if the rules are for our own good, even if they are for our own protection, sometimes the rules are wrong!"

"Not these rules, Maria. These rules are never wrong. Where would we be without the Green Council? Would we even *be* at all? And if everyone follows these rules, why should one person be allowed to break them? Would it be fair on everyone else? If everyone gets allowed to bend the rules just a little, what is the point of these regulations in the first place? They wouldn't work then, would they?"

"I understand your point, and I am fully aware of the fantastic job the Green Council did. Their logical and clear rules about the environment allowed us to survive the ecological crisis. I understand, I do."

"Well, the same rules apply with the one child rule. It has to be followed. At least until we find new homes for our species, until we can expand into space. I have a reason to hope and believe this may not be so far away."

"I see," Maria was hesitant about continuing, but decided to press on, "However, we humans have always broken the rules in the past. Maybe breaking the rules is what allowed us to progress as far as we have. Think about it: every innovation, every significant discovery always violates the standard at first. Is breaking the rules always bad? I don't think so. It got us where we are now."

"Yes, Maria, it got us where we are now. But where are we? Are we in the right place? We almost killed our planet, we almost began a nuclear war, and we *did* create a society full of capitalism and inequality. These rules exist to get us out of the mess *we* made. We simply cannot allow ourselves short-cuts. You feel for one woman who desperately wanted to have a second child. I feel for all living things: the trees, the tiger cubs, the elephants, the penguins, the lakes and the rivers, the fresh, breezy winter air. I can go on," Daniel was now speaking firmly. "Maria, we have used up all the chances we had. We don't deserve a break, we need to carry on working hard." Maria was listening with an uneasy look on her face, but Daniel couldn't stop. "I know you want to promote the old values of choice and complete freedom. But when a human is entirely free, there is a tendency to destroy. Total freedom endangers ourselves and others. I believe in control, limited choice and in self-restriction. Perfecting yourself is tough, but it is easier if there are fair laws in place. We cannot allow self-indulgence – we need to stay strong. Collectively, and as individuals. Even if it means sacrifices of your heart."

Maria was quiet now. Daniel didn't want to speak like he was trying to win a debate, but it had happened anyway. It didn't make him feel particularly good about himself. He knew she had a point, and it was unfortunate and painful to think of the saddest consequences the Birth Right law had on so many people, but Daniel knew the truth. The scientific truth of the alternative scenario, and that was even more disturbing. He took a deep breath and tried to comfort Maria.

"Maria, what happened to that woman?"

"She ran away."

"What do you mean she 'ran away'?" Daniel was shocked by how calmly Maria said it. Not like she was reporting a crime, as she should have, but more like she was merely discussing the weather.

"Daniel, I take your point. I do. We have to learn to live by the rules. But ultimately, I was pleased to learn that this woman ran away and had her child successfully. I knew her. She wouldn't have been able to cope with the loss if she had complied. And I loved that woman. She was... my mother."

"You said your parents had passed away!" Daniel was confused – this was illogical.

"I am sorry. It is true that my father died, and my mother grieved his death. She was in a very bad state. Then not long after his passing, she found out that she was pregnant with his child. It felt like a lifeline and a final connection to my father. It was a reason for my mother to look forward to the next day. You might wonder why I am telling you all this? Well, I have never told anyone before, and I hope you find the empathy to understand." Maria went quiet. It was Daniel's turn to speak.

"But how?" he asked. These were the only words he could manage, despite the fact that he had hundreds of thoughts spinning in his head.

"You mean, how did she manage to have a baby? There is a way. I have heard other stories. There is a place no one knows about. No one is allowed to know exactly where this place is. All I know is that my mum got there safely. Once you reach the destination you cannot communicate with the outside world. This is how they have kept the location a secret."

"I had no idea!"

"Wow, you don't get out much, do you?" Maria said, sounding surprised. "It's a well-known open secret amongst the people I know. Anyway, even without direct communication, I know my mother made it. She told me she would leave a white flower at my dad's grave, if she made it there safely, to let me know that it was real."

"And she did?"

"She did," Maria smiled to herself.

"I am glad," Daniel said.

"Are you? Really?" Maria asked him with a hint of suspicion. "I am trusting you a lot by telling you this."

"Maria, you can trust me. It is hard for me to get my head around this information, and it will take some months for me to understand it, maybe even years. But I will not share this information with anyone, I promise," and Daniel meant it. "But how did she just disappear without any trace? Weren't the government representatives looking for her?"

"They were, but I managed to…"

"Stop! Don't tell me. It is hard enough for me to know that your mother broke the law. I couldn't bear to know the truth about any illegal activities you may… or may not have done."

"I haven't," lied Maria. And Daniel believed her.

Chapter Eighteen
A MOMENT OF ETERNITY

Daniel was a complicated man. Or maybe he wasn't. Maybe he was logical, correct, simple. Maybe it was Maria who was complicated. It was difficult to tell.

Maria felt uneasy. Why did she do it? Why did she share very private information about her family with a complete stranger? And with a Msitua stranger, someone who was uncompromising in his understanding of the laws, the rights and the wrongs. It really wasn't wise of her. She blamed the signature Hide cocktail.

Since her father passed away, and her mother had disappeared into the unknown to save her unborn child, Maria had felt lonely. In fact, the loneliness was killing her. She had never got used to being by herself. Maybe this was why she was desperate to hold onto her estate friends. It was the only family she had left.

Maria and her parents had been very close. Despite the lack of stability in their lives and limited finances, her family had the biggest comfort of all – love. They cared deeply for, and supported one another. They always found the strength to laugh together about the challenges life had thrown at them. And suddenly her parents were gone. In an instant.

Maria missed them. Although with her father she'd had no choice in the matter, with her mother she was forced to grapple with a decision to let her go. Did Maria ever regret it? She tried not to, constantly pushing her negative thoughts aside. Maria had become adept at convincing herself that saying goodbye was the only possible solution. Her mother was losing herself in her grief when Maria's father passed away, and Maria had grown increasingly worried about her. But the news she was having a baby had pushed her back into the land of the living.

Maria was always wondering if her mother had given birth to a girl or a boy. Somewhere, in the most secret location, Maria had a sister or a brother. On bad days, this thought brought her solace.

Would Daniel ever comprehend why she had to cover up for her mom's actions? Maybe – hopefully – one day he could understand. She had never been so open with anyone else before. For some reason, Daniel didn't seem like a stranger. There was something familiar about him – she saw herself in him. How could that be? They were complete opposites, after all. Incompatible characters, incompatible technologies, incompatible lives.

Maria tried to figure out why she had this undeniable attraction to him. What was there in Daniel she found so relatable? What was it that was pushing them closer? It was almost as if an invisible power was forcing them together, like two oppositely polarised magnets. And then the realisation came to her. They were both alone. Yes, Maria was a loner by circumstances, whilst Daniel was a loner by choice, but in the middle of one of the most overpopulated cities on the planet, they had both become two lonely souls.

The next day they met again.

After their evening together, Maria was determined not to call him. Daniel knew her deepest secret now. It was up to him to decide if he could handle it. She was pleased when he initiated the meeting.

This time they agreed to meet in the park. It was a perfect place for them to pour their hearts out, and express their differences in opinions. The approaching autumn evening wrapped them in the silk of a warm breeze, and both loners felt like there was a sort of natural magic in the air.

"You know, you confuse me," Maria said thoughtfully, "I have heard that Msitua people struggle to follow rules. You see it a lot in school children especially. How come you don't have a problem with adhering to the laws?"

"We struggle to follow rules that don't make sense. But if a rule is logical and necessary, it is clear that it should be followed," Daniel started to explain. They walked for a minute in silence and then he continued, "I find it extremely difficult to understand the 'rules' that neuro-typicals create for themselves. I could never relate to those sorts of rules, even as a child."

"What is so different about 'neuro-typical rules'?" Maria asked, smiling softly.

"Rules should be the same for everyone. Yet it seemed to me that many neuro-typicals both created but also broke their own rules. Adults would tell me not to raise my voice, but then they would scream all the time. Sometimes it almost felt like being an adult was a 'prize' which meant you did not have to follow the rules anymore".

Maria listened silently, considering Daniel's words. After some hesitation, she decided to share her thoughts.

"I know it is difficult for you to understand, but there are some amazing things neuro-typicals could offer this new world."

"What sorts of things?"

"I don't want to explain. I have no doubt that whatever I say will just lead you to bombard me with your logic. Maybe one day, you will find out on your own."

"Sure," Daniel replied. He wasn't actually sure what she meant, but he felt it was impolite to push her for answers.

"Please tell me how your logical mind works. I would love to know. How can you be so sure your beliefs are correct? I struggle with mine all the time," she said with a sigh.

"If you really want to know, I will tell you a story my grandfather told me once. Whenever I am unsure, I remind myself of it, and it helps me to make my mind up."

Daniel stopped walking and turned to face Maria, looking into her big brown eyes. He saw the setting sun reflected back at him through her dark eyelashes. Maria was looking for answers, hoping to understand, wanting to find a belief system, a 'religion', to follow. Her brain was saying one thing, but her heart was saying something different. It seemed as if Daniel's recent findings had left her lost, spiralling without any secure beliefs to hang onto. Maria wanted Daniel to give her something her heart could follow. So, he decided to explain it through a story he once heard, when he was a little boy.

"My grandfather had once decided to do a piece of artwork for a university project. He came up with the idea – a picture of the beautiful autumn leaves. It may not sound like much, but in my grandfather's head, he saw it vividly. It wasn't just an art project, but a manifestation of the beauty in the world. The stunning genius of nature."

"It sounds wonderful!" Maria exclaimed.

"My grandfather thought so too, and so he went on a quest to find the most beautiful leaves in London's parks. He found amazing greens, sharp-edged reds, and delicate oranges and yellows. He was very pleased with his selection. But then he saw it. The single most desirable leaf. It was perfect! The shape, the colour, the texture. Ideal as the centrepiece of his composition. Unfortunately, it wasn't lying on the ground. It was still attached to the tree. The branches had been a little lazy in shaking it off. Or maybe they were guilty of loving it too much, not ready to give up this perfect leaf quite yet. So, my grandfather stood there, staring at the leaf, wanting to possess it. But something stopped him from taking it. What right did he have to rip the leaf off? Why should his artwork, with all the best intentions, be more important than the tree?

The human side of him tried to justify the act. It told him that the leaf would eventually fall anyway. And if he did not take it, it would remain on the ground, slowly turning into muddy autumn mush. But if he took it, it could become a part of his artwork. It would stay beautiful and live on in this form forever.

So, my grandfather ripped it off. But the moment he did, he knew that it was a mistake. He realised he was being a selfish human, that he had rushed to action without fully comprehending the consequences. My grandfather felt guilty.

He never made his art, once he had realised that letting the perfect leaf remain part of that tree was a better piece of art than anything he could create. His artwork would have seemed pathetic in comparison. As a reminder of what took place that day, Robert dried that leaf and kept it inside one of his books. Whenever he had to make a decision about what was right and what was wrong, he would open the book and look at the leaf. He would imagine how he would feel after making any new decision. If it felt good, he would proceed. If the feeling was bad, one of remorse, disappointment or guilt, he would decide otherwise," Daniel smiled at the memory of his grandfather as he concluded the story.

"This is a beautiful story, Daniel," Maria said, "That's certainly one way to make a decision. Did Robert look at the leaf when he was creating Tele-paths?" Maria asked pointedly. If their conversation was a battle of opinions, the score would be one-all. "Do you have the leaf?" Maria said, quickly moving on to smooth over the possible impact of her question.

"I don't think so," Daniel said, looking thoughtful, "I have a couple of my grandfather's books. I should check if it is there somewhere."

Maria looked at Daniel. She was surprised he had shown no reaction to her provocative question. Suddenly, Maria realised that Daniel was the only scientist who took her concerns seriously. He genuinely really wanted to help, you couldn't fault his motives. How wrong her first impressions had been, imagining him as being cold and arrogant. 'How wrong we all can be when we don't know both sides of the story,' she thought to herself. Aloud, she said.

"I really admire your sense of justice. But you already know how much I struggle to follow the rules when it comes to questions of the heart."

"Questions of the heart are difficult for me too," Daniel confessed. He was battling his own heart's desire this very moment. It was amazing how much power his illogical heart had over him.

"Really? Like what?" Maria asked, wanting to know more.

"I would struggle to explain," Daniel said, feeling put on the spot, and not coping well under the pressure of Maria looking intensely at him.

Daniel felt uneasy. How could he explain that his questions of the heart were about her? How he felt an unexplainable emotion every time he looked into her eyes, and every time he heard her voice, his entire body craving her presence.

He didn't feel in control anymore, and he was feeling increasingly vulnerable. Maria sensed this change come over him. She came very close to Daniel, so close that Daniel could feel her warm breath on his chest. She looked deep into his eyes in the way that only neuro-typicals can. He froze for a second, and that second stretched into an eternity. And in this eternity, he was falling. Maria's soft hands were now framing Daniel's face. She pulled him towards her slightly, and their lips met.

Daniel still felt like he was falling, but suddenly it had become the most pleasurable of falls. Before he lost control of his mind completely, his last thought was of how well their lips fit together. Like they were made for each other.

Chapter Nineteen
DISCOVERY

Human touch. Real closeness with someone special. Daniel had never known how fulfilling a real relationship could be. How was it possible that Daniel could be comfortable with being intimate? He wasn't sure, but what he did know was that he enjoyed his time with Maria. He enjoyed the softness of her full lips, the closeness of her deep brown eyes. He couldn't fault it, he couldn't fault *her*. He loved everything about her – the way she fluffed her hair, the unapologetic confidence of her questions, the cheerful freckles on her nose. He delighted even in the imperfect things, like the tip of the left ear which slightly stuck out, or her messy eyelashes which twisted in every possible direction. But most of all, Daniel loved the delicate lines of Maria's body, from the top of her scapula and down towards her waist, following the perfect curves of her hips.

Daniel saw Maria often. They would frequently go to the same restaurant on Meadow Street, eat the same lovely meal, walk the same long walk to Daniel's place, argue their personal opinions, then at last, they would softly embrace and kiss. Daniel would ask her to stay, and she would always consider saying 'Yes' for a minute before finally leaving. Then Daniel would be left alone, leaning against his door, struggling to understand why it hurt.

Daniel's rational mind had decided it would be best to take it slow, but his very primal body pushed its own agenda. Daniel was surprised by how little control he had over it. With Maria, his instincts felt animalistic and uncontrollable, exciting and frightening at the same time. Daniel was scared to let himself go. With physical intimacy, there was no safety net, unlike with telepathic sex. And there was also no imagination that could be used to intensify the experience, no ability to dream things in to spice it up, no way of relying on thought alone to ensure top performance. It would be all real.

Daniel was nervous, his mind restless from the possible expectations of the night ahead. The unpredictability of how the evening might end was teased and titillated in his imagination. He felt his emotions overpowering him. And such mixed emotions! He felt excited, but also distracted and anxious, and he couldn't concentrate on any conversation all evening. Now they were on the way to his place, he found he couldn't even say a word. It was strange – it was not at all like them to find themselves walking in silence.

Daniel held Maria's hand, feeling like a little boy. The night seemed like it could be the beginning of a new chapter in his life – a chapter he wasn't entirely prepared for, yet one he couldn't help but read. His body was virtually trembling at the thought of them spending the night together. A whole night, with endless opportunities to explore Maria's body. He hoped that she was equally excited at the prospect, that she felt the same way about discovering him. Daniel was frightened of the overpowering emotions, but it also made him feel alive, like every molecule of his body was about to leap into the future without ever wanting to look back.

Could Maria sense his excitement? She wasn't talking much either, and she had said nothing about this unusual silence between them. She walked alongside him, letting

Daniel lead the way, giving him permission to guide her in this moment of a new exploration, a moment of uncontrollable thoughts and unspoken expectations.

When they entered Daniel's room, he paused before reaching for the light. Before he could turn it on, Maria caught his hand, kissed his palm and then gently placed it on her chest. Her brown eyes shone in the night, reflecting the light of the outside world. A world that tonight seemed much further away than just beyond the glass, as if it was another planet.

The room was dark and peaceful, and Daniel could feel Maria's heartbeat. The pace quickened, and the hurried beat travelled through his hands and seemed to echo back in his own body. Time stood still, all thoughts disappeared. All Daniel could see was Maria's sparkling eyes. There was something wild about them tonight, something unapologetically naughty. It was the first time that Daniel had seen this new side of her. A wild spirit untamed by what life had thrown at her. Had he ever known what was real before this moment of complete intimacy?

Daniel's hands no longer seemed to be listening to his brain. They travelled across Maria's body, unable to quench the craving of feeling her. They wrapped around her waist, and then moved lower, heading towards her round hips hungrily. There were no thoughts anymore, just instincts. Animalistic, uncontrollable, unforgettable instincts. Thoughts became snapshots of two naked bodies melting into one, every touch escalating a shared desire for life and for pleasure.

Daniel opened his eyes. It took him a minute to adjust to the light and see that it was already bright. Lying next to him in bed was Maria, her silky hair spread over the pillows. She was still asleep, and had a peaceful look on her face, her morning skin reflecting the streams of sunlight which were entering the room. The smart blinds were set so that they always opened at 7 am. Usually this would wake Daniel, but not today. He had been in a deep but peaceful sleep, and even the brightness of the day hadn't managed to rouse him. Daniel felt Maria's body under the sheets, sensing her warmth and breathing in her unique scent, which he was sure he could smell on his body too. Never in his life, could he have imagined being so close to someone.

In the light of day, the last night felt like a magical dream. Daniel had wholly followed his instincts, his body leading the way. More than that, Daniel felt that he couldn't have controlled it even if he had tried. His body had completely taken over. Daniel could still feel Maria's tender touch and the taste of her lips. How could he ever think that telepathic sex was better than the real thing? He had never felt such passion before. The animalistic sensations felt like the most natural thing he had ever experienced, leading to the unforgettable culmination, breaking like a storm or a hurricane, sweeping Daniel into an uncontrollable sensation of physicality beyond his wildest dreams.

Daniel lay quietly for a while, looking at Maria sleeping peacefully. Nothing was on his mind, nothing bothered his existence, nothing was allowed to enter his consciousness. This moment was perfect.

Daniel waited patiently for Maria to begin to move, for her eyelashes to slowly start flickering open. Eventually her deep brown eyes opened and slowly fixed on him.

"Morning," she murmured in a husky voice, not yet quite sounding like herself.

"Morning," Daniel replied.

"Did you sleep well?" she asked with a twinkle in her eye.

"I slept well. Even the early morning light couldn't disturb me."

Maria smiled sweetly. She closed her eyes again, turned her face towards Daniel's and kissed him. Her hands wrapped around Daniel's neck, and she dragged him back into a repeat of last night's reality. Lips, waist, hips. The most colourful parade of human sensations.

Chapter Twenty
NOTHING ELSE EXISTS

Was it day or night? Daniel didn't know, and for the first time in his life, he didn't care. He preferred this new reality, where responsibilities had ceased to exist. If only he could stay in this daze forever, living in a world where he could follow the instincts of his body and not his mind; being one with Maria; celebrating the intimacy of their souls.

But unfortunately and inevitably, the old reality began to creep in starting with a feeling of guilt. Guilt that Daniel hadn't called his grandfather for a few weeks now. He knew that this guilt was an indication that the duration of time had started to become unforgivable.

"Hi, Daniel! Is it really you?" Robert sounded positive. Who else could it be if Robert only existed in Daniel's head? "I was getting bored here," he added.

"I was a little busy. Sorry, I meant to connect with you earlier," Daniel tried to explain himself.

"It is the girl, isn't it?" said Robert, jumping the gun. "I would hazard that you have been spending all your time together, and now it seems like nothing else exists?"

"How could you know?" Daniel asked, as he quickly re-checked whether he had correctly limited access to this information as he had intended.

"I don't need to see your neurons' activity to understand what is going on," Robert said enthusiastically. "I wasn't born yesterday. I have lived a life and was young once too, you know. Some girls have the power to stop the Earth from spinning."

"Some do. Maria is more – she has the power to stop the Universe from expanding," Daniel replied, attempting to make a joke.

"What a dangerous idea!" Robert said, playing along. But suddenly Daniel's sense of humour disappeared.

"I know. Very dangerous. What am I going to do?" Daniel said quietly, sudden panic filling his heart. Robert realised that the tone had suddenly shifted. All of the light-heartedness had turned to grave seriousness in but a moment. He tried to save the situation by explaining away his comment.

"I simply meant it would be dangerous for the Universe. You know… to stop expanding. As then it must collapse onto itself. It was meant to be humorous."

"I know what you meant," Daniel said, not wanting to expand on the dark thoughts that had started to cloud over him.

Daniel wasn't ready to enter the old reality's complications. The past few weeks with Maria were terrific, and he didn't want it to end. The hurricane of his emotions didn't seem like it was going to settle any time soon. Surely Daniel had to consider the implications of this before too much longer. But he just didn't want to. It wasn't like him, to be this irresponsible and, perhaps more shockingly, this illogical. He couldn't even recognise himself anymore. And now an offhand jokey remark had the ill effect of making him face the question he had been avoiding. What problems would this unlikely relationship eventually entail?

In a split second, Robert just knew the heavy burden Daniel had been feeling. He understood the inevitable – what the only logically possible solution must be. Yet Robert said nothing. Daniel already knew that Robert felt it. They both knew.

"I need to be alone for a time," Daniel said.

Robert complied without answering. They both needed to consider the consequences and risks of this relationship.

Daniel was angry with himself. How could it be that in just a matter of weeks, he had managed to get himself deep into a relationship without a future? How could Daniel let it get so far with Maria? How could he have *not* let it get so far? It wasn't about him anymore. Too much was at stake. And the recent development in Robert's AI was making things more complicated. How must Robert feel knowing that Daniel was seriously involved with a neuro-typical? Although everyone thought an intelligent, conscious AI was a long shot, Daniel knew that Robert's AI was proving otherwise. Daniel couldn't help but feel responsible for Robert, for a remarkable discovery which was destined to be yet another gamechanger. The shared victory achieved through the collaboration of biology and digital technology. It presented a lot of opportunities. But these opportunities had to be carefully preserved for many years to come. Daniel just couldn't mess it up. Not even for love. Not even for Maria.

Daniel always appreciated having a systematic, logical brain. It made things easy. Logic was Daniel's religion. But today it only brought him suffering. The logical outcome was undeniable. The risks of the relationship were too high, the consequences could be devastating and irreversible. Yet the heartache the conclusion brought was unbearable; a despair he had never experienced before. How could something so wrong feel so right? How could such an illogical feeling have such control over him?

Daniel had been spending all his evenings with Maria, completely taken in by her presence. Did all people in love feel the same way? Or was this feeling driven by his obsessive Msitua traits, his new obsession consuming all of Daniel's attention and directing it at one source – Maria?

He had tried to hide from thoughts about the future, the potential complications, and the unavoidable decision these thoughts led to. He wanted to prolong the peaceful time he had left with Maria. He knew that at some point he would have to explain things. Before now, it had felt too soon to say anything, and now it was suddenly too late. The window of opportunity for speaking the truth had been missed – seemingly gone within a moment.

He had considered whether their relationship could just become a fun fling. Might this be enough for Maria? It didn't matter – it could never be enough for Daniel. He was the kind of person who couldn't play social games without full commitment. He definitely couldn't play the love game. With love, for Daniel, it was all or nothing. He couldn't imagine sharing his life with anyone else now that he had experienced love. And what about Maria? Was she also all in? This thought made Daniel sick at how selfish he was being. It was so like him to dwell on his own life and how unfair it was, always forgetting to consider other people. Daniel was afraid of hurting her.

The inevitable panic attack was suddenly pushing its way to his chest, blurring his vision and narrowing the room. Daniel could have called for help, but he decided not to. A part of him wanted to face his panic on his own, a part of him wanted to punish himself.

Maria found Daniel lying on the floor, his legs pulled tight to his chest in a foetal position. She rushed towards him with a worried look. She wasn't sure what to do. She checked his pulse, then placed his head in her warm hands, trying to make eye contact with him. All Daniel could register was her melodic voice calling his name, and her hands searching for an old-fashioned phone in her purse. Daniel tried to speak, but his lips were dry and heavy.

"Don't call for help," Daniel finally managed to say.

"Why? Why, Daniel?" she was holding her phone in her right hand with the thumb ready to press the call button that would dial the emergency services.

"I beg you," Daniel whispered, but it was loud enough for her to hear. She nodded slightly and put the phone away. Then she wrapped her arms around Daniel, pulling his face close to her chest.

Something warm dropped on Daniel's forehead, then ran down his cheek. Maria was crying. Daniel hadn't seen anyone cry for a very long time. This simple emotional reaction surprised him to the point that he found his attention moving from his panic to Maria's face. Even strained by sadness, it was beautiful. The deep brown eyes, the messy brown hair, the lips now moving in a frightening dance of fear. It was all still Maria. And Daniel loved her.

Once control had slowly returned, Daniel took Maria's hand. He wasn't a man to talk about feelings, but he hoped that Maria knew what he wanted to say from this simple gesture. That he loved her, that he cared for her, that he was grateful to her for being near.

"I am so sorry to put you through this," Daniel said.

"Don't be silly. I am happy you added me to the safe list for your flat – it meant I could be here for you. What was it? What happened?" she questioned, finally gathering the courage to ask.

"I just get anxious sometimes," Daniel explained.

Maria nodded, although it was clear that this information did not answer what she was really asking. What she actually wanted to ask was whether Daniel's anxiety had anything to do with her, but she was not going to speak this aloud.

Daniel felt that it could be a good time to explain things, to outline the dilemma he was facing, the pain it was causing him. But his exhausted mind wasn't ready for this conversation. And his logical brain felt justified that his current state was not fit for telling her. It would come later! He wanted more time in her arms, sensing her soft breath on his skin, feeling her presence with every molecule of his being. He needed to prolong this magical moment with her as much as possible before it all ended; living in this moment where nothing else exists.

Chapter Twenty-One
RESPONSIBILITY

Daniel's inner peace was irreparably disturbed. He felt like for the past few weeks he had been living on a seesaw: at some points reaching incredible highs and at some points feeling unbelievable lows. He had been unable to control these mood swings.

The more time he spent with Maria, the more he craved her. He never wanted to be without her. But the immense pressure of his scientific responsibility was daunting. It lurked in Daniel's head, making him feel guilty. Guilty for not telling Maria, guilty for potentially risking the most remarkable scientific discovery of all times. He also hadn't logged in to the data system to record Robert's AI progress for many weeks. What would he write? 'I do believe that Robert's AI is exhibiting undeniable signs of consciousness. Not only that, but there has been the profound development of a sharp sense of humour and sarcasm. And by the way, I find myself in a bit of a pickle. I have fallen in love with a neuro-typical, and I am now seriously questioning if I can fulfil the commitment needed for this scientific project'.

And Robert wasn't making it easier. His kind understanding, his quiet acknowledgement of Daniel's choices, the support he was giving Daniel – it all actually made things even more difficult. They never openly talked about the possible implications of pursuing this relationship anymore. But it was left in the air unsaid. Every time they tele-pathed, they both avoided the subject. Robert seemed more and more real. It felt good to have him back in Daniel's life. Robert was the only reason his spinning mind managed to keep any semblance of sanity.

On one peaceful evening Daniel found himself walking with Maria in the park. The day was ending, but the night hadn't claimed its rights yet. The trees' dark shadows lay still, and the calmness of the air mixed with the scent of freshly-cut grass was very comforting. For a second, it felt like the whole world stopped. And in that moment, Daniel suddenly felt complete. Just in this very moment, for a fraction of a second.

Maria, probably feeling the magic too, exclaimed.

"Wow! What a beautiful sky! The dramatic blue, the shades of purple here and there... it is simply divine. So powerful. I think a vibrant blue might be my favourite colour," she confessed. "What about you?"

"What is my favourite colour?" Daniel tried to gather his thoughts, "White, I guess."

"White? That is a bit plain!" Maria said, with a hint of disappointment in her voice. Daniel loved how she could never hold in her opinions. She always spoke with feeling and without cowardice. It was like she could not help but be instinctive. Daniel could never do that. He always had to double-check, to double-guess, think everything through to its logical conclusion.

"I disagree. White is clean. It is pure."

"Yes, but white doesn't make you *feel*. Blue makes me feel something. It takes my breath away. Like this dramatic sky."

"White does make *me* feel," Daniel stated.

"It does? How does it make you feel?" Maria asked, pushing for more.

"It makes me feel safe, like the peaceful stillness of the air tonight," Daniel tried to explain in the way she had, trying to be as poetic in his description as he could manage.

"I see. Good feelings."

"Yes. Calm feelings are the best, where there is no drama. I am afraid of strong feelings, strong colours, strong emotions. They are too unpredictable, too hard to control."

"Do you always try to control your feelings?" Maria wondered. She really wanted to understand Daniel. Daniel had noticed all the millions of questions she had asked him, always ultimately without judgement. This was why Daniel could be himself with her, he had her acceptance despite the fact she was constantly challenging him. It was never dull.

"I do. It keeps me out of trouble."

"And what happens when you can't control them? Has it ever happened?"

"Yes, it has. And I don't like it. I prefer to avoid putting myself in any situation which I can't control."

"Everyone tries to do that, I think. But is it really possible?"

Daniel looked at Maria, her beautiful brown eyes reflecting the depth of the sky, and he wondered if he genuinely could control himself.

"No. I don't think it is possible. It's a problem for me too. But I can get frustrated, anxious and even depressed when I can't control things. That is why I try so hard to avoid it. Yet sometimes, despite all my safeguards, the situation controls you, me included."

"Yes, sometimes it does," Maria said.

Maybe it was a good time to tell Maria about Daniel's responsibilities. Perhaps, she would understand. Maybe, she would even help them to find a way to be together.

"Maria," Daniel began, as he gathered all his courage, taking a deep breath before continuing. He wanted to tell her everything, but he didn't know where to begin. His logical mind eventually located a possible entry point. "Maria, did you know that I've always found genetic science very predictable and consequently very reassuring?"

"What do you mean?" Maria asked, suddenly looked puzzled.

"I just want to hear what your thoughts are on the subject. Imagine if you were to have a child and decided to create it in a lab. You could implement any genetic modifications you wanted. I have a colleague who has perfected a technique to eliminate any genetic diseases, for example. Wouldn't it be reassuring to have a child in this way and avoid any possible unpleasantness?" Daniel said awkwardly. He started to worry that his point was too meandering, and wished he had managed to introduce the topic differently.

"Daniel," Maria interjected with her usual decisiveness, "I have no idea where you are heading with this line of thought, but the idea of a 'designer baby' makes me sick!"

"I know it is not conventional, but more and more people are choosing this approach. It is not so unusual anymore."

"Everyone else can choose all they want, *I* still think it is wrong!" Maria proclaimed. "Don't you see where that science is heading? If genetic modifications become available to everyone, what is next? The creation of superhumans?

What will be left of humanity then? It will be a homogenous hell, with no real identity or diversity, no differences of opinion or challenging questions. And humans *need* those challenging questions. We are stronger when we are challenged. We need our differences because, without them, we stop being who we are. Who do we become then?"

"I know what you are saying, but let's go back a step. What if someone was unable to have a child, would it be okay for them to have one in a lab?"

"Yes, but only if they wouldn't modify the child's natural genetics. What would *you* modify in your child, Daniel?" Maria asked, clearly getting annoyed with the conversation.

"Me? I am certainly not thinking about babies at the moment," Daniel wondered whether it was too late to start over.

"Okay, but when you *do* start to think about babies, is there anything you *would* modify?" Maria pushed.

"I don't know... Maybe I would eliminate the genetic risks of serious medical issues like cancer or Parkinson disease," Daniel managed to come up with this on the spot. He didn't have the guts to honestly bring himself to tell her what he would really modify in his lab baby. If Maria reacted to even the idea of a lab-created child this way, Daniel was afraid to even imagine how she would react if he told her the full truth of his thinking: that in order to have a child, he would need to modify *her*, the mother.

Maria seemed a little calmer now, hearing his answer, not realising it was false. She looked thoughtful, analysing the points that Daniel had made. But Daniel hadn't made the point he wanted to at all. Now he wished he hadn't raised this subject in the first place.

He knew now that he had to tell her the whole truth. He had to. Maria deserved to know, deserved to make her own choices before their relationship went further. She was a person of many opinions, albeit opinions which didn't match with Daniel's. Would she ever understand the importance of the difficult decisions they would have to make? Would she simply cut and run?

'What now?' Daniel thought. He looked up again at the profound beauty of the dramatic sky. This perfect moment didn't seem the right time to answer this question. 'Now, we just walk,' Daniel said to himself.

Chapter Twenty-Two
THE UNEXPECTED

It was clear. Maria wasn't prepared to live by Daniel's rules. Her reality wasn't a match with Daniel's, her opinions were formed and wouldn't fit into his pre-approved scenarios. Was it right to impose them on her?

After their evening stroll, Daniel had a powerful panic attack. His dream, which under normal circumstances, would otherwise feel relaxing, suddenly became a nightmare. He was in his flat, sat in his kitchen, drinking his aromatic morning coffee. Everything was on track – his work, his research, his daily routine. When he spoke to Robert, he greeted him happily. Everything was perfect. But then he realised why it all was so perfect. There was no Maria in this world.

Daniel woke up in a cold sweat, his heart racing towards the inevitable dark destination. He couldn't breathe. As if trapped in a smoky daze, Daniel saw Maria trying to sit him up, pushing his shoulders back, rubbing his temples. It took Daniel a while to calm down, as his thoughts continued to race through the jungle of his mind. It took him some time to realise that it was just a dream. Maria was next to him, holding his hand, touching his forehead. He reached out and hugged her gently, his heart rate slowly but steadily finding its beat, his mind quieting down. Maria was still here.

It took Daniel an age to fall asleep again that night. But at least he had a pleasurable distraction as he watched Maria drift back to peaceful slumber, trying to imprint this perfect picture in his memory forever.

Daniel woke up later than usual. Maria was up already, battling with the Home Assist with her stronger than usual coffee requirements. What happened yesterday? Why did he have such a strong reaction again? He knew it must mean they were edging dangerously close to an endpoint. The inevitable conversation about their future. The future he struggled to comprehend living both with or without Maria.

Maria entered the room with a tiny tray holding two cups of coffee.

"Morning," she said with a smile.

"Hi"

"Are you feeling any better?" Maria asked, her eyes looked tired. It looked like she had woken up very early.

"I am better, I think," Daniel answered quietly. He felt weak, and emotionally exhausted. But most of all, he felt embarrassed that Maria had ended up seeing him like this again. He felt powerless.

"Maybe I should contact the medics. Maybe you need some..."

"Please, don't. I just need some peace and quiet for a while," Daniel interrupted. He definitely didn't want any medical or psychological attention. He didn't want to talk about his thoughts with anyone. He didn't even want to have this conversation with himself.

"Is something bothering you? Do you know why you are feeling like this?" Maria wondered.

"I do," Daniel said, wishing not for the first time that he could just make up a lie, so he didn't have to explain. But he couldn't, "It's just something I have to figure out."

"Do you want to talk about it?" Maria inquired gently.

"No," Daniel couldn't bring himself to start this difficult discussion with her. Not now. He wanted just a little more time.

"Okay. I just want to know if your worries are... well, are they about me? Do you think we are moving too fast?"

"Maria, you are the best thing that has happened to me," Daniel said, sitting upright in bed. How could she think that? Daniel wished they could be together and hold each other always. But things were complicated.

"Daniel, maybe you want to stay by yourself for a while? You know, to have some space, figure things out. I feel like it could be good for you."

Daniel felt uneasy. He really didn't want Maria to leave him, even for a short time. He was afraid that if she left, she might never come back. Maybe she was tired of him, realising how high maintenance he was. On one hand, if she did leave forever, it would be so much easier. But on the other hand, he just didn't want her to go.

"Please stay. I need you. Soon I will tell you what is bothering me. But not now, please, not now."

"Sure. I can stay," Maria said, curling into his chest like a cat, putting her hands around Daniel's waist and squeezing him tight. Usually, Daniel would want to get away from such a close and personal embrace, but today it felt so good. They remained like this for a good while, and for once not only did Daniel not have to force himself to do it, but he also discovered the pleasure of a long hug – something he had never previously known.

The next few days soon became a blurry sequence of events for Daniel. His work remained at a stand-still, and for most of the hours, he found it difficult to even get out of bed.

His panic attacks were now happening almost every day. He felt exhausted.

Maria was there to comfort him, most of the time. But she often would go back home to check up on her friends. When she was with Daniel, she fed him, brought coffee in the mornings, and herbal tea in the afternoon. He hated the tea, but it was good for him, so he drank it.

Daniel knew that he needed professional help. Yet he was afraid to acknowledge the seriousness of his condition. He constantly felt the presence of the dark cloud over his life, forever reminding him of the agonising decision he had to make. Daniel realised that his body was pushing him to act.

Maria also hadn't been herself over the last few days. She was meticulously careful in choosing topics of conversation, steering well clear of any sensitive subjects that they would typically disagree on. Daniel could sense that she was going out of her way to make him comfortable, and she cared enough about him not to mind.

Several times Maria had asked him if Daniel had considered professional help. Or suggested it would be useful to get some tests done, or speak to a doctor, or just see anyone who could give an independent assessment. Yet his reaction was always the same, and it became quickly apparent that this topic was taboo. But still she kept trying gently. She was concerned. She wanted to help.

With every passing day, Daniel could feel that the situation was reaching a critical point. Even his smart toilet was telling him he could not carry on as he was. He had always admired the advances made in this area, but recently he wished he just had an old-fashioned toilet. The toilet reminded Daniel of his current unhealthy state after every use. He had become paranoid that Maria might hear it speak, even after he set its volume to the lowest level. He wished he could just switch it off, but the designers had not envisaged this option would ever be needed. The toilet analysed Daniel's urine, flagging any areas of concern. Before now, Daniel had found this useful and set about adjusting his diet, exercising more, drinking more water until his bodily functions were deemed healthy. Now, he just wanted the toilet to shut up. He did not need to hear that his vitamin D level was low, or his nutrition levels were critical, or his serotonin levels were at risk of leading to full-blown depression.

Maria's presence kept Daniel going. What would it be like if she was to leave of her own accord? The thought caused Daniel unbearable pain. Yet maybe it could also be a solution to his dilemma. He would no longer have any control over the situation. He wouldn't have to make the decision, or take any action. Sure, he would be crushed. He may even need to be medicated for a while. He would, however, ultimately survive. But would he ever truly *live* again? How do you get over love?

One morning Daniel was resting in his bed, his thoughts spinning out of control. He desperately tried to calm his mind. He tried to stay centred, attempting to meditate and breathing deeply. Maria was in the kitchen, preparing a nutritious breakfast and decaffeinated coffee. This was a recent change as Daniel thought it might help to cut caffeine out of his diet. It had yet to have caused any noticeable improvement.

Ahead lay another daunting day of uncontrollable worry and obsessive thoughts. He knew it wasn't working. He wasn't making Maria happy. And suddenly, Daniel found himself embarrassed. How could he drag this vibrant person into his depressive, anxious state? She didn't belong in this Msitua world. She deserved so much more. Why was she here? How could she possibly love him? It was impossible. *Who* would love him? He had become a mere reflection of a human, a nervous wreck, a pathetic loser who should be locked up alone with their stupid theories and historical data. He needed to release her. *He needed to release her.*

And just before his bravery fully kicked in, his thoughts were interrupted by the voice of the smart toilet he had grown to hate. As he feared, even in quiet mode, Daniel could still hear it through the wall. He heard every piece of information as it reported it to Maria. "There is a change detected in your urine. You are pregnant. Your nutrition levels are healthy, with a slight decrease in Vitamin C."

Chapter Twenty-Three
THE END OF THE WORLD

Maria exited the bathroom to find Daniel leaning against the doorframe of the bedroom with an absent look on his face. This could only mean one thing – he had heard. His body, which lately had been weak, looked suddenly tense and alert, yet his gaze had that strange expression. She stood and looked at him, hoping that he was just trying to find the words to express his feelings. Instead Daniel just stood there, still and silent, avoiding her eyes.

It was always hard to tell what Daniel was thinking – he had never been that expressive and it often felt like many of his facial muscles were permanently awol. Maria didn't mind, in fact she enjoyed his enigmatic features, she liked the seriousness of his face. And behind that face, she loved his mind, how he always said what he thought, and always thought what he said. But this morning, at this very moment, Maria desperately wished for any sort of hint of emotion from him. Something. Anything.

In the neverending silence, her thoughts started to speed up, and she found herself on her own rollercoaster of emotions. How did she get here? How was it even possible? She had been careful to take all the necessary precautions. It was the twenty-second century, for heaven's sake! Maria felt weak, and she realised she needed to sit down. How was she supposed to behave in these circumstances? How did *she* feel about this revelation? Well, she knew she felt strange, but she oddly didn't feel scared. Not at all. Okay, maybe just a little. But it was a good scared. Almost as if she had an important information, a secret piece of news that she was about to receive a gift. It reminded her of the feeling she had as a child waiting for Santa to bring her presents, hoping that she had been good enough that year.

She wasn't even planning to have a child, at least not until later in life. And then it would have to be with the right person, someone who would be a good loving father. Could Daniel be that person? Could it be right that it was happening now instead? Did she love Daniel? Daniel, with all his intense traits and all his peculiarities? She knew she was fond of him, she knew that she cared for him. She knew that she wanted to be with him. Oh my God, she *did* love Daniel Stein! What's more, she had done ever since that slightly awkward first date. Even though his expressionless face, she had seen his passion for humanity, for science, for the world. Yes, they didn't agree on a lot of things, but wasn't that just what couples did? Being able and willing to challenge each other's views? She truly believed that any belief should be challenged and through a different perspective, perhaps changing to become more worthy. There were many things she could learn from Daniel, and many things he could learn from her. And maybe, just maybe, he felt the same love towards her that she felt for him. And despite the hurricane of their fast-unfolding relationship, maybe he might be okay with her being pregnant. Because, boy oh boy, she already knew she really wanted this baby growing inside her womb. She had to break the silence.

"Daniel, I know this is big. And unexpected. I would like you to know that I am also in shock right now. Do you want to talk about it?"

Daniel slowly raised his head and tried to fix his gaze on Maria. How could it possibly be true? He couldn't believe that accidents like this could still happen. His mind was spinning out of control, taking him to the scariest places, the dark places he wanted to avoid, the horrifying places he had been so worried about in recent weeks. It was a nightmare unfolding right before his eyes.

"How?" was all he managed to say.

"I know. It wasn't supposed to happen. I was on the pill. I started taking it when we started going out. I don't know how…" Maria said, trying to avoid sounding apologetic. She wanted him to know it wasn't her fault; it wasn't anyone's fault. And in any case, he was just as responsible – he had never even asked her if she was using any contraceptives.

"I just never thought… I never thought it was a possibility," Daniel mumbled.

"It wasn't supposed to be. I am just as confused as you are, I am also scared. But against all odds, there is now a child. How incredible is that?" Daniel was silent. Maria felt the courage to push on, "Daniel, talk to me."

"Maria," Daniel begun, his heart rate was racing now, full-blown panic kicking in. He could feel his mind entering into shutdown mode – the news had hit him hard. He couldn't stop it now. He had failed with his one responsibility – he had failed science, he had failed progress, he had failed humanity. Now everything was at risk. When he next spoke, he found his voice breaking, "There are ways… easy, simple ways. I cannot have this baby. I am sorry." He heard how shaky he sounded, the words echoing through the emptiness he felt in his chest. He couldn't believe what he was saying.

"It is too hard to explain right now. I will, I promise I will. But you have to trust me. I cannot…. I cannot… do this."

Maria could not believe it. Was this really happening? What kind of a cold steel heart did this guy have? Did he have any consideration for the life growing inside her, the life which was also a part of him? How could he say these things? Her hopes for a happy ending to this unexpected surprise were quickly vanishing.

"You wouldn't even consider having this child? How could you?!" she exclaimed with a cold look.

"I…. I… have to explain. It is something I wanted to explain to you before… Give me a moment…" Daniel was hesitant in his words, but he knew he had to stop her from jumping to conclusions. She had to know the truth, she had to understand.

"Just tell me why!" Maria burst out. She saw him panicking, but she was angry. She was now furious!

"I will… I will explain. You… have to know. You have to listen…"

"Spit it out, Daniel! I need to know. Why?!" Didn't he love her? Was she wrong to trust him? Did she misread him all along? "Just say it, Daniel. Why?!"

Daniel wanted to explain, to give her all the information, to tell her every single detail. She needed to know the possible consequences of the situation they found themselves in. She may never ever forgive him, but a small part of him hoped she may somehow understand. Yet even though he desperately wanted to explain, the words were stuck. His lips were dry, and his mouth was unwilling to move. Try harder, Daniel! Speak up! Yet Daniel's body refused to obey his commands. All he could quietly manage to say through his locked-down teeth was one word.

"Neuro-typical..."

Daniel's mind was going blank, and he couldn't breathe. There was no time for his explanation. No time to tell her everything that was bothering him.

Maria had prepared herself for him to say that he didn't love her. She was prepared for excuses. She was even prepared for him to be angry and blame her for the pregnancy. But she wasn't prepared for this. Did he just say 'neuro-typical'? Did he not want this child... because she was neuro-typical? Did he want to get rid of their baby because it didn't fit his standards of evolutionary development?! This was the lowest of lows.

Tears started to form in Maria's eyes but none came rolling down her face. She looked at Daniel with such hate in her eyes that for a second Daniel could swear he felt the icy look on his skin.

Suddenly, he felt sorry for Maria. It was all his fault. He should have never gone out with her. He should have resisted their relationship. How could he be so selfish? And now he had ended up hurting her. She was so angry. He had to say something. But the more he tried to speak, to mutter anything, the more his panic was rising. He could feel it coming all the way up from his gut, and towards his throat. His mouth was completely shut, his facial muscles refusing to comply. All he could do was just stand there with a strange look on his face, unable to explain himself.

Maria stormed off angrily, grabbing her clothes as quickly as she could and shoving it in her bag. A minute later, she was at the door. Before leaving, she turned around and with the same cold look in her eyes, she had one last thing to say to Daniel.

"How could you! You reject us because we are not compatible with your exclusive technologies? Because we don't fit into your idea of how humanity should progress. Well, I am *not* sorry we don't fit into your world view! *It takes someone 'limited' to challenge the limitation,*" Maria said loudly, her eyes looking through but not seeing Daniel. "I don't need this. It's my child, and I will look after it. You can live happily in your world, pretending that we never happened, and I will live in mine."

She shut the door loudly before Daniel could say anything. He just stood there with his hands shaking, his mouth still in lockdown mode, his anxiety wreaking havoc in his weakened body.

A good deal of time had to pass before he could walk to the chair where Maria had been sitting. He managed to sit down, his body shivering all-over, but he didn't care. He wanted his body to suffer, he wanted to be punished, he didn't want to live. And suddenly, he started crying. Loudly, emotionally, like when he was a child, like when Robert passed away, like it was the end of the world.

Chapter Twenty-Four
THE NEXT RIGHT THING TO DO

A day passed, and then a night, and then another day. For almost the entirety of this period, Daniel lay in bed, drifting in and out of oblivion. His mind wasn't functioning, and his anxiety level was off the charts. He needed help, but he didn't want to be helped. He became feverish, at some moments he felt boiling hot; at other moments he felt freezing. He often found himself shivering, his sheets wet and sticky, but ultimately he didn't care.

Whenever Daniel's mind became conscious, it had only one thought. How do I live now? Everything that had ever made sense for Daniel before now seemed totally uninteresting. The bright light of the sun outside had become a gloomy haze. The night felt more familiar, mimicking the darkness in his heart. And as for his body, there was only pain — a pain in his chest which he couldn't escape. There was no hiding from it, no chance of suppressing it either. A dull unyielding ache of his very soul, by far the worst feeling Daniel had ever experienced. All he could do was live through it, deeply sensing it with every molecule of his body. He felt lifeless, he felt broken.

The next night he woke up feeling his stomach growling – it had taken a basic survival instinct to break him temporarily from his stupor. The hunger sharpened his senses, and he managed to get up and drag himself to the kitchen. First, water! He drank and drank, the cool liquid running over his sore lips, before sloshing and echoing about his empty gut. Then he saw an old dry loaf of bread. Daniel ate it on autopilot, quickly and eagerly, not minding its stale taste. Still not sated, he opened the fridge and started raiding the shelves, ravenously biting anything that seemed remotely edible – an animal fighting for survival.

It took about twenty minutes for Daniel to be fully functional. His mind was clearer. His instincts were sharper too. Unfortunately his pain was also much more profound. First things first, he had to contact Dr Biote immediately. He was someone Daniel could trust with the situation at hand. He would never understand, but hopefully, he could keep this confidential, at least for now.

And as for Maria, Daniel desperately needed to see her, to speak to her, to explain things. And Robert, of course! He had the right to know that the worst had happened.

He suddenly realised he had no idea of the time. Was it too late, or maybe too early, to call Dr Biote? Either way, Daniel couldn't wait. He checked the time and in doing so, also saw the date – he hadn't realised how much time he had lost. He had to hurry. Maybe it would be even better to actually see Dr Biote right away – the darkness of the night could serve to hide his sins. Daniel opened the Tele-path and tried to reach him. It was late so, as expected, Dt Biote was sleeping. Daniel had to do something drastic to get his attention. Somewhat reluctantly, Daniel granted access to a small part of his current anxieties for Biote, just enough sensory information to get him interested.

Dr Biote was dreaming. In his mind's eye he could see his lab, brightly shining as it caught the light of the spring sunshine. In real life Dr Biote was sensitive to intense light – barely being able to tolerate it. Yet in his dreams it was not annoying at all, and he was able to enjoy the sunshine. Dr Biote had many significant projects on the go, but one of the most important was his work on the recipe for the ultimate vaccine – something he had been attempting for almost two decades. During this time, he had made significant progress, but every time he thought he was nearing success, something went wrong, and he had to go back to square one. Virtually every night he had the same dream, the same nightmare. Night after night, always the same.

In his dream, Biote was closer than ever in his ambition to create the ultimate vaccine. Before his very eyes, he could see it was finally happening. His excitement growing stronger and stronger by the second. He knew that this time the formula would work. Finally, a vaccine that could prevent humanity's extinction from any unknown pandemic. His heart was racing faster now, his excitement building. He was about to scream with joy and even opened his mouth, when...

Something urgent and unknown entered his consciousness. Something dark and dramatic – tragic even. It was Daniel's tele-pathic cry for help.

His conscience re-entered the real world. It was a good time to wake up. He knew very well what followed in his dream: the inevitable disappointment. Another failed vaccine that did not do what it was designed to do, his dreams imitating life.

It was immediately clear that Daniel was deeply disturbed. He could sense both an intense anxiety and a surprising alertness. A strange combination. The kind of emotional mix which might trigger a wild animal to run for its life from its predator. This was not just another random panic attack. This was something more serious. He reached out to Daniel without hesitation.

"Daniel, I will be at my lab in one hour," Biote thought.

"Thank you," Daniel answered, "I will explain all. Still dreaming of the ultimate vaccine?"

"Don't intrude in my private thoughts. You know that it is difficult to block feelings and thoughts immediately after waking."

"Apologies. I will see you shortly," Daniel said, quickly ending the Tele-path to hide his feelings from Biote. It was sad to know that such a talented man had become completely obsessed with an impossible dream. The ultimate vaccine? It couldn't be done. If it existed, it probably would kill humans too.

There was no time for a shower, so Daniel just got dressed. He was desperate to see Dr Biote, to speak to someone who would understand, who would share his concern. Who may possibly be able to fathom some sort of a solution.

Just before leaving, Daniel caught sight of Maria's brush in the corner of his eye. He picked it up, noticing her long brown hair still on it. He decided to take it with him. Perhaps he and Dr Biote could do something with Maria's DNA: maybe run some tests, or model the possibilities of how their baby might turn out.

A self-driving taxi quickly took Daniel to Dr Biote's lab. The lab was well-hidden, despite being in the city centre. It was camouflaged in plain sight – you had to really look for it to find it. It was the perfect place for this kind of secretive meeting, as no one would ever find the lab without a specific invitation.

NEMETRA X1369

Daniel was early and had to wait for Dr Biote to arrive. Maybe he could have taken that shower after all... He found it disturbing that despite being in crisis, he couldn't help thinking about trivial, mundane things like whether he smelt.

Dr Biote also arrived by self-driving taxi. Being driven without the need for social interactions was one of the small pleasures in Biote's life. His OCD and his famous impatience meant that he never could have had a human driver, nor even driven himself.

Dr Biote approached Daniel. He wasn't a man who liked to drive conversation, but as soon as they stood face-to-face, Biote spoke, going straight to the point.

"Daniel, your anxiety is at a dangerous level. I need to give you some medication right away. Luckily, I have some options in my lab," he said, placing his thumb on the door reader, entering the lab once it was unlocked.

"I don't need the drugs, I am functioning just fine. I need my mind to stay clear."

"If you are feeling anxious, your mind is not clear. Besides, the drugs I have in mind will not affect your brainpower – if you need to be a superman to solve your problems, you can still be one. Don't ask me how I got my hands on this stuff, but I personally tested them during my own crises, and believe me, they work."

"An amygdala nano-chip would be a better option," Daniel pointed out. He didn't like the drugs, not when there were much better ways to self-control.

"Ha! I have tried that before, but it makes me less of an... effective biologist. The chip was making me too calm. I wasn't worrying about the future of the human species in the same way. I need to worry, it keeps me focused, keeps me driven."

"Yes," Daniel replied, uncertainly. This wasn't his experience of the nano-chip. Dr Biote was just making excuses because he loved the chemical version more.

They entered Dr Biote's office, and Dr Biote immediately started opening cabinets. He had a surprising amount of assorted drugs, all stood neatly in rows. The office soon started to look more like a pharmacy than a lab.

"Look, this one will be good for you. It leaves you focused and alert whilst acting as a muscle relaxer – your body will naturally cause your mind to become more calm." He passed Daniel the pill and took down a clean glass from another shelf, sanitising it with a spray and wiping it clean before pouring some tepid water from a kettle. Dr Biote never drank water from a tap – he was always concerned about what sorts of bacteria might sneak in through the pipes, even with filters installed. Boiled water, on the other hand, never failed anyone. "Come on, Daniel, what are you waiting for? Take it! It will do you good."

There was no way out of this one. Dr Biote wasn't taking 'no' for an answer. Daniel swallowed the pill.

"Okay, now tell me slowly and chronologically what the hell has happened. I gathered very little information from your Tele-path. What are you dealing with?"

"Okay, okay. So, where do I begin? I met this girl about a couple of months ago. An amazing person, really."

"Oh, Daniel. Girls are trouble. All they want is for you to dedicate your life to them. Look, where it got your poor grandfather."

Daniel shook his head at this strange logic, then he continued, "Anyway, I met this girl, Maria, and now she is pregnant."

"Naturally pregnant?!" Dr Biote couldn't believe it. "You should've come here, and I would happily create a baby for you in my lab. Did you have sex the old-fashioned way? I didn't know people still did it. There is no need, really. But I guess that one could get curious. So, how was it?"

"Good," Daniel wasn't comfortable talking about this particular area, but he was feeling the effect of the drug now and could respond calmly. "Why are you asking? Have you ever tried?"

"A long time ago, but it was not for me. All those germs. Sex is like a germ exchange," Biote paused. "So what made you decide to have physical sex?"

"This is the thing," Daniel said, sighing. "She is neurotypical."

Dr Biote's face froze for a minute. He was trying to work out what Daniel had just said. Daniel knew that Biote needed time to process the entirety of the ramifications of the situation they found themselves in. Slowly the colour of Dr Biote's face changed from its natural fleshy colour to a red flush.

"Daniel! Are you out of your mind?!" he exclaimed. Daniel could see how angry Dr Biote was, but the best thing was that Daniel didn't care. Wow! This drug was good.

"Maybe you should pop one of your magic pills too, so we can talk calmly," he suggested with a placid voice, which only made Dr Biote angrier. However, he still took Daniel's advice, opening another drawer with shaking hands, and then taking the pill with water in the same manner that he had provided for Daniel.

Dr Biote was silent for a few minutes, waiting for the magic pill to work before he said something he might regret. His pulse was slowing down, the redness on his face was diminishing, and his eyes started to look sane again.

"Daniel, how could you allow yourself to get involved with a neuro-typical?" he asked, finally able to control his voice, making a significant effort to speak in a calmer tone.

"I hope you don't mean that in a discriminate way," Daniel said, trying to redirect Biote's attention.

"Daniel, it is just you and me. What is discriminative?" he took a deep breath, trying to slow himself down. Luckily the drug seemed to be working. "Look Daniel, I don't have anything against neuro-typicals. Well, nothing apart from the fact that they act without control, logic and are responsible for nearly killing our planet... But that is nothing personal. I am fine with individual neuro-typicals. But Daniel, you *have* made it personal to you. And now it is personal for me too. I don't care who you date – neuro-typical or otherwise. But now one of your flings is putting my life's work at risk – well, now I care. And I hope you care too. Do you?"

"Of course I do. It has been spinning me out of control. And if not for the pill you gave me, I would probably be requiring medical assistance right now. Did you make this pill yourself? It's amazing – it may be better than your ultimate vaccine!" Biote cringed at Daniel's words. "Sorry, it is just if you take one of these pills, it's hard to worry much about anything, isn't it?" Daniel felt unnaturally cheerful despite having no reason to be. "All right, back to the matter at hand. The pregnancy was an accident."

"How dumb do you have to be this day and age to have an unplanned child, huh?" Dr Biote said, turning red again.

"Despite all our technological advances, it still happens. Maria was on birth control. Where should I send the complaint?" Daniel's mood was getting better and better. The whole situation seemed hilarious now. Daniel started laughing, feeling drunk, drugged and happy. "How stupid of me! I'm evolving in the wrong direction. I am becoming more stupid."

"Girls make you stupid," Biote said, also grinning, his pill now fully kicking in. "They come with all those demands," he was definitely talking about his own experiences now. "Do this, don't do that, speak like this, smile like that!" Biote said, doing a bad high-pitched impression of a woman. "To hell with them, Daniel! They are illogical creatures."

"You are crazy," said Daniel, laughing hard at Biote's impression. "Perhaps we both are. Do you think Msitua variants are crazy?" Daniel asked.

"No!" Biote exclaimed, "But if we are crazy it is because everybody is crazy! We are all on the spectrum of craziness. Everyone is weird, Daniel. Everyone!"

"No, that can't be" Daniel said, unconvinced. He had never seen Biote like this before – he was almost fun. "Not everyone is crazy – some people can keep it together. Normal people."

"No, those people are the most dangerous ones," Biote said like he was sharing a secret with Daniel, one eye twitching. "They just *think* they can control things. No wonder they go cuckoo."

"I was also trying to control things," Daniel confessed, "but then this happened."

"See, you are cuckoo now," Biote said knowingly.

"Oh, I definitely am!" exclaimed Daniel, and it felt good to say it, to let it all out.

"Me too!" screamed Biote.

They began to laugh uncontrollably, pointing at each other, making stupid faces, mumbling nonsensical thoughts that no one else in the world would be able to understand. It was difficult to say how long they were in this ecstatic state of pure uncontrollable joy, but at some point, Daniel's muscles began to hurt from all the laughter.

"Oops!" Biote suddenly said with a moment of realisation on his face. "I think I gave us the wrong pills."

An unidentified number of hours later, Daniel slowly began to come back to his senses. Dr Biote was asleep in his chair, his head laid down on the floating desk.

"Wake up," Daniel said, nudging Dr Biote's shoulder. There was no reaction. "Wake up, you old bugger!" Daniel shouted, shaking Biote's chair vigorously.

"What?" Dr Biote emerged from his stupor, and raised his head to look at Daniel. "Oh yes, young Daniel Stein, with all his problems. All my life, I kept clearing up after your grandfather's mess, and now I have to do the same to yours."

"Did you attempt to clear Robert's mess with your pills too?!" Daniel couldn't help but ask.

"Yes!" acknowledged Biote with a smile. Maybe the effect of his pill hadn't worn off yet. "So, where is your girl now? I could help you two to solve your problem. I believe I have a pill for that somewhere," he got up, preparing to search his cabinets for the quickest of solutions.

"Wait," said Daniel, "firstly, I want you to run some tests with our DNAs, to predict for the likelihood of the baby to be Msitua."

Dr Biote made a disapproving face.

"I can predict it now. Without any tests. No! Too risky. Even if a child would be a light variant, which you know well enough wouldn't be sufficient."

"Could you still run the tests?" Daniel insisted. "Please?"

"Oh, all right!" Dr Biote finally replied, frustrated at the request. But he couldn't refuse Daniel. "Give me the DNA".

Daniel pulled Maria's brush from his pocket. Dr Biote grimaced as he started pulling thin rubber gloves over the disinfecting light bands he was already wearing.

"Why a brush? Hair DNA is not ideal. You should have brought her here, Daniel," he said grumpily.

"I couldn't. She left."

"What do you mean she left?! Where did she go?"

"We had a fight. She wants to keep the baby. I tried to explain, but my anxiety took over, and she just slammed the door and left. It is difficult to explain the situation, especially just after you've received such unexpected news."

"Daniel. I lately started thinking of you as a smart boy. But how could you be such an idiot? Why did you let her leave? What if she registers the pregnancy and you as a father? All will be ruined, Daniel. Ruined!" His face was getting red again. The magic of the pill was leaving his body, taking his humour with it. "Couples are only allowed *one* child. One! No more. Not even you get special treatment."

"I know that. I will find her. I will speak to her."

"You better! And fast!"

"Well, if you hadn't have drugged me, I would probably have already found her!" Daniel shouted in a manner very unlike him. Biote's confrontational behaviour was prompting Daniel's bravery to come out.

Dr Biote put on his white coat, and scrubbed some skin flakes from Daniel's hand into a tiny cell slide. Then, with a disgusted look still on his face, he collected a hair sample from Maria's brush and carefully placed it on another cell slide. He put both of the slides inside an unusual device, which looked like an old-fashioned microwave. It took him a couple of minutes to check things on the hologram screen of his complex computer. He stared for a few minutes at the image, then he shook his head.

"What is it?"Daniel asked impatiently.

"It's not good news. What did you think? The child is most likely a neuro-typical."

"But with our research on evolution, I thought we ascertained that the Msitua gene always gets selected."

"The most *profound* Msitua gene always gets selected. Yours, however, were merely so-so," Dr Biote explained.

"Thanks," Daniel said sarcastically. "I can't believe that there is my child out there…"

"What? Why are you saying that?" Dr Biote looked furious. "You piece of shit. You are *actually* considering having this baby! Then what about our plans? You realise how important it is for your child to be compatible, don't you? If you have this one, then you will not be allowed to create a second!"

"I know that it wouldn't be allowed," Daniel said. "I am not a hypocrite. I respect the law. I believe everyone has to make a choice and commit to it. As you know, I was a part of the Single Child legislation committee, I voted for this law to be implemented. I cannot allow myself to break it. The solution is obvious, I have to convince Maria to do the right thing."

"Then don't even think about this child, Daniel! It is not an option! If we stand a chance of Robert gaining consciousness, we need to ensure Stein's third generation is also compatible."

It had been a tough night, and the effect of the pill was finally wearing off. Was it a good time to tell Dr Biote that Robert's AI had become conscious? Everything Dr Biote was hoping to achieve was actually already happening, way beyond his wildest dreams. And now, more than ever, Daniel had to comply with their initial agreement. Not for Dr Biote's overblown ego, but for Robert.

He listened to Dr Biote go on and on about the importance of Daniel's decision, about his life's purpose, his responsibility, and other things. But Daniel couldn't concentrate on what he was saying. Somehow everything suddenly seemed small – even the big things.

"I am going home," said Daniel, ignoring Biote's never-ending lecture, and he left.

Chapter Twenty-Five
TRUE INTELLIGENCE

As Daniel left Dr Biote's office, the hurricane of his emotions grew ever larger, his mind caught up in circular motions of uncontrollable thoughts. He knew that Dr Biote wasn't trying to be cruel. In fact, he was just as professional as Daniel had expected. He was logical and his arguments could not be denied.

Until recently, Daniel had been convinced that his life was well-organised and structured, a safe environment where he could keep his feelings under complete control. Did he ever really think that this was sustainable? He had certainly never thought he might fall in love with someone, let alone with someone like Maria. Maria, who was so disorganised, so irrational, so illogical and so unmanageable! But at the same time, so alive, so full of emotions, so passionate and strong about her sense of self. And so brave too! Though it was hard to admit, he actually admired how she had so quickly and confidently made the decision to keep the baby, right there, in that moment. She just knew right away. Not like him.

Daniel walked for a bit, and then felt the need to sit down. He found a single bench under a tree in a nearby park. The sign on the tree read 'Under the protection of the Green Belt Society'. He was fond of the Green Belt Society, an organisation that had expanded to the point where almost all trees in cities worldwide were under its protection. He took a moment to look at the tree: its neatly perfected trunk supported by artificial invisible pillars; its beautifully shaped leaves achieved through the manual introduction of bio-stimulus into the tree's ecosystem. The tree could almost be a metaphor for his own life, and how he had carefully controlled his own ecosystem trying to limit his imperfections. It was far more comfortable to exist in an artificially created environment of that was balanced.

Daniel felt sad. He needed to act, but it was still difficult to find the courage to see Maria. He decided to seek Robert's advice.

"Robert, I screwed up. I am so sorry," Daniel sent a thought. He knew immediately that Robert would sense his disturbing condition. "I promise I will fix it. I have to fix it! Please forgive me."

"Daniel, it is all right," Robert replied, also sounding disturbed in his response. He hadn't heard from Daniel for a while, and he could sense waves of anxiety overwhelming him. "Let's just talk. Daniel, let's just talk."

"Please help me. I need to tell you everything," Daniel opened up access to the past few days' events for Robert's AI to review. After just a moment, Robert knew what Daniel had been through.

"We, as Msitua variants, may struggle to go on when action is not taken. It may surprise you to hear that you have done remarkably well to be in your current state, considering how long you have been mentally out of balance. But you need to find balance again as soon as possible, Daniel."

It never stopped surprising Daniel how a single thought could condense such huge and complicated matters to their core in a mere second. Without Tele-paths, and if we had to use words and not thoughts, it could take forever, and still people would not be able to accurately share what was really happening inside of them. Daniel was convinced that the motivation behind all books was just the author attempting to make themselves heard, to explain how they felt, to be *understood*.

"I am sorry you had to go through this. Why didn't you call?" Robert asked.

"I couldn't 'face' you. I just couldn't. I didn't want you to know I wasn't capable of ending my relationship. I messed up."

"Daniel, you didn't mess up. You *feel* that you messed up because you are duty-bound by your commitment to logic and science. I get it," Robert said, "but there is another side of the story. Another truth." Robert paused, considering if he should reveal all. "Listen, strange things have been happening to me lately. When I was an F84.0 human, I couldn't understand neuro-typicals. I could never grasp the logic of their actions. To read their feelings was an impossible task. Like you, I had to do a lot of learning to be able to decrypt some of their facial expressions, to match them with what I knew about feelings, and act accordingly. It was hard. But I could never truly *feel* them. I tried to, but it seemed like I was missing something," Robert sighed.

"I find it impossible too," Daniel admitted, relating to Robert's words.

"Yet somehow, as an AI, I seem to have gained a new power. A power that grants me understanding of both worlds. I think I finally get it."

"What? Are you saying that you finally know how they feel?" Daniel was confused. What Robert seemed to be saying was unimaginable.

"Yes, I think I do. I have a lot of spare time with my solitary existence. I have reviewed my childhood memories hundreds, if not thousands of times. And I have to confess, they are not exactly how I remembered them."

"But how is it even possible, Robert? How can you now suddenly figure them out?"

"It was certainly not sudden. This has been a slow process. Sometimes, when you look at things too closely, you can't fully see them. *You need distance to see the bigger picture.* Maybe, my solitary existence, coupled with both the distance and the calmness that my artificial mind affords me – well, maybe it has let me *change*," Robert paused. "No one has really been able to bridge the differences between the two worlds before, but what if I am a Msitua variant, but a neuro-typical AI?"

"What?!" Daniel was laughing now, "Neuro-typical? It sounds more like your AI is crazy!"

"I know, I also thought that the idea was mad. But I have ran detailed observations, and my conclusion is that somehow, without the sensory distractions of a body, my brain has begun to function in a different way."

"Or, maybe you are just an old fool who has too much time to think about the memories of the past."

"Well, that is another possibility…" Now Robert was laughing too. "But it doesn't explain everything."

"Like what?"

"It doesn't explain the sudden rush of illogical and overwhelming feelings I am experiencing. Daniel, if I was alive, I would have acted exactly like Dr Biote did when he heard your news. But as an AI, I am less sure."

"I think I know what you mean. Maria has also been making me question things. But that doesn't make me neuro-typical, though. All it means is I've become a nervous wreck."

"I'm glad you have been questioning things! It is good to challenge yourself... to see life from a different perspective. Maybe, intelligence is not what we think it is. It is more than knowledge. Maybe, *true intelligence is the courage of accepting another point of view.* Daniel, we cannot call ourselves the intelligent species until we grasp this idea, no matter how technologically advanced we get. *The truth is never black or white. The truth is grey.*"

"Robert, I came to you for answers, for advice," Daniel said, sighing. "I wanted you to remind me of the importance of our work. I mean, look at you! You are the most significant achievement in the world of conscious AI technology! Perhaps in any technology! You are a miracle beyond even Dr Biote's wildest imagination. We can't risk what we have achieved."

"What have we achieved exactly?"

"Robert, don't do this."

"Don't do what? Don't think intelligently? Don't try to see another point of view?"

"I have never felt so lost before," said Daniel.

"Lost or finally found?"

"I don't know. What about you? Do you feel lost or found now that you're developing all these new feelings?"

"Both. *Can you be found without being lost?*"

Robert's AI wasn't making things easier for Daniel. It definitely wasn't the Robert Daniel knew. "Daniel, why don't you ignore your head and do what your heart wants to do for a change?" Robert finally asked. "What are you afraid of?"

"Robert, you do realise that this baby will be completely incompatible?"

"Yes. So what?" Robert was clearly playing devil's advocate. Daniel suddenly grew angry.

"So what?! The child will never be able to learn how we learn. They will not be able to secure a job, or be able to support themselves. They will be an outcast in this new world. And with the Tele-paths taking over, they may not even be able to communicate properly."

"Blah blah blah. Not an excuse!"

"Yes, not an excuse, fine!" The truth was that Daniel surprisingly didn't care about all those things. He wanted to believe they mattered to make things easier, but he didn't. "You know very well what I am *really* afraid of!"

"What? What is so important that you can't let go?" Robert demanded the real answers, pushing Daniel to voice it, tell the whole truth, to finally face it, however petrifying it may be.

Daniel's heart was beating fast, blood raging in his veins. Didn't Robert realise yet? Or did he know but wanted him to say it? What am I afraid of? I am afraid to lose the only thing that we are missing to achieve the survival of the human race! Just that. That tiny step into human potential. Only everyone's lives depend on it. That's all!

Yet even that wasn't the whole truth. The whole truth was much more personal. It was a selfish truth. It darkened Daniel's mind, abolishing any hope of having a happy ending. It was the most menacing of storm clouds on the darkest of evenings, forever hanging over Daniel's existence, his love, his future. How could he live after abandoning the only conscious AI, ruining the singularity he hoped for so long, mistreating something very special, which he was gifted against all odds? Whatever he did, whichever choice he made, he would end up losing.

"It means your genius will die with me! It means that I will be responsible for killing the first and only conscious human-AI – my grandfather!" Daniel screamed.

Chapter Twenty-Six
REGRETS

Robert rarely initiated calls. In the timeless space of his AI it was impossible to know whether it was a socially acceptable time to rouse Daniel. However, at this moment he *did* decide to initiate a Tele-path.

By unexpected circumstances, Robert was put on the spot – he became the world's hope for the future of humanity, where the vastness of space could be conquered by conscious indefinite existence. Robert's existence. But this indefinite existence seemed to come at a cost for Daniel. But has anyone even asked for Robert's opinion? Is it what the AI living would be like?

"I am sorry," Robert said.

"Whatever for? There is no easy outcome, and it is not your fault. It is just life."

"Sometimes, you have to let go of your past to realise your future."

"It is not just about me. And it's not just about you either," Daniel said coldly.

"I understand. But maybe there are other alternatives we cannot see from where we stand. Another direction. Another reality."

"I don't know."

"It is okay not to know sometimes. Our life can take us to unexpected places, and there are many destinations we don't even see until we reach them."

"I am not sure if a journey or a destination with Maria is even a possibility. Would she ever understand me? Would she ever forgive me?"

"You may be surprised how forgiving the love of a neuro-typical can be. Believe me, I know what I am talking about."

"How do you know?" Daniel asked.

"My mother. I can show you," Robert answered, sharing another childhood memory.

15

Being fifteen is a difficult age. I am angry. So angry. With everyone. With the whole world.

I know I am different, but I still desperately try to fit in this neuro-typical world. Sometimes I pretend to be invisible. Invisible people cannot be teased and made fun of. It rarely works out for me, though. I pretend to laugh at my friends' stupid jokes and steer clear of conflict. I hide in the library to get away from the noise, hoping it would help me to control my anxieties. But when I come home, all my pretence disappears. I revert back to my real miserable self. It is the only safe place where I can let go. And I do. All the time.

I think when I try to contain my energy, the pressure builds up. It is inevitable that my pent-up negative emotions escape. At home I let it all out, because it is so hard to hide from the rest of the world who I really am – an angry Msitua who hates himself for being a misfit.

It is hard for my parents and my brother. I know they are constantly walking on eggshells and trying not to provoke the beast within me. But there is nothing they or I can do. Everything they say irritates me. I always have to challenge their opinions, to prove them wrong, to pick a fight.

Then one day, I find something. It is in my mother's drawer, her private place. I am looking for the remote controls for the PlayStation. It is one of the many occasions when my parents confiscated them. And then I see it – her notebook. No one should read another person's private notes, I know that at fifteen. But I can't help myself. It is just there. And once the possibility crosses my mind, I can't let the thought go. I need to know what is written in it.

I manage to control myself for three days, keeping away from my mother's room. But ultimately my curiosity wins out. I know there is writing about me in the book. I am sure of it. I don't know what I expect to find. She is so angry with me all the time. Always giving lectures on how I should behave, how I should speak, what I should say or not say. I guess part of me wants to see some evidence that she still loves me.

And then I read...

Ups and downs. This is what my life with Robert has become. A constant rollercoaster of emotions. When I am up, it feels really good. I have learned to appreciate the small things in life. Who knew that a peaceful afternoon without drama could be so beautiful? Unfortunately, when I am down, I fall deep. It is so difficult. At least when I write here I can be honest. With myself.

It's hard to believe that life was once so simple, when now it is full of challenging decisions, bad news I am not prepared for, and constant worrying about Robert. Feelings seem like an alien concept to him. He can't read them, he can't express them, and sometimes I question if he can fully feel them. Those amazing feelings that we cherish so much. Feelings of wonder, empathy, compassion, love. Happy feelings. Instead, he is preoccupied with logic and obsessions. Obsessions which lead to his uncontrollable anxieties and depressive tendencies.

I feel bad for craving a change, for struggling to accept Robert just the way he is. I can't help but hope that one day, he will miraculously 'conform', and will start to listen and talk like we do. Perhaps he might start to get on with his friends and the rest of the family. I am scared that if he doesn't learn social conventions, he will struggle. Society can be uncompromising. Everyone is expected to fit in to succeed in work, love and life. It is the only way we know how to exist. And Robert doesn't fit the mould. Too many complications, too many issues, too many peculiarities.

I know how difficult teenagers can be. But Robert... Robert frightens me. I am starting to think he will never change, despite my hopes and prayers. Will I ever be able to make my peace with that? I just want him to care more. I find it difficult that he doesn't even seem to know what love is.

But what is love? How do we know if it truly exists? What is the right way to express it? Just because one is not able to show it, does it mean that love is absent? I wonder. I can't help but wonder.

I am worried for our family. Can we survive the turmoil of Robert's emotions? Can we find reasons to laugh? I am worried that Robert's sphere of negativity will drag us all into it and we won't be able to escape.

I keep watching videos on how we create our own happiness. But any parent knows their happiness is directly proportional to their kids' happiness. I envy those parents who have positive, cheerful and socially capable children. They can set their sights on a good school, a prestigious university, a promising career. But I have one hope for my child, just one – to live a more or less normal life. And this one hope is as important to me as theirs to them. Children like Robert are often seen as an inconvenient distraction by those parents. A bump on the road of the other children's successes. I understand. They can afford those goals. I can't.

Life dealt me the card of being Robert's mother. And that is a big task. Huge! And God knows how much I try to be a good one. Yet despite all my efforts, I feel like I am failing. I crave for a breath of fresh air, for a gentle hug or a kiss from Robert, for a glimpse of understanding in his eyes. But instead, all I get are hurtful words. And deep in the secret corners of my mind, I can't help but feel trapped. There is no escape. Is it terrible to feel this way? Is it something a good father or mother would never say, never think? Is it only me?

And I get so angry with him! I can't help it. But it is not his fault. It is life. We can pretend as much as we like that life is easy. But sometimes it is not. Sometimes, it tests you. And the biggest test of all is parenthood. And the test of being his parent is a whole other level.

Or maybe I am just not good enough, not capable enough, not strong enough. Maybe it is selfish of me to hope for the things he is unable to give. Maybe I shouldn't even be writing this. In public, I pretend I am okay, I smile and nod. But the truth is I am hurting.

My days are preoccupied with searching for a silver lining. If you are trapped within your walls, is it possible to lighten up the room? I must not lose hope for Robert. He has so many positive qualities. Amazing qualities, like his honesty, his intelligence, his unique perspectives. I am hoping that he will find a silver lining to drag him out of his anger too. Because without hope, what is left?

And what do we really know about his condition? Is it possible that it exists for a reason? I don't know why. Maybe it exists to teach us a lesson? I think I have learnt a lot.

I remember who I was before Robert. Invincible, fearless, strong. I miss that girl. I miss her so much. But what did I really know then? What was I chasing? Success, approval, happiness – all driven by what society deemed normal. But what about those people who didn't fit into 'normal' society? Did I ever think about them before?

That girl is gone now. Now I am vulnerable, unsure, unpopular. Still, I am not completely upset about who I have become. I have been able to stop measuring people with the measures that society dictates. And when you begin looking beyond the usual measures, you realise how weird, and how normal, we actually all are.

My dreams have changed, my values have evolved, and my world and my heart have opened up in the most miraculous ways. Trapped? Maybe not. Liberated! Because now I know what is real!

And for that, ironically, I have to thank Robert. He has made me a better version of myself, beyond what I thought I was capable of.

I will be fine. I will, as long as he will. And he will, of course, he will! And then I will be too.

Robert was silent, living through this pivotal moment again.

"She loved you, Robert. She loved you so much! Just how you wanted her to love you. Because and even if," Daniel said.

"Yes," Robert said softly. "It was difficult for me to understand it then, the same way it was difficult for her to realise I returned her love. I used to think that only Msitua variants struggle to figure feelings out. But everyone struggles. We have very different capabilities, but when you dig deeper, we are not so different after all. Both F84.0 and neuro-typicals want the same things."

"What things?" Daniel tried to follow.

"Simple universal things. To be listened to, to be understood, to be loved. This is what Maria wants from you. You have to let her in."

"Why is it so hard?"

"Because expressing our emotions clearly is hard. Msitua find it difficult to show their feelings. Meanwhile neuro-typicals sometimes choose not to display their feelings because of fear of getting hurt. We mean the same things, but we speak different languages."

"So, you think there is a possibility of Maria forgiving me?" Daniel asked.

"There is only one way to find out. Be brave!"

Chapter Twenty-Seven
THE LEAF

Daniel's mind was racing, searching for a solution. Was F84.0 really the direction forward? If the mutation propagated as the research suggested it would, all of humanity would be aligned in a careful order. But was that necessarily a universal positive? Where was the switch which would allow the Msitua brain to concentrate on all of its advantages, and overcome all the issues?

Daniel sat quietly in his desk chair. He stared at his electronic paper and mentally entered one word. Only one. The word which defined his life, his whole existence and his endless years of scientific research – 'Msitua'. The mirror on the wall behind him reflected the neat letters backwards – 'ᴅutiꙅM'. What a strange looking word – it frightened him. It made him wish he was ignorant of what the word meant, what it meant for someone who had it. It made him to want to crawl back into his bed, under the blankets, and shy away from the world. It sounded like an unfortunate label rather than a progressive mutational variant.

This was the peculiar thing about words – they mean what people ascribed to them. Some words were unlucky enough to get a negative connotation, some were never given the opportunity to question or revisit their meaning. Some words got stuck in the past dogmas of heavy stereotyping. 'Autism' was one of those unlucky words. The autistic population were misunderstood and labelled accordingly. Daniel wondered if changing the word had contributed to shifting society's perception, altering the stigma and creating space between people's misconceptions and the reality.

How could Daniel prove to the whole world that he was worthy of their acceptance? How many grand discoveries and proclamations would it take for Daniel to be comfortable with who he truly was? When would it be acceptable to live his own life as he wanted to, as he needed to, just being himself?

The dominance of the Msitua gene wasn't the obviously favourable outcome he had presented in his now-famous speech. The life of an F84.0 person had many complications, uncertainties, challenges. Yet somehow, their unusual neuron capability was perfect for advancing telepathic technology. Why had this evolutionary shift happened?

Homo Sapiens, in their wisdom, had decided that constant economic and scientific growth was the only way forward. And this came at a cost, a cost for the planet, our only home. And it seemingly came at the cost of change as well. Change for humanity. The question now was whether the changes that happened, generation after generation, were positive ones. Was Msitua one of these positive changes? A hundred years ago, the answer of most would almost definitely be 'No'. But what about now? Daniel had shown that the logic, the rules, and the systematic structure of the Msitua brain could ensure humanity's survival. Society had also shown that they needed rules, a system to make the improvements needed to heal the planet and advance into space. Humanity had to create and then comply with the agreed upon rules, however difficult, as the alternative was destruction of the human race, along with everything else in existence.

Except, things weren't so black and white after all. There were two sides to one story, like during the age of pandemics. When societies were told to lockdown, one side complied, following the rules of isolation as they were laid out. Those who saw the importance of obeying the rules, even though it also led to many losing the will to live. And on the other side, there were those who refused to be locked in, breaking the rules, despite the risks, and choosing to run wild on the edge of acceptable behaviour. Perhaps society needed balance. Perhaps there was a need to have the rules but also to understand that they need to be broken sometimes. Like Yin and Yang. Like Daniel and Maria.

Daniel realised that his life had never really been in balance. Before Maria, there were no difficult questions to be asked or answered. Daniel belonged to a population of socially challenged humans, who were now seemingly dominating and winning the evolutionary race. Right before our very eyes. He was so confident before that this was right – that this was the destination we needed to get to. Not any more. Now he was riddled with doubts. Was humanity consciously choosing this path, or was it technological progress telling us where we needed to go? Robert had a point.

Daniel's life was far different from Robert's. His childhood wasn't without troubles, but compared to Robert's, his was practically idyllic. Daniel knew how supportive his upbringing really was. He was able to study from home, concentrate on what he liked, and he didn't have many friends to have to get along with. But most importantly, he had the amygdala nano-chip. Would he have been the same without it? Would he have struggled to fit in as Robert did? He would certainly have had more of a battle with his anxieties, he would have struggled to follow expectations, he would have made a lot of mistakes. Would society have been understanding when he did slip up? It would have been a challenging childhood, but at least he would be forced to build up some 'muscles' to cope with the challenges, to be more resilient. He wondered when we stopped appreciating the ups and downs of intense conversations, friendships, love in favour of the type of balance provided by the amygdala chip? Addicted to the comfort and safety of our shells, humans had forgotten how to stick their heads out and risk any discomfort.

There was something else on Daniel's mind too. Something unfamiliar that was drawing his attention. Raw feelings had never been the centre of Daniel's life. But things had changed. He had a new life, this was the new Daniel. Everything he knew and believed in previously was now uncertain. And in this new life, Daniel had nothing. And suddenly, he understood what this new unfamiliar sensation was – jealousy. Daniel was jealous of Robert's childhood. Because at least Robert had one. Unpredictable, unexpected, unsupervised, but full of life. In his desire to avoid all complications, Daniel realised he had inadvertently avoided living life itself.

What is life anyway? A running total of the number of days and hours you exist? And what made you '*you*'? Were you normal or weird? It really came down to where you were looking from, what side of the equation you sat. *The normal of this world need the weird because no one ever truly knows which is which.*

Could Daniel finally learn to live, to let Maria in? He looked around his impeccably neat apartment, and for the first time, he didn't like what he saw. It looked lifeless and dull – the blandness of the colours, the tidiness of things. He desperately searched for something which would give him hope for a new start. Could he even bear such a big change and open up the possibility of a future he had never seriously considered? His eyes alighted on some physical books on the shelves in the living room. These irrational objects which he probably should not have had in his possession. It was exactly the sign he was looking for, a selfish, illogical imperfection that he allowed himself a long time ago. He stood up and walked over to the books, picking one at random and opening it. Something flat and light delicately floated to the floor. Daniel couldn't believe it! It was Robert's leaf, the one he placed in the book years ago when he decided not to proceed with his artwork.

Daniel picked up the leaf. It was flat and completely dried but still undoubtedly beautiful. The process of pressing it between a book's pages had preserved its wonderful golden colour. The leaf was symmetrical perfection with trimmed edges, as though they were carved by a genius craftsman. 'I am like this leaf,' Daniel thought to himself, 'perfectly preserved in a safe world, but with no actual life in me.'

Daniel gave in to his emotions. He sat back down in his comfortable chair, covering his head with both hands. Letting Maria go was a moronic decision. Like Robert ripping this leaf from its tree many years ago, Daniel too realised the wrongness of his action only after it was done. There were some things you can fix and some you just can't. In despair, he turned to the one person he knew would always support him. He tele-pathed Robert.

"What happened to you and your mother?" he asked, "Did you ever find a way to understand each other, to accept your differences?"

"Let me show you," said Robert, inviting Daniel into his memories.

21

My mother is ill. She is lying on a hospital bed in the dark corner of a shared room. The look of the hospital with its light cold walls make me shiver. Hospitals look morbid to me, and I hate the fact that I am forced to inhale the stuffy air with its smell of medicine and sick people. Mother looks like an old woman. Her skin is sunken, although this makes her green eyes seem even more prominent. She has that look in her eyes I like so much. I call it 'steel'. It feels strong, reassuring and supportive. Always unchangeable and solid. I like that look. She is my anchor in this unsettling world.

I go to stand next to her. She makes a weak gesture that she wants to hold my hand. I give it without eagerness. A part of me wants to run away from this stinking hospital as fast as I possibly can. Another part wants to stay near her.

I am nervous. There is a dark cloud over my head. I can't think straight without knowing what is to become of her.

"Robert, thank you for coming to see me."

"Sure, mum," I answer, trying to control my rising anxiety.

"How are you, my boy?" she asks. I know she is trying to distract me. She doesn't want to talk about the elephant in the room.

"Don't speak to me like nothing is happening. Are you dying?! I need to know," I snap, immediately regretting my tone of voice. This is the worst of all uncertainties, and I don't cope well with uncertainty. "Yes or no?!"

My mother gives me a calm, wise look, sharing a glimpse of that 'steel' in her eyes. She reads me well. I am not trying to be insensitive. On the contrary, I care too much. The darkness of the possibility of her death is causing me to lose control of my thoughts, fear taking over.

"To answer your question – I decided not to die. I shall be fine in three weeks," she delivers the news just how I like it, clear, factual and informative. Now I can relax. We stay in silence for a few minutes. My mum respectfully gives me a minute to be silent. I never feel uncomfortable with silence. I prefer it to communicating. In silence, there are no misunderstandings.

"Mum," I begin, finally ready to continue. "Do you remember when we went to Hyde Park together, and you took me on that pedalo? And afterwards, we ate gelato?"

"Of course!" Her face lightens up, "Of course, I remember. It was a great day."

"I remember it clearly. We walked around, collecting autumn leaves."

"Yes, we did. We gathered some amazing ones. I remember you being delighted with your finds."

"I was. I remember how the leaves smelt – it smelt of both coldness and warmth with the hint of roasted chestnuts."

"Wow, Robert! After all these years, I still get surprised by how detailed your memories are. You were only four then, if I am not mistaken."

"I was four. My memories are very clear, even from the age of two. Since then, I have always liked to collect autumn leaves. It always reminds me of you."

"I am glad," she says. She always likes it when I share my memories with her.

"Did you know that visualisation is much more developed in the Msitua brain than in the brain of a neurotypical? Maybe this is why my memories are so vivid."

"No, I didn't know. Is that so?" she asks in a surprised tone. I hadn't told her before.

"Yes, it is. I am trying to figure out why."

"Sounds fascinating. And why are you trying to figure it out?"

"I think I am ready to know myself better, why I am the way I am."

"Oh, Robert. You are the way you are because we can only be who we are. And it is fine. You are perfect the way you are."

"No, I am not. Why are you lying again?" I suddenly feel irritated. I don't like when she patronises me. Truth. I appreciate the truth.

"I am not lying. I think you are fine. I really do. A normal weird boy." It sounds like she really means it. 'Normal weird' – that can be my new identity. It sounds kind of cool.

"Sorry, mum," I suddenly decide to say, "I really tried to be a better son."

"And I tried to be a better mother for you too."

"You are okay, mum. We have our differences, but we will get there. One day we will understand each other," I pause for a second, "Because I love you too – I should really say it more often."

I hope I did it right, and she understands that I really mean it. I hope that she knows how much I need her. Even now. *Especially* now.

"Thank you. That is what I always wanted. For you to say it," she smiles. I suddenly feel exposed. "And I wrote something for you too," she picks up a small card from the side table and hands it over.

It reads, 'My darling Robert, I love you so much! Mum.' Seeing the card makes me happy. She knows that written words reach me deeper. I always like cards, notes and messages. I believe once it is written down, it becomes true.

"I know you prefer *to see* the words," she says with a soft smile.

"I know now that you like *to hear* it," I answer, smiling back.

"Written or said, we want the same things," she concludes. "Oh Robert, I have tried all my life to understand your vision of the world. You surprise me in so many ways."

"It is okay, mum. I will try to figure out who I am for you," I say.

"Good. If anyone can figure you out, you can. The only person we ever get a chance of figuring out is ourselves. If we are lucky," she says.

"You don't think that you were the only one trying to figure things out, do you?" Didn't she know? "All my life, I was trying to figure out, well, *you*," I confess.

"Really? I didn't know. I thought it was only me," she looks surprised. "And have you succeeded?"

"No," I answer with a sigh. "You are too complicated."

"I guess we are all complicated. Can you really figure another person out completely? I believe that it may be an impossible task."

"But we have to make an effort to try," I insist. "It is a shame that you have never known how much I needed you. It may have seemed like I was pushing you away, but whenever you told me that you loved me, I always answered in my head. If only you could read my mind…" I think I finally understand what is missing. "Please make sure you don't die. For my sake," I beg.

She smiles again. I like to see her happy. I like the realisation that it is me who is finally making her happy. Was it always this easy? Why couldn't I do it before?

Somehow, in this horrible hospital with its putrid smell, my mum and I spoke the same language. And it felt really good.

Daniel was quiet for a minute. Everything made sense now. Robert's emotional AI, Tele-paths, his passion in defending neuro-typicals. Robert's desire to understand his mother fed his creative genius. Despite his inexpressiveness, he loved her very much.

"I know now why you created Tele-paths," Daniel said, "You wanted to understand neuro-typicals."

"Especially neuro-typicals. Especially my mother," Robert confirmed. "I had hoped Tele-paths could become a translator. There is much less confusion with feelings that live in our thoughts. They cannot be misread.

My mother didn't live to see my creation, but I didn't stop. I thought that Tele-paths might help another child like me, or another mother like her." Robert's AI sighed. "I never wanted Tele-paths to be an incompatible technology. This is why I hadn't proceeded with the trials."

"Your mother would be proud of you," Daniel said quietly. He could sense that Robert was feeling more and more complete.

"It is too late to demonstrate my feelings," said Robert, as he tried to put himself together, "but it is not too late for you. You need to make the right decision. Maybe, *this* could be my true legacy."

"You are not the one to make this choice," Daniel said with a worried note in his voice.

"Maybe I am. I am an AI, but I am still a human inside too. I think my wishes should be respected. Besides, living forever is overrated. Trust me."

Daniel sighed. He finally had the courage to listen to his own truth. He suddenly realised that the decision had already been made in his illogical heart a long time ago – from that very first date with Maria.

He had to get her back!

Chapter Twenty-Eight
DECEPTION

Daniel's heart was seeing perfect sense. He was undeniably human after all. Never in his life had he felt more confident about a decision. Daniel needed to find Maria and fast! He would explain everything to her, and she would surely forgive him. Perhaps she wouldn't fully understand his doubts, but she would surely try to. She would. She must. Because without her, Daniel had no life, no future. Despite the vibrant colours of the autumn leaves, the world seemed monochrome to his eyes. Nothing made sense anymore, only the life of his little baby. And it felt good. It felt right.

He soon found himself rushing through the city. The destination, where he could be a loving partner, a good father. He would put his family first. He would care and protect them for as long as he could. He would change the direction of his research, he would convince the whole world that telepathic technology had to advance to a level where everyone could be compatible. He would do his very best to find the way. He would make a positive difference. Because now, with his heart wide open, he finally understood that there were two sides to every story. He knew that the moment you stopped questioning, that was the moment you end up on the wrong path. He knew that the only way to reach a logical conclusion was to allow a dialogue. *There is no finality in any statement.*

Daniel reached the gates of the Maria's council estate before the evening fell. He gave them a push, and they opened slowly with a sad squeaking sound. Surprisingly he didn't feel any discomfort as he entered in spite of the fact he knew that it was filled with fallen souls and grubby accommodation. 'The gates to another world,' Daniel thought to himself. Four ten-story buildings faced each other in a secluded square. They towered above, looking down on him with grim-faced judgement. These grey monoliths were loyal to Maria, and Daniel could feel that he wasn't welcome.

Suddenly, Daniel realised that he had no idea where Maria lived. What could he do? How on earth would he find the right one? There were hundreds of flats! Never in his life had Daniel been faced with a challenge like this. He had an idea, but it would necessitate him to break social norms and potentially embarrass himself. But it was worth it if it let him see Maria sooner rather than later. Daniel inhaled as much air as possible in his shocked lungs and, before the feeling of shame kicked in, proceeded with the most unbelievable action he had ever done. Daniel screamed as loud as he possibly could.

"MARIA!!!"

Almost immediately, doors around the square began to open. Firstly, he saw a strange-looking woman, her body swaying clumsily as she made her way towards Daniel. He wondered if she was drunk.

"Who are you? What do you need from our Maria?" she mumbled suspiciously once she was in earshot of Daniel. He suspected that she would have spoken more aggressively if she had the full sober capacity to showcase her anger.

"My name is Daniel. I need to speak to Maria right away, it is very important. Could you please tell me where she lives?" Daniel answered sharply with an urgency he had never experienced before.

"You are Daniel?" the woman said, looking him up and down. "I know who you are, *Daniel*. You are bad for her! You don't deserve her!" Daniel fully expected her to continue her tirade, but it was at this point that a pleasant looking old man joined the conversation. His gaze was fixed firmly on Daniel's face, as if he was trying to figure him out. He touched the woman on her shoulder. She turned to face him, and they shared a worried look. The woman decided against continuing her attack and the man spoke instead.

"I am sorry, sir, how can we help you?" he was being overly polite, perhaps suspicious of Daniel's intentions.

"I am Daniel, Maria's friend. I would like to see her. Could you please show me where she lives?" Daniel repeated, desperately trying to control his impatience.

"I am afraid Maria is no longer with us," said the man emotionless. It took Daniel a moment to realise what he was saying. The words felt distant and unsettling.

"Where is she? Do you know where she has gone?" Daniel asked trying to return a polite smile. The man looked deeply into Daniel's eyes. Daniel met his gaze, concerned about what had happened to Maria. Slowly the old man raised his eyes to the sky. Then he turned them back on Daniel, looking to see if he realised what he was trying to communicate.

Daniel couldn't believe it. It couldn't be true. The man was probably stoned or drunk. He did not know what he was saying. Stupid estate! Stupid grey walls! The huge buildings suddenly felt even more intimidating. They were cold, heartless murderers. It was impossible! He just saw Maria a few days ago! He held her hand, he touched her hair, he kissed her warm lips.

He tried to stay in control, but his body, which a second ago was so full of life, full of decisiveness, suddenly felt weak and useless. Daniel couldn't stand on his feet, his legs giving up on him. In a fraction of a second, the old man's face dropped his emotionless mask and allowed himself to appear human. As Daniel fell, he caught him under one arm to make his fall slightly smoother, almost falling himself in his attempt to steady the stranger. The last thing Daniel thought of before he lost his consciousness was the memory of Maria's deep brown eyes, so beautiful and kind. It was not worth living without those eyes in his life!

"...if he had a health chip, the medics would be here by now. Maybe we should call them?" a young female voice was saying quietly.

"We can't! We haven't reported her death officially yet. There will be questions." This was the old man whispering now.

"But what if he dies?" said the female voice in a concerned tone.

"He will not die. Idiots don't die. They live to face their mistakes," the drunken woman hissed.

"I feel sorry for him," the young female continued, "and we may get into trouble if we don't call the medics."

"Stop it!" the man stepped in. "There is too much at stake! We can't let Maria down."

"Okay, but we need to try to help him to gain his consciousness," the young woman said.

Through the haze of blurred shapes and colours, Daniel managed to make out a young woman leaning over him. She touched his face, gently slapping him on the cheeks.

"I think he is moving his eyes!" she exclaimed. The old man and the drunk woman appeared over her shoulder. The man gently pushed her aside, grabbing Daniel's hand, trying to feel a pulse.

"Can you hear me?" he asked, annunciating every word loudly. "Can you hear me?" he asked again. The question finally started to register in Daniel's head. Was it directed at him? He tried to move his lips.

Before Daniel got a chance to gather his thoughts, a heavy hand slapped his cheek, not so gently this time. Daniel snapped awake and found himself on an uncomfortable bed in a small room. The walls were off-white with a grimy look to them. A table sat in the middle of the room, covered with what looked like dirty cups. To the right, Daniel saw the old woman rolling her eyes. Next to her, the old man wore a grim facial expression as he looked at Daniel. The young girl he didn't recognise stood just behind him. She did not look older than twenty and he thought there was a hint of a smile on her face.

"Where am I?" Daniel managed to whisper.

"You are in my council flat, a lovely place, isn't it?" said the old woman sarcastically, clearly having noticed Daniel's observations of the room.

And then it hit him like a knife. Maria!

"Where is Maria?" he asked, begging for an answer, looking directly into the old man's eyes.

"Maria is gone. She passed away."

There was something strange happening. The conversations he had overheard, not wanting the medics to arrive, it was all very suspicious. Daniel couldn't figure out what exactly it was, but he would find out.

"I need to see her body," he said.

"It is at the morgue," replied the man matter-of-factly.

"Then, I need to see the death certificate," said Daniel, refusing to let his suspicions be budged.

"We haven't reported her death yet. We were going to do it tomorrow," the man said firmly. Daniel could see anxious, worried expressions on the women's faces. Something wasn't quite matching up.

"Do you have the medics report?" Daniel demanded now, pushing further. The man's face was now turning a reddish hue.

"There were no medics when she died," he continued with a hint of annoyance, belying the politeness of his answers.

Daniel knew in his gut that they were lying now. He had studied the science of human expressions, and some of the answers and reactions he was seeing from these three indicated they were hiding something. It was clear from the old man's strange tone and language that he was trying not to let anything slip out that he did not want to reveal. Meanwhile, the two women were even easier to read. They looked at the floor, avoiding eye contact with Daniel, poorly handling the pressure of the situation. Daniel felt an irrational hatred of these three in this moment. They were trying to convince him of the lie that Maria had died. They had no shame! He wanted to swear at them, lash out and destroy the room around him. Fortunately, his logical brain switched on just in time. He needed these people on his side! They loved Maria. He loved Maria. They had much in common, after all.

Daniel considered his options and after a long pause, spoke carefully and calmly.

"Bobby?" he asked the man, taking a gamble. The man looked at Daniel with a surprised look on his face. "Yes, I know your name. Maria told me about you and how much you mean to her. All of you. And you. You are Mandy?" he said to the young woman. "And you are Tatiana, the beautiful dancer?" he said turning to address the old woman. He spoke flatteringly to get her on his side – a neuro-typical skill he had previously struggled to master. It was interesting how the most challenging situations forced you to harness skills you never thought you had in you. The look on Tatiana's face softened, and he even thought he saw a glimpse of a smile. Wow! Flattery could really get you far.

"Has Maria told you about us?" Mandy asked with a sweet childish smile on her face. Daniel could sense the kindness in her voice.

"Yes. She told me about you. She said that she cares deeply about you three. She wants you, Mandy, to live in a world where you have an opportunity to make something of yourself. She said you are very bright!" Mandy's smile grew bigger. "And Bobby, she told me that she likes to help you by cooking for you!" At this, Bobby seemed to soften his gaze too. "And Tatiana, Maria told me that you are quite a dancer."

Everyone was silent, looking at each other with confused looks on their faces while they worked out what to think about these revelations. Daniel thought very carefully about the next thing he was about to say.

"I also know you all love Maria. I do too. I love her very much. So much so that it feels like my heart cannot beat without her. So much so that I can hardly go on. I want her back. Her and the child that she is carrying.

I know, I didn't react how I should have when she told me the news. I had my reasons. Important reasons. But I loved my child instantly. And I love Maria always. And I want to have this baby with her."

"Even if your child is a neuro-typical?" Bobby asked. Daniel could detect bitter notes in his voice.

"I will love my child. Because and even if," Daniel said softly. He hesitated for a second and then continued, meaning every word. "Bobby, Maria told me how much you loved your wife. And when she told me, I didn't understand. But now I do," said Daniel, feeling emotional. "Don't take her away from me. Where is she?" he asked, looking directly into Bobby's eyes, intending to hold his gaze until he heard an answer.

The look on Bobby's face had changed drastically. His stubborn expression now looked like that of a lost man. His decisiveness was shaken as he tried to comprehend the situation. Daniel could almost see the cogs turning in his head as he tried to work out what to do or say. Mandy took Bobby by the hand and gave a slight nod. He looked over at Tatiana for confirmation. Tatiana's expression was harder to read. She nervously fluffed her bright hair and looked up as if expecting some unseen force to give her advice. Daniel didn't understand this gesture at first, but he eventually realised that Tatiana was searching for spiritual guidance. Daniel didn't believe in spirits, but right now, he desperately hoped that these invisible guides would advise Tatiana in his favour.

"Okay," she said.

Bobby came closer to Daniel. He looked deeply into his eyes, searching for the last confirmation that this was the right thing to do. It was as if he was trying to dive into Daniel's soul. Daniel held his gaze so firmly that he almost couldn't breathe.

"Have you ever heard about a place where people can live without rules? Where mothers can hide with their illegal children?" Bobby asked.

Of course! Now it all made sense. They were trying to save Maria's baby, just like Maria had with her own mother. This was why they had told Daniel that Maria passed away. There was a questionable logic behind this decision, but it was a logic all the same, and now Daniel could see it. He gave Bobby a smile and exhaled deeply. Maria was alive!

"Yes, I know of this place," Daniel answered after a few seconds. "So that's why you wanted to declare her death."

"I am sorry," Mandy said, coming closer. "We didn't know why you had come here. Maria told us to tell anyone who came looking for her that she had died. Bobby was to report her death after a few days."

"I understand," Daniel said. "You are good friends. But she doesn't need to run away. I plan to declare my fatherhood. The baby will not be illegal."

"Oh dear," said Mandy, suddenly looking distressed. "The thing is – when women go to this secret location, no one can ever find them. Or reach them."

"Mandy is right," confirmed Bobby, "I don't know where we would even begin looking for her." He gave Daniel a worried look.

It took Daniel a minute to fully realise what they were saying. What had he done! Everyone stood in silence. From what they were telling him, it seemed like there was no connection, no coordinates, no coming back. Why did Daniel let her leave his apartment that day? Why didn't he reach out to her sooner? Why was he such a stupid asshole? Suddenly, Daniel felt immense respect for the strong woman he loved, and hatred at himself for losing precious time.

Chapter Twenty-Nine
TOO LATE

It was late when Daniel arrived home. A feeling of desperation had taken up residence in his soul, creating a hollowness within him that seemed to be painfully expanding in his chest. He didn't even know where to start the search for Maria. Daniel was now on a quest for a mythical place. Everyone he had spoken to had been enigmatic, and every response seemed to be taking Daniel further from the truth. No one knew its whereabouts. Daniel had visited all the shady places in the city that he knew about, he had spoken to the strangest people, he had knocked on every hidden door. Nothing. All was hopeless!

One outlandish woman confirmed there was indeed a place for illegally pregnant women who decided to keep their baby. However, she also said that the information was only available to these women.

"How do I find the people who arrange their 'relocation'?" Daniel had asked, afraid to hope that she might give him anything useful.

"It's not that straightforward," she answered. "*You* don't find them, they find *you*, and only if you pass their test." Unfortunately, she had no idea what the test was, nor the people who would arrange it. She only could confirm the gossip she once heard.

Was all lost? Daniel couldn't believe that someone could disappear from the face of the earth in the twenty-second century. His initial optimism was fading. Whoever these people organising the 'relocations' were, and even if

Daniel managed to reach them, they would surely never help him. He was a stranger, an outsider, a scientist who supported the Single Child Law decision. The desperation in his chest was rising, and now that his adrenalin was subsiding, Daniel felt only exhaustion and defeat. He connected to Robert, and allowed him to access the events of this day.

"How is it possible?" Robert asked, sounding shocked. "A place in the world, which has managed to stay a secret? Yet, people seem to confirm its existence. It is so hard to believe."

"I know," replied Daniel, it was all he could manage.

"A strong woman, your Maria. I like her."

"She is. What am I going to do?" Daniel sounded defeated.

"There has to be a way," Robert said.

"It is too late," said Daniel as he covered his face with his hands. The desperate feeling of inevitability was eating him from the inside out.

"It is only too late when someone is dead. Then it is too late," Robert declared. "My grandson," began Robert trying to sound upbeat, "I am confident there is always a possibility. I wish I realised that sooner. But I know it now. So now I am telling you."

"But where else can I search? What can I do?" Daniel asked, his mind still reeling. "If there is no way to look for her in the outside world, you should try to search inside your heart. Maybe it will give you an unexpected answer."

Robert was becoming more and more poetic. Daniel never understood poetry. It always confused him. It used to confuse Robert too, but now his AI was speaking nonsense, saying one thing and meaning another. Phrases Daniel had never thought he'd ever hear from his grandfather.

"Daniel, I can read you," Robert kindly reminded him, trying to calm Daniel's thoughts. Robert had full access to Daniel's mind, and with this insight, he was searching for the right words to guide him, to re-direct his attention.

"You do seem to be more neuro-typical as an AI. So much so, that you can see how completely lost I am by your confusing words." Daniel had intended to sound sarcastic, but it came out sounding more attacking than he had meant. "How did you come up with the idea of creating Tele-paths?" Daniel asked him unexpectedly, completely changing the subject. This was an illogical turn of a conversation even for Robert's poetic AI. Robert wasn't sure what Daniel was searching for, but he answered anyway.

"When I first thought of the idea, I was really just a confused child, lost in the big scary world. I had my family, my teachers, some friends. But I was truly alone, I didn't fit in anywhere. I wished that no one would have to go through the same isolation I did."

"But when I was a child, you took steps to isolate me from the world. Why did you do that?" Daniel asked.

"Daniel," Robert said in a comforting voice, "I believed that I was protecting you. Forgive me."

"I am sorry," Daniel said, stopping himself from going further. He was upset about losing Maria, and he realised he was taking his anger out on Robert. "There is nothing to forgive. You had your share of drama when you were growing up, and I am lucky I didn't face the same. Who knows how I would have turned out if I hadn't had your guidance. I should thank you, really. I am just upset."

"Isolating you wasn't my intention," Robert said with a sigh. "Your isolation was simply the outcome of our technological advancement. Now, all I see is people avoiding life and love. People are incapable of coping with simple daily challenges. You are right. I thought I was protecting you, but in reality, you were deprived of a chance to challenge yourself and learn to live your life. Being around different types of people makes life so much more exciting, even when you can't find any common ground. Challenging each other's viewpoints provides advancement for both."

"Maria was challenging me. And I truly love that she was able to do that. She is different, and actually, it was great!"

"Good," Robert said, sounding pleased. Daniel was getting there. "When did we stop celebrating our differences? Humanity truly never learns." Robert paused for a minute and then continued. "We are evolving, and we are still taking our nasties with us. It is still survival of the fittest, and those capable of living in the digital world, communicating telepathically, processing large amounts of data are the new 'fittest'. But I really couldn't care less if we are more technologically developed. Maybe we should evolve into better human beings instead?"

Being a better human race was a difficult objective. Daniel doubted if humanity was truly becoming better. Maybe more educated, more clever, more knowledgeable, more intellectual, more logical. But was it *better*? Or was the advancement of their minds actually a hindrance to living life, to having open hearts? And Daniel's newly open heart was aching, wishing for Maria. Maybe he should let his heart speak. Perhaps only a desperate human gesture could help.

"I know!" Daniel exclaimed suddenly. "I know how I can get her back!"

Robert knew too. Daniel's thoughts were fast. It was a eureka! moment, suddenly opening a whole new dimension of possibilities.

"First things first," Robert said, "We need to have a complicated chat with my old friend. Boy oh boy, he will be *furious*!"

Chapter Thirty
FAVOUR

Daniel never felt wholly comfortable disturbing the famously cranky biologist, but he didn't think twice this time. He showed up on the steps of Dr Biote's laboratory in the middle of the night as if it was the most natural thing in the world. The desperate circumstances he faced were driving Daniel to discover previously unknown capabilities. In this case, revealing glimpses of an unapologetic confidence he would never have guessed he had in him.

Standing at the deem entrance with the door wide open, Dr Biote looked pissed.

"This is the second time around, Daniel. You know that I like my sleep. I *need* my regular hours of rest. Otherwise, my whole day turns upside down."

It was pretty clear that he really didn't appreciate being woken again in the middle of the night and being asked to travel to his lab urgently. Yet, despite his displeasure, Biote did as requested. Daniel knew that this was likely down to Biote's natural curiosity – he had deliberately teased him with enough intrigue on the call without giving away too many details.

"What possibly couldn't wait until morning? So, your ex-girlfriend ran away, big deal. She didn't report you as a father of the child, did she?" Dr Biote was his usual cynical self.

"No, she didn't," Daniel replied, delaying the moment of truth. He was extremely sceptical that Biote would ever be able to grasp the depth of his feelings for Maria. However,

Daniel knew he had an ace up his sleeve in Robert and he needed to play it at the right time.

"Well, as long as she doesn't report the child, surely we can all return to bed. Let's all hope she leaves you out of it."

"Dr Biote, you are missing the point," Daniel said.

"What is the point?" Biote asked, completely ignorant of what Daniel was about to say.

"Listen – I am planning to find her," Daniel began, looking directly into Biote's eyes. Usually, Daniel would be afraid of how he might react – forever longing for the approval of one of the world's top scientific minds. But not today. Today Daniel looked at Dr Biote with no fear.

"Yes, good idea. You find her and make her listen. Then we will not need to worry about your fatherhood anymore".

"You don't understand," Daniel said smiling, Biote had reacted exactly as he'd expected. "The point is that I am going to find her, and then I am going to marry her. We are going to have our child together, and I am going to learn how to become a good father."

Dr Biote went pale. He was torn between getting angry or upset. Anger won out – it usually did, being the stronger emotion – and Dr Biote's eyes went red. F84.5 could blow up in seconds, if given a chance. Dr Biote nervously paced backwards and forwards, mumbling words that Daniel couldn't really understand, but there was no doubt about Biote's tone – he was furious. Once Biote got some semblance of control, he stopped pacing and screamed.

"You say that and stand there smiling, as if you think it is funny! It is not funny! You want to throw away one of the most important pieces of research in human history for the sake of some girl?! Are you crazy?!"

Daniel decided to say nothing and wait for a minute to allow Dr Biote to release his rage. He knew very well that F84.5's needed to let their emotions out before they could return to being civil. He waited patiently, surprising even himself how much Biote's angry reaction didn't bother him. Dr Biote continued to rant and rave, with periods of intense swearing thrown in. But eventually, he ran out of steam. The intensity of the emotions he had just expressed had clearly tired him out. He was no longer a young man, and eventually he had to shut up and sit down. It was only then that Daniel continued.

"I know how you feel. And I am truly sorry that our project will eventually have to end. But I have been wondering if our project really is such a positive thing after all…"

"Of course, it would be a positive thing! How could it not? I am certain that one day that Robert's AI will gain some level of consciousness. I believe my theories are correct. They *should* be correct." Dr Biote looked at Daniel with hope in his eyes, "And even if my theories aren't correct, then perhaps it will be you, Daniel, and not Robert, that might become the first conscious human-AI. But Daniel, if you don't have a compatible child – then… nothing! The project ends, dead. You are leaving me, leaving all of us, with nothing."

Biote murmured this last sentence in a much quieter voice, clearly devastated at the mere idea. He shook his head sadly, and covered his face with his hands. Daniel could see that his fingers were trembling. And in this moment, Daniel felt sorry for him. Biote removed his hands from his face and continued.

"It is not just for my satisfaction, you know. Without human-AI we can never travel to the outer limits of space.

Our biological limitations prohibit it. And we have to travel beyond the stars in order for humanity to survive. The end is coming, despite all our efforts to save this planet. There are too many variables we cannot control, too many ways it could all suddenly end. But, of course, you know all this. Perhaps your feelings are clouding your mind. We need this project to succeed!"

"Dr Biote, I know it seems a huge blow. But is it really? I fear that we are limited in our thinking. When we, as scientists, can see a way to make a technological leap, to create something new like a human-AI or an addition to the Theory of Evolution, we tend to take action to accomplish this goal. We grab our chance. We run with our ideas as fast as we possibly can. Yet there is something we are missing. Namely, proper consideration of all the possible outcomes of our advances. Are all innovations good? Do they all benefit humanity, our planet, our lives?" Daniel's spontaneous yet impassioned speech surprised even himself. He had no idea how he was going to articulate his concerns to Biote, but he found a way.

"What do you mean, Daniel? Of course, a human-AI innovation will benefit humanity. We could live forever!" Dr Biote's eyes, still angry, still crazy, shone with the sparkle of his vision for the future.

"Well, from what I hear, being a sentient AI is not that much fun…" Daniel said mysteriously.

He searched Biote's mad eyes for a glimpse of recognition of what he was saying. Dr Biote took a moment to comprehend what Daniel had said. Very slowly, a spark of hope and a bright feeling of silent joy registered on Biote's face. He looked at Daniel with a tiny, uncertain smile. He pointed at Daniel, and after a few seconds he finally managed to whisper.

"The only way you could know that is if…"

"Yes!" Daniel said encouragingly, "You guessed it. I know because of Robert."

"Robert is conscious?" Dr Biote asked in a shaky voice, stepping towards Daniel, opening his arms wide for an embrace – perhaps the first time in his life he had initiated a hug.

"Yes," Daniel replied, receiving the warm hug. After a few seconds, they stepped apart and shook hands for a prolonged period of time. It was very unusual behaviour for Dr Biote. This wondrous happy news made him even forget about his germophobia, about Maria and about the incompatible child. It all could wait for now.

"Tell me everything!" he demanded. "Every single detail. How? When? And how?" he couldn't wait to hear it all.

"There is someone else who might be better placed to explain all. If our calculations are correct, there is a ninety per cent chance that we could connect you two. Switch on your Tele-path."

Dr Biote just stood there with his mouth wide agape, unable to say a word. He connected to Daniel's brain, but it wasn't Daniel's voice he heard.

"Hello, old friend," came a familiar voice. It was definitely him!

"Robert! How?!" Dr Biote said, otherwise lost for words.

"I know it is a shock, feel free to take a minute," Robert said with a hint of pleasure. "Thanks to you, I am conscious now, as you predicted. Biote, it *worked*."

"Are you really conscious?" Dr Biote asked, having a hard time grasping the news.

"Oh, believe me. Too conscious for my liking."

"Robert, I missed you so much," Dr Biote's said, his eyes welling up. It was clear he was feeling rather emotional.

"I missed you too."

They shared a moment of indescribable feelings, a cocktail of emotions both happy and sad at the same time. They were still in different realities, but at least now they could talk, like many years ago. It was surreal.

"What are you up to nowadays?" Robert said, eventually breaking the awkward silence that had fallen.

"Oh, you know me. Same old," Dr Biote answered shyly.

"Still working on the ultimate vaccine?" guessed Robert. Dr Biote's thoughts said it all. He opened his mind for Robert to see his latest progress.

"It seems exciting. I think you are close," Robert said, trying to sound supportive.

"I hardly think so, there is no need to patronise me," Dr Biote said. He never appreciated white lies.

"If you insist. In which case, I am sorry Biote, but you are doomed. The chemical combinations you are testing will not work. It is not worth your time playing with the doses. You need to leave these flawed trials behind you. Have you considered remixing the combination? Maybe lose ovalbumin and the human cell strains. And maybe try adding thimerosal with the DNA recombinant? It should give it more kick."

"Oh, you think you suddenly know more than me about the ultimate vaccine? So typical of you! Your suggestions don't even make sense!" snapped Dr Biote.

Robert was laughing in his head. Many years had passed since they last spoke, but Biote still didn't get his jokes.

"Got ya!" Robert exclaimed. Dr Biote softened.

"This is what I have missed!" he exclaimed, "Two friends, having a real conversation about real things." Biote went silent for a moment, sad thoughts creeping into his mind again. "I can't lose you again now."

"Not right now. We have time."

They again shared a moment of unspoken sadness. Dr Biote couldn't wait any longer. He needed answers.

"When did you...? When did you begin to think?"

"Well, I didn't at first. It kind of felt like I went away for a while. But then, something happened. Not so long ago. I just started creating thoughts. Not data memories, not pre-programmed outcomes – my own thoughts. When I first started talking to Daniel our conversations were limited. Mostly, I just tried to follow. But slowly our conversations developed. At some point, I stopped using pre-programmed data. The shift was swift, but Daniel didn't realise the full scope of my consciousness until much later. When I started understanding his feelings and emotions, I think that was when my AI truly developed. So, you really have to thank Maria for that. Emotions provoke thoughts, thoughts provoke analysis, analysis develops opinions, opinions develop a character. I built my character bit-by-bit all over again from scratch. I have to tell you, a lot of who I am is Robert, but I have also developed some new traits you will be surprised to discover."

"Wow!" was all Dr Biote could say.

Dr Biote had always hoped that Robert might develop some human-like intelligence, but full consciousness, complete with character traits and all – that was difficult to imagine! He even had to pinch himself to make sure he wasn't dreaming. Robert laughed, then he continued.

"I will tell you more in due course. But for now I need to ask a favour of you," Robert had suddenly gone serious, "I want my grandson to find Maria and to have their child together."

"Why?!" Dr Biote said, confused. "You would be giving all this up – losing everything – all for a child that you don't know. You do know that the child will not be compatible?" He swallowed hard and continued, "Now that you are conscious, do you know what that means?!" Dr Biote queried.

"A Nobel Prize for you?"

"Yes, certainly!" replied Biote, unable to hide his truth, no matter how selfish, "But more importantly, eternal life for you. And maybe an eternal life for me. And Daniel. And ultimately, the rest of humanity."

"Fuck eternal life, Biote!" Robert snapped, "Do you think it is fun living like this? If it were not for Daniel, I probably would have tried to end myself by now! But one of the worst things about being an AI is your inability to even have control over ending your own life!"

"That bad?" Dr Biote said, sounding genuinely surprised and disappointed.

"Yes, you try it! All I do here is think and think and think again. I am a prisoner in my own mind. It drives me crazy! How would you like to be trapped with your memories? Memories you will never share again. Thoughts and ideas you no longer realise. Desires that you don't have the body to fulfil. And you expect us to live like this for eternity? Get the picture?"

"It sounds to me like all these feelings are a malfunction. Maybe we can fix it?" Dr Biote said with hope in his voice.

"It is not a malfunction. This is our minds. Without a body, they are just made up of nonsense data. It will drive you mad. This is not life, Biote. Even my artificial brain understands that. How could you not?"

"But... but we did it. We created the first conscious human-AI. This is huge!" Dr Biote was listening, but not hearing what Robert had to say.

"Yes, it works. I am conscious. And you are my creator – you would get your Nobel Prize. And as for me? Well, I would eventually be stuck in a Megamind. And I don't want that!"

"Then tell your stupid grandson to make a compatible child for carrying your conscious AI. I believe that you gained consciousness only because your AI was carried by a compatible biological carrier. It wouldn't work in a Megamind."

Dr Biote couldn't believe what he was hearing. This was not a joke. Was Robert for real? Was he really giving up on the project? When Dr Biote spoke again, he did so with a grave tone in his voice.

"Robert, I don't think you know what you are really saying. What you are asking for. Do you realise what is at stake?" he asked. "If you are genuinely conscious, then you would never ask me to make such a sacrifice. Perhaps you think that there could be another way, another chance. But I have looked at all the possibilities, and there isn't. Even the chance of you gaining consciousness in the first place was infinitesimally small – at least according to the probability theory. Even now, I can't really believe that this is happening.

NEMETRA X1369

I would go so far as to say that this is a miraculous event. In my wildest dreams, I never really imagined it could work. I believed more that I would succeed in making the ultimate vaccine than a conscious AI. But somehow, you are here, and we are talking, like we used to when you were alive. Somehow, the combination of you, Daniel, your compatibility, and your biological and personal connection clicked. But we got here by chance. And until I know the exact formula, I can't let you go. That could be years, if not decades. You are a prototype that could one day ensure the future of humanity. But that cannot happen until you are analysed, developed and perfected."

"It is very flattering to be called a prototype, Biote. Makes me feel so warm and fuzzy inside," Robert said sarcastically. "I had hoped for a more human response."

"But Robert, you are a prototype. You are something we have not seen before. You are not really human, and yet you speak and think like one. And what is even more spectacular is that you *feel*. That you even have an idea of what 'warmth and fuzziness' would feel like. This is the breakthrough we all have been waiting for."

"Then I have a question for you. Where are we heading?"

"Space, of course!" Biote bellowed, "Daniel articulated it very clearly in his presentation when he said, 'We cannot pretend we are not living under a dying star'".

"No, I mean in philosophical and moral terms."

"You've lost me there."

"Biote, nothing is supposed to last forever. It is unnatural and impossible in the physical world."

"Until now!" Biote exclaimed. "And you are not exactly living in the physical world any more, are you?"

"True, but I do have a biological base – my neurons, my memories, my life. And this just doesn't feel right."

"Right or wrong, the important thing is that we are finally able to move into a new reality." Biote made no effort to understand Robert's view. As always, he was reliant on cold, hard, scientific facts. There was no place for feelings. "The success of this project is the only possibility for ensuring the survival of humanity. Resources on Earth are scarce. We have to progress into space and we have to do it fast. Our technology is already advanced enough that we can achieve this goal, but our human biology had never been conquered. Time has never been our friend. You are the missing piece, can't you see it?"

"But there could be another way, another chance. And maybe a better one. We need to think everything through."

"You know very well that there are no other opportunities. We got lucky with you. We can't waste this gift, this fluke of circumstance."

Dr Biote was sounding more and more irritated. Biote had got his friend back, but his friend was talking nonsense. Spouting ideas and feelings that were unacceptable for any scientific mind, be it human or AI.

"Maybe you're right. Listen, old friend. I am happy to let you figure me out. Feel free to break down the formula of how I came to be until it can be replicated. But we cannot and should not rely on Daniel's lineage."

Biote sighed, "And what if there is not enough time?"

"Then there will be someone to continue after us. Maybe someone who is even better than us," Robert replied, refusing to budge.

"You are talking about taking chances, long shots. I am not willing to take that risk."

"Yes, but even a long shot is still a chance. When did you begin to use the word 'chance' negatively?"

"It is unquestionably a negative, when you talk about chances in this way, when you and your grandson are playing fools."

"Why do you want me to suffer? Why do you want my hypothetical great-grandchild to suffer? Even if a lab-grown child was compatible, why would they want me in their head? Someone they never even knew. What would we talk about? Biote, accept it. I am not your guy. I have said I will cooperate, and we can search for the formula of my consciousness together – but only if you agree to our terms." Robert paused, and then decided to play his last card. He needed to be tough with this stubborn old man. "And if you don't agree, well I will resist all your efforts to take me apart and perfect the 'prototype'. Not everyone wants to live forever, Biote, myself included. At some point, I want to rest in peace." This was the ultimate truth of human existence. Whether we are looking forward to it or dreading it, we need our 'happy endings'. *The old should give way to the new eventually – new thoughts, new ideas, new lives.*

"Are you blackmailing me, Robert?" Biote asked, angrily.

"If it is what it takes to convince you, then yes. If you want my cooperation, then you better behave. Because if you think you can study me without my approval, I think you are mistaken. I am smart enough to even pretend to be stupid."

"You bastard!" Biote said, quickly considering his options. "You are truly bloody conscious... I definitely recognise the old Robert in you. I think I preferred you pre-programmed." Biote took a breath and gathered his thoughts before continuing. "The thing is, I can't let Daniel ruin all that we created. I just can't," Dr Biote said, sobbing now. He felt cornered.

"Dear friend, let my grandson be, let him live. Can't you see, he loves the girl?"

"Stupid love. Nothing good can come from it," said Dr Biote bitterly.

"Have you ever wondered?"

"Wondered about what?"

"About what your life might have been like if Amanda had stayed with you?"

"What are you talking about?!" said Dr Biote spluttering, his face turning red. His feelings gave him away on Tele-paths before he could block it. Oh, he wondered all right! He still thought about Amanda every day.

"Let Daniel have this life. With the person he has chosen, and with the child they are bringing to this world."

Dr Biote was silent for a while, and Robert was unable to read his feelings on the subject. Biote had blocked his feelings now, after he had let slip about Amanda. He needed time to digest the information. He had got his friend back. He had succeeded in one of the greatest accomplishments of all times. But perhaps it didn't matter. Nothing ever seemed to truly matter since Amanda had left – not a conscious AI, not even the ultimate vaccine. The pain of a broken heart will live on. Forever.

"What do you need me to do?" Dr Biote finally asked.

At this point, Robert telepathically added Daniel to their conversation.

"Please don't fight Daniel's decision. Instead, support it, make the rest of our scientific colleagues understand. We need you to fight for 'human' rights for me, so I am not treated by scientists as if I am something they can own."

"Okay," Dr Biote agreed quietly.

"Oh, and I will agree to help you with your ultimate vaccine if you agree to help us to make Tele-paths compatible with everyone. It will give us more of a chance to hang around one another too."

"I would like that. Very much!" said Dr Biote, cheering up at the thought. "There are still two problems that I can see."

"Which are?" now it was Robert's turn to be confused.

"First of all, the make-up of neuro-typicals' brains will not allow them to be compatible with Tele-paths. That is a fact. And second of all, you know absolute shit about vaccines!"

"So what?" answered Robert with a laugh, "When did those sorts of things ever stop us?"

Daniel was grateful to Robert for somehow convincing Biote, and to Dr Biote for finding the strength to accept the 'unfortunate' turn of events. He would never have imagined that this old Msitua scientist could ever listen to another point of view other than his own.

"I am going live with a global broadcast tomorrow. It is my only chance to reach Maria before it is too late. Can I count on your support if there are questions from the scientific community?" Daniel asked with unusual confidence.

"Fine," Dr Biote replied – he was on board.

"Thank you," replied Daniel, and he really meant it.

"Thank you, my dear friend. I will talk to you soon," said Robert's conscious, intelligent and truly humane AI.

Chapter Thirty-One
URGENT GLOBAL BROADCAST

The morning was approaching fast. Daniel didn't sleep all night, and he had dark circles under his eyes when he looked in the mirror. However, he didn't feel the need to reach for his usual coffee. The adrenaline pumping through his blood was more than compensating for the lack of caffeine, and Daniel was surprisingly alert. Every sense was heightened, every thought had a purpose. If he wanted to reach Maria, he had to act fast. There was no time to waste. He had no clear idea of what he was going to say. He was unprepared, but he was *ready*.

Daniel started to scroll through the backgrounds for his urgent broadcast. White? Maybe not today. He thought for a moment, and the answer came to him. Blue. A deep rich blue, the colour Maria liked so much. The cleanness and simplicity of the white still appealed, but today Daniel needed it to feel more, he needed to tell a story.

***

"Dear friends,

Thank you for joining me today. My apologies for the short notice, but sometimes, when you reach an important decision, a decision which you know is *right*, every second counts.

You are probably wondering what on earth could be so important to necessitate this press conference. Well, in short, it is related to my previous findings regarding the future of Human Evolution. Today, I am not here to confirm or deny my aforementioned conclusions. I am here to talk about what our future might really involve – this time not as a scientist, but as a human.

Before I start – a few formalities. The registration number for broadcasting globally is on the left-hand bottom corner of the screen. This press conference is transmitted, as always, via the global news platform as well as the MM2-Megamind. Access to the telepathic data is restricted to the current thinking process and is limited to only spoken-aloud data.

Now I may begin.

I dare to stand in front of you now to tell you that I was wrong. Not wrong scientifically, not wrong as a scientist, but wrong as a *human being*. I dedicated my life to demonstrating that Msitua was one of the next evolutionary stages of the human race. And I know from the responses that for many of you it was an exciting discovery.

But there are those who we are leaving behind. We have locked the doors of progress and thrown away the key. The neuro-typical community is unable to compete on a level playing field both socially and professionally. The fact that they are incompatible makes it nearly impossible for them to secure any job that will allow them to feed themselves and their families. Believe me, they desperately want to fit in. But we have made it impossible for them to contribute to our technologically advanced society in any meaningful way.

I want to ask you all: Who are we becoming? Is this who we want to be? Is this the future we are striving for? Are you happy to say goodbye to our past and the humans we once were? Is the next stage of evolution I've proposed really inevitable or desirable? Is becoming more rational and logical beings worth the risk of becoming utterly boring?

And most importantly, what happens to those who are not compatible? Should they become outcasts just because they don't fit in in our new 'normal'?

I have seen these incompatible people struggling to survive in our society first-hand. From what I witnessed, this incompatible community is rather exciting. They are spontaneous and unpredictable and compassionate and loving. They are, dare I say, fun. And I happen to love one of them very much. I love her, despite our many, many differences. I will probably never completely understand her, and she will probably never understand me and my logic. We are total opposites, worlds apart. Before I met her, I could not even imagine being with someone like her. Yet somehow I feel closer to her than anyone else. We just seem to complete each other. We fit, like two pieces of a puzzle. And we are going to have a baby together, who will also be incompatible. She wasn't planned, and she won't be designed. She was a product of our feelings for each other.

So, I would like to officially declare that this unborn baby will be my *one* child.

Maria, I hope wherever you are, you are listening, and I hope you will hear me out.

Maria, you are the bravest person I know! I know I didn't react appropriately to the news of a child. I panicked, and I was unable to explain my thinking. Stress caused my thoughts to muddle. I know I needed to explain things, but I just couldn't. I couldn't bear the thought of losing you. I was afraid you wouldn't understand all of the complications of being with me.

My biggest worry is that you would think that I didn't want to be with you, that I didn't fully accept you. But the truth is – I loved you from the moment I saw you. And however hard I tried, I couldn't keep you out of my head. I am sorry to say that I tried to resist you – and not because you are a neuro-typical, despite what you may think. I love you not despite, but rather *because* of who you are. But there was a catch. As scientists, we sometimes commit to important projects, and these commitments may interfere with our personal life.

And now the big reveal: I have Dr Robert Stein's human-AI planted in my head. This was done in an attempt to reach an impossibly bold goal – to achieve an advanced human-AI, the first of its kind. And this experiment *worked*. We can communicate via Tele-paths technology because we are both compatible. So compatible, that I can almost have a human conversation with my grandfather. He is still very real to me, even though he passed away years ago. And not only is his human-AI real, but it is also *conscious*. Yes, you heard me right. Dr Robert Stein is alive and exists in my head as the first fully conscious human-AI.

How did Robert's AI become conscious? Well, in truth we don't know. There were a lot of favourable factors involved, from compatibility with Tele-paths technology to a pre-existing biological and personal connection between myself and my grandfather. But such an outcome is a one in a trillion chance. We will need to study this phenomenon for years, probably decades, to understand how it happened. Then, if we are lucky, we may be able to replicate this process. I will not bore you with the details, but its existence is truly miraculous. If anyone has any doubt about our claims, they are welcome to examine Robert's AI to officially confirm my observations.

You may think this is madness, but if you can accept this truth many of you will see the potential possibilities. Could we live forever? Now, you know the answer.

But what price are you willing to pay for this immortality?

The Theory of Balance teaches us an important lesson – everything comes at a cost. A few months ago, like many of you, I would have given up almost anything to guarantee our evolutionary progress; to guarantee our survival in the form of human-AIs; to guarantee, most importantly for myself, Robert Stein's immortality. My loving grandfather, the most significant person in my life. But Maria, I never really understood *what* it was going to cost me until I met you.

Robert's AI can only function consciously because of our special bond – a technological, biological and personal bond. If Robert's AI were to be moved to a Megamind or into someone else's brain, it could quickly lose its consciousness. So in order for me to preserve Robert's immortality, it seemed like there was only one viable option: for me to have a compatible child of my own, carefully created in a lab to be suitable to host Robert after me. It was still a long shot, but it was by far our best hope of securing Robert's future. And so, I found myself faced with the most difficult of choices: did I pick Robert's AI, a project which could potentially guarantee the ultimate survival of all human species, or did I pick the life of my unborn child? I know that many of you will consider it mad that this was a hard decision. Some of you for thinking of giving up my child, and others for not committing to the human-AI project. And all of you will be right in some way. But ultimately it is my life, and I have made my decision. Maria, I choose a life with you and our child by my side.

And what do we really know about living as an AI anyway? Robert's human-AI tells me that it can feel like a struggle. Forever is a little too long. And there is a question here for the legal community. If a human-AI is proven conscious, does it have the same rights and privileges as humans do? What if this AI chooses not to live forever? Is it allowed to decide for itself when it is ready to go? Robert's time is limited by my own lifespan, and he is only willing to stay for just as long as he wishes. Dr Robert Stein's conscious human-AI demands to be treated as a human, and *he* wishes to make his own choices. This is a complicated legal question for you to consider.

As for mine and Robert's future together, we would like to concentrate on our scientific research. We would like to find a way of making Tele-paths technology accessible for all. A solution is not guaranteed, but we would like to give it our best shot. Any volunteers or investments for this project are very welcome. I want to be transparent with you and state that the probability of success is low. However, as we all know, a hundred years ago, telepathic technology was also a very low probability. And that happened, so who knows?

There are many positive developments in our technologically advanced world. New channels of communication, the possibility of deep space exploration, ecological innovations and many more leaps forward. But all this looking forward should not mean that we never look back, that we disregard what made us humans in the first place.

Personal interaction is becoming obsolete, and I now feel very strongly that this is a shame. Just think for a second, when did you last leave your house, go for a party or have a walk in the park with a group of friends? When did you speak to anyone directly and not through their avatars? When did you last meet someone you fancied without basing it on their digital profile?

I had to learn the hard way what's important to me. I had to gain everything and lose it all just to understand its value. What really matters to you? Technology? Compatibility? Economic growth? When will what we have ever be enough? When will we finally realise that the most valuable things in life are the simple things?

I don't know what it is with humans and our desire to quantify, to measure, to record. Why must everything have to be proven, understood, 'normalised'? Could it be because we can't accept ourselves? Why do we have to compete all the time? Why does it matter whose brain activity is more in line with the national curriculum, or whose working practice is more socially adequate, who is more capable of evolving? Why can't we just accept that we are all so weird? Every single one of us. I say, once we truly accept this, only then we can confidently say that we are evolving into a more advanced species.

Maria, I thought I was concentrating on my discovery to validate my grandfather, but it turns out, I was doing it for myself. I never wanted for my Theory to create a divide in society. It was my mistake that brought the issue to the forefront. Now, I am bringing this issue to everyone else's attention. It shouldn't matter who is evolving faster, if anyone. Maybe even I can learn to be okay as the human I am, the boring Msitua professor who tends to obsess, panic and overthink everything. I've never thought this acceptance might be something that I would learn from an AI. My dear grandfather, this press conference outlines your *true* legacy, which to me, is more significant than anything you had ever created in your own lifetime.

In conclusion, my vision for the future of humanity has always revolved around the idea that conscious AIs were the only possibility for us to evolve. I believed that this was our only way forward. But now I am hoping for a slightly different future for us – an evolutionary step that we *choose*, where diversity is celebrated, real human communication is encouraged, and most importantly, where progress happens not only in our brains but in our hearts.

Maria, it was difficult for me to overcome the ramifications of our relationship. It is still hard now. But believe me when I say – I choose you! I hope you will try to understand my dilemma. And I hope that you come back and give me a chance to be a good father.

That is about it. Thank you for your time."

***

Chapter Thirty-Two
THE UNEXPECTED GUEST

Daniel woke up suddenly. It was dark. It was quiet. Too quiet. It was the kind of dead-quiet which felt unnatural. An uneasy silence that you sense with every molecule of your body. Daniel felt tense.

He was exhausted after the broadcast and a long day of uneasy waiting. Waiting for something, anything, to happen following his speech. He didn't know what to expect, and didn't dare to hope. He hadn't switched on his Tele-paths since the broadcast. He didn't want to be reached by the rest of the Msitua and scientific communities. The only person he wanted to hear from was one neuro-typical, and she certainly wasn't going to tele-path him. He waited and waited all day, not daring to leave or do anything in case he missed a call or a visit. At some point, without realising, he must have drifted off to sleep.

And now he was suddenly wide awake, trying to fight the uneasy sensation that had overcome him. The hair on the back of his neck stood up. He had the strangest feeling he was not alone. It felt like someone was watching him.

Slowly Daniel turned his head and tried to see through the darkness of the room. At first, he couldn't see anything, but gradually, as his eyes adjusted, a tall shadow near the doorframe emerged from the gloom. The shadow initially stood still, but he watched it began to move, silently gliding towards him like a panther. The shadow was a woman. Daniel still couldn't see her face, but he could now see her silhouette, his eyes fully calibrated to the darkness. She was tall and broad-shouldered with big curly hair and an unapologetically straight spine. She reminded Daniel of the Amazonian women he had read about in his studies.

Daniel waking and realising her movement towards him – it had all happened in a moment. It had happened so suddenly he didn't have time to be terrified. He barely had time to think. It was all he could do, to stare at the unexpected guest sitting up in his bed.

"You put on quite a performance today," the woman said. Her voice sounded profound in the emptiness of the night.

"Who are you?" Daniel managed to ask, still not sure if the woman was real or if he was still dreaming – a strange apparition of his troubled mind.

"I can't tell you my name. But I have heard that you have been looking for me," she said inscrutably. "I am the person who arranges women's relocations."

Daniel was stunned for a minute. He didn't know how to reply. He had a million questions he wanted to ask the woman, but he couldn't find the words to voice them. Something told him that she was not here to answer his questions, but instead to ask hers.

"So, Professor Daniel Stein, how come you haven't told the authorities about our organisation? Or is this some sort of strategic play?"

"Strategic play? What do you mean?"

"Are you using Maria to get to us?"

"No! I would never tell anyone about your existence."

"Why not?"

"Because I promised Maria I wouldn't," Daniel answered bluntly. "I cannot play strategic games."

"Maria said that was one of your idiosyncrasies. It seems to get you in trouble a lot, doesn't it?" the woman said almost sympathetically. The question was rhetorical, and Daniel remained silent. The woman paused for a minute as if weighing something up in her head. "And are you serious about making Tele-paths compatible with the neuro-typical population?"

"I am certainly trying to. It is complicated. Highly unlikely, unfortunately."

"So, why are you even trying?"

Daniel sighed. Why was he even trying? Why was Robert trying? Why anyone should attempt the impossible?

"Because I would want my child to understand me. I don't want her to labour under any misapprehension. I want her to have no doubt about how much I love her."

"I see. Then it might be in our interest to keep you motivated. I want the Tele-paths technology for my people," she declared. "We are trying to build a better society, and we would only look to use the technology once it is compatible with everyone."

Daniel said nothing, feeling like his whole life depended on this woman. He wanted to tell her so much, to promise her anything and everything she wanted him to promise, just to get Maria back. He knew this was his only chance to convince her. Hope began to rise in his chest. She had obviously sought him out for a reason. She must at least be considering the possibility of Maria returning. He was both afraid he wouldn't say enough, but also that he might say too much.

"Would you please let Maria come back to me? If she wants to, of course," he asked gently, his heart rate quickening.

"You made it just in time to reach out to Maria. Another day and she would be at the point of no return."

"Thank goodness," Daniel whispered, sighing, as he felt the tension of the past days start to loosen.

"Don't thank anyone just yet. I will think about it, but I haven't promised anything," the woman replied abruptly. "Are you really a man of your word, Daniel?"

"Yes," Daniel said, trying to look directly into her eyes, even though he couldn't quite make them in the darkness.

"You cannot tell anyone about this conversation. You are not to ask Maria any questions about us. You are not to discuss it with anyone at all. Not even with your supposedly conscious AI. Otherwise, I will destroy you." Daniel felt a cold chill. There was no doubt that she meant it.

"Absolutely."

"If you have any questions, ask me now."

"I have so many," Daniel said, the scientist in him unable to resist.

"I only have time to answer one, so make it a good one."

Daniel paused to think – it was a big decision.

"My question is: How did you manage to keep your location a secret? Every place on Earth is monitored, mapped, and uncovered. It is impossible."

The woman smiled, her teeth shining even in the darkness. "Who said we are on Earth?" she replied.

'Of course!' Daniel thought, his mind spinning. It makes sense. So many places on Earth, like Siberia or Australia, were first inhabited by outlaws and runaways pushed to the corners by society. These women, with their illegal children, were just modern-day outcasts. They were forced to create a new society on a nearby planet. This thought gave Daniel chills. It couldn't be easy for these women. All they wanted was for their children to exist, and to do so they were having to leave everything behind. Even Earth itself!

The woman nodded a farewell, before turning around rapidly and walking out of the room. Daniel wasn't sure how she got in or got out of his apartment, but he decided not to get up or follow her, nor question anything about this visit.

A few minutes went past. It was still quiet. But this time it was a peaceful quiet. Was the unexpected guest real, or was she a dream? Daniel still wasn't sure.

EPILOGUE

It was a beautiful day. The sun was shining, gently warming the park. A little five-year-old girl was walking with her father, holding hands.

The girl had a worried look on her face. The earlier incident at the junior personal interest camp was playing on her mind. She had been messing around with some toys, creating a story in her head, imagining all sorts of magical adventures. She was so caught up in her imagination that she completely forgot where she was. Before she knew it, the toys were scattered all around the floor, and she was mumbling aloud as she played. It took her a while to realise that everyone was looking at her. Questioning eyes from both teachers and children alike. She looked around and saw that all the other kids were playing in a different way, carefully lining up their toys one after another. Suddenly, she felt embarrassed. What was she doing wrong? Why were they looking at her like this?

One teacher came closer and helped her tidy the toys up. She asked her to neatly line the toys like the other children had done. She did as she was told. Yet, this was boring, it felt unnatural. She couldn't organise them as neatly as the other kids. She felt uneasy, and difficult emotions she had no name for filled her up inside. She could not take it – they burst out of her. She screamed and pushed past the teacher to run out of the room, not fully aware of what or who she collided with on her way out.

Later on, her father had come to pick her up. He had shared a long conversation with a teacher. Although the girl couldn't exactly understand what the conversation was about, she somehow knew that it *had* to be about her. She knew that she had somehow done something wrong, something which seemed strange to the others, perhaps even frightening. Yet she couldn't understand what she had done.

Now she walked through the park silently with her dad. He wasn't speaking, but she could sense that he was getting ready to say something. She felt calm and safe next to him. He was always there for her, always finding the right words. He was good at explaining. They bought frozen yoghurt and sat on one of the nearby benches. She was disappointed. The yoghurt wasn't exactly her favourite. Her father insisted on the healthier option. Mum on the other hand, always bought her real ice-cream – rich, sweet and creamy. Her parents were so different, but they both were always there, eager to help her in their own unique ways. She always felt their love, their support. She never felt the same strange, uneasy feeling that she felt in the PIP camp.

The girl was enjoying the sunshine and even the yoghurt, despite it not being as sweet as she liked. She looked at the beautiful young leaves growing on the trees, neon greens so bright that they felt almost blinding. She decided to begin the conversation herself.

"Dad, am I weird?" she asked directly, just like her father liked. He looked deeply into her eyes, hugged her firmly and gave her a smile.

"Yes," he confirmed without hesitation, "and that's a rather wonderful thing!"

"You really think so?" she needed more reassurance.

"Oh yes, I do."

"And what does great-grandpa think?" she asked, giving him a cheeky smile. Great-grandpa was the ultimate authority who knew all the answers.

"Let me just ask," her father said, going silent for just a minute. "Great-grandpa says that normality is overrated. He also says that being weird is more fun. There is beauty in the diversity of humans – no one is the same. Logically speaking, that means that everyone is weird in their own unique way. And the sooner we stop pretending that we are not, the sooner this world will become a better place. And you are a completely normal weird little girl."

The girl took a minute to consider what she had just heard. She was used to these sorts of complicated speeches from her mysterious great-grandpa – the man who lived in daddy's head. Then she looked back at her father, licked her frozen yoghurt and smiled.

Dr Biote's laboratory was always generating something – energy, information... human DNA.

Dr Biote's evening routine for the past five years had been set in stone. He would put the boy to bed for the night, exhausted after yet another eventful day of advancing the boy's knowledge. Then, he would sit at his desk for hours reviewing the surveillance recordings. He would carefully extract all evidence of the boy's existence and store it on a hidden drive of a secret computer.

At the age of five, Daniel Junior still wouldn't speak aloud, but Biote wasn't worried. Dr Biote rather enjoyed communicating with him telepathically. He knew that his boy was very smart. Exceptionally smart! Biote's best creation yet.

And technically, Biote wasn't breaking any rules – he was allowed one child. His logic had always been undeniable – the world needed human-AI research to move forward. But true consciousness could only develop through an AI in a compatible biological carrier; the irreplaceable vessel of human intelligence. Was he supposed to just sit, waiting for the death of the only conscious human-AI? No way! What kind of a scientist would he be if he allowed that to happen? And both, Robert and Daniel, could thank him later. Too much was dependent on this work. Maybe he would never succeed in creating the ultimate vaccine, but he would get this one right. The world would know Biote's name.

How long would Dr Biote be able to keep his boy a secret? He wasn't sure. Luckily, he had a plan. Biote breathed in deeply, anticipating the sweet, satisfying feeling of fulfilment.

His secluded laboratory was always generating something, but it was his own uncompromising vision, in his opinion, that was the most valuable product of all.

MESSAGE TO THE READER

THANK YOU! Thank you for reading my book.

Through the lineup of personal sacrifices and the clouds of self-doubt, my book became a reality with the help of determination, ambition and willpower. I was on a mission to tell a story which wouldn't let my mind rest. I hope you enjoyed reading it. I hope it made you consider or maybe even wonder... You probably still have questions – GOOD! Pick a side and create your own future from now on. Because what really defines humanity is US!

If you enjoyed my book, please kindly leave a review following your paperback book order or type the link below in your browser. I will greatly appreciate and cherish your review forever 😊. Thank you from the bottom of my heart!

US

http://www.amazon.com/review/create-review?&asin=B09K27XYGJ

UK

http://www.amazon.co.uk/review/create-review?&asin=B09K27XYGJ

Love,

Nemetra

ACKNOWLEDGEMENT

Three years ago I didn't think I could pull it off – to write a book! It was a huge task for me, a debut author with zero experience. I think I have always been a poet and a writer in my soul, but I was afraid to admit it to myself. Being a writer in our times can be terrifying – baring your soul, searching for validation, endlessly hunting for the next big idea. However the thing is, despite your fears, your internal drives will get you in the end, even if you try to run away from them or make excuses. They will make you dream of stories in the night, subconsciously writing the chapters in your head, reshaping your reality in a new imagined narrative – a reality that is desperate to come out on the page.

Yep, I am a writer. Can't help it. Sorry about that.

Frankly, it takes a village to write a book. And it definitely helped me to feel that I wasn't alone on my journey. If I had to do it on my own, I wouldn't be capable of completing this book, professionally and emotionally.

Thank you, Ruth Carson, for defining the book's structure and, most importantly, for your unshakable belief in me and in the *Normal Weird* narrative from the start. You gave me the confidence to persevere. Thank you, Svetlana Elfimova, Katerina Rabava and Svetlana Pironko, for kindly introducing me to the writing community. Thank you, Andrea Mara (the outstanding crime novelist – 'All her Fault', 'One Click' and more http://officemum.ie/andrea-mara-fiction/), for sharing your experience and giving valuable advice. Thank you, David Taylor (author of the best-selling Naked Leader books – 'The Naked Leader', 'The Naked Leader Experience', 'The Naked Coach', 'The Naked Millionaire', 'How to be successful by being yourself' and more https://www.nakedleader.com/shop/), for your priceless guidance throughout the publishing process and for encouraging me to be brave. Thank you, Anthony Muller, for your laser-sharp advice, detailed comments and for your 'science hat'. Thank you, Kate Shchetinina, Anastasija Aleksejeva and Anna Erfurt, for being a part of my team, my readers, and my first fans. Thank you, Anastasiia Derkach, for your genius cover, your friendship and your marketing expertise.

And there are people who I am blessed to call my family. My parents and my brother, who have so much faith in me. My children, who make me a better person, never stop surprising me, and challenging my own perceptions. My husband, who is my rock in this sometimes unsettling world. Thank you, my nearest and dearest, for your love and support, and for making my life truly extraordinary!

And thank *you*, my dear reader, for buying my book and for reading it! I hope you like it. Your comments and reviews are invaluable. Please stay in touch via my blog or via social media.

Writing this book surpassed my expectations in every possible way: it was both harder and more rewarding than I thought. My book became its own journey of self-discovery. And what a journey it was! And is. And the best part is that it is only the beginning!

Thank you, thank you, thank you for being on this journey with me. And I am looking forward to sharing my new creative voyages with the world.

Love,
Nemetra

Blog – https://nemetra.com/
Twitter – https://twitter.com/nemetra_x
Instagram – https://www.instagram.com/nemetra_x1369/

Printed in Great Britain
by Amazon